HARD FIX

MCCULLOUGH MOUNTAIN 7

LYDIA MICHAELS

BAILEY BROWN PUBLISHING

Lydia Michaels

Romance
HARD FIX {McCullough Mountain 7}
Copyright © 2019 Lydia Michaels

All characters and events in this book are fictitious. Any resemblance to actual persons living or dead is strictly coincidental.
www.LydiaMichaelsBook.com
First E-book Publication: August 2015 as HOLD ME FAST
Cover design by Lydia Michaels
All cover art and logo copyright © 2019 by Lydia Michaels

To moms... All of you.

Especially the ones that have touched my life and guided me in some way...

Mom
Aunt Linda
Aunt Carol
Aunt Donna
Both my grandmothers, Mary & Mary
Lori L'Heureux
Aunt Joanne
Sue Hume
Ronda Slager
JoAnn Perotti

You are all a part of Maureen McCullough.
Thank you for countless moments of inspiration.

Listen to the McCullough Mountain Playlist!
Click Here to Listen!

McCullough Mountain
Publication Order

Almost Priest 1
Beautiful Distraction 2
Irish Rogue 3
British Professor 4
Broken Man 5
Controlled Chaos 6
Hard Fix 7
Intentional Risk 8

Find more McCulloughs in Jasper Falls!

Wake My Heart 1
The Best Man 2
Love Me Nots 3
Pining For You 4
My Funny Valentine 5
Side Squeeze 6
And more…

PART I

THEN

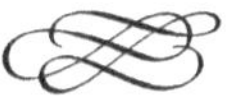

CHAPTER 1

"Move your arse, Maureen, or we're gonna miss it!" Colleen's voice pitched from the school parking lot, her rump balanced on the window of their father's hand-me-down Ford Falcon as her skirts bunched over the mint green door, her other sister, Rosemarie, thumping the horn repetitively as she waited behind the wheel.

"Late for what?" Maureen called, her books weighing down her right arm as she bustled to the car.

"They're takin' O'Malley's!"

Maureen's steps staggered at the fender of the old Ford. "What on earth are you talkin' about? Who's taking it? And where?"

Colleen's beanpole body slithered through the window and the door popped open as she scooted to the other side of the white leather seat. "Liam Cloony, that's who! Now get in!"

As soon as the door shut, Rosemarie gunned the boat of a

car into drive. Pedestrians on an unhurried journey scowled and dodged the rambling vehicle in favor of life over death.

"Move your bloody arses, people!" Rosemarie growled from behind the wheel.

"I don't understand," Maureen repeated. "How does someone take a bar? There isn't far you can take a place cemented to the earth."

"Don't be daft, Maureen," Colleen said, balancing her elbows on the back of the front seat so she could stare out the wide windshield. Whoever gave her sister a driver's license should have been driven to the middle of Center County and shot. Maureen remained safely in the back, her white knuckled grip glued to the handle on the door.

"They aren't takin' it anywhere. They're claimin' it. Liam won it fair and square in a game of poker and it's too good of a price to let go."

"You think Caleb O'Malley is going to just hand him the keys?" They were nuts and Maureen wasn't much in the mood for an Irish brawl.

Colleen's grin was pure evil, her eyes set with dumb love. "That's why Paulie's going."

Maureen rolled her eyes until she saw brain. "You think every Italian has a mob connection. The only thing Paulie Mosconi's good at is pronouncing pasta and doing whatever his mean old mum wants."

"His mum wants him makin' a living for himself," Colleen argued defensively. Chances were she'd end up marrying the poor sot. There wasn't much Colleen wanted that she didn't get.

"Workin' as what, a bar back for Liam?"

"They're going to be partners, isn't that right Rosemarie?"

"I don't know why you're bitchin', Maureen. They get this bar, you'll get served."

That was true, but not something Maureen found remarkably persuasive. True, her sisters were adults, while she was still a seventeen-year-old senior in high school, but there wasn't much they did apart. While some girls went off to finishing school, her father was old fashioned and of the mindset a woman didn't need much more knowledge than how to change a diaper and read a recipe.

It wasn't always fair, but it was all she'd known and after seventeen years, she'd grown used to his dated philosophies. Maureen didn't think herself overly qualified for things outside of the home anyway—nor was she overly motivated to seek higher education.

She wanted one thing and it wasn't part of any curriculum. She wanted to fall in love.

The tires squealed as her sister took the bend and yanked the wheel. Hand over hand, she directed the Falcon into O'Malley's parking lot.

"There's Paulie," Colleen sighed and fluffed the curls of her fiery red hair.

Rosemarie slid the car into a slot and quickly adjusted her breasts in her blouse. They sure did get ridiculous around boys—well, men. Paulie and Liam were close to twenty-five years old, which wasn't too much of a difference considering her sisters were both in their twenties now. As far as age differences went, Maureen sometimes wondered if she were an afterthought or an accident where her parents were concerned.

"Who's that tall guy?" Maureen asked as they climbed out of the car.

Colleen blew a large bubble, the gum sweetening the dry May air. "That's Frank McCullough. He and Paulie are old friends. Good thing he brought him. Frank's built like an ox. Works for his dad up at the lumberyard. Quiet. Sort of dull, but he'll definitely be the muscle we need if Caleb O'Malley tries to pull any shite." She blew another bubble and proceeded to chew like a cow as they approached the trio of men.

Maureen's voice shriveled to something irretrievable and delicate, lodged in her chest as she stared at the dark haired man. The dark denim of his Levis almost matched the pressed black cotton of his shirt. The sleeves were bunched and rolled casually up his thickly muscled arms, already tanned in a way that told Maureen he spent a lot of time outdoors.

His collar was open and his neck wore a layer of dark stubble, something unarguably sloppy, but she liked it for reasons she didn't understand. Her classmates didn't have facial hair like that. *This* was a man.

His hair was beyond windblown, a mess of strands flipped and quaffed like a collection of broken blackbird wings. It was atrocious and unkempt, yet, she couldn't stop covertly admiring it. Her head remained tilted down as she studied him from under her lashes, her body facing Paulie so her attention wasn't too obvious.

He grinned at something Paulie said, but made no comment. While the other's prattled on about the events that brought them there, this man remained silent.

She found herself waiting for the slightest show of emotion. When he finally laughed, her heart seemed to leap into her mouth as her palms suddenly moistened with dewy sweat. His teeth were perfect, his lips full and tanned with the rest of his face. She never saw such rugged beauty. He was like a bear in the wild, gorgeous in his own right, but intense and deserving of space.

Slowly, he turned and Maureen froze as two of the bluest eyes she'd ever seen rested on her. Breath turned hot and heavy in her lungs. With each slow pull she became aware of her breasts pressing against her cheaply made dress. His lips closed over his teeth, hiding his smile as he stared at her. Her mind demanded she look away, but her body was frozen, literally held in place by that intense stare.

The others continued to discuss their plan of overtaking the bar, but this man just stared. His inspection, so unyielding and concentrated, became too much and she snapped her gaze away, severing the connection.

But she still sensed his eyes on her. So many men had come home from the war amputated and her father said some men claimed to still feel what was no longer connected. She felt him, felt the weight of his stare and the strength of his regard. Nothing had ever felt so vacant and so extreme at the same time.

"Let's move," Liam said, his words finally penetrating her bewildered mind.

She turned and frowned as her sisters fell into step after the men. Reaching out, she grabbed Rosemarie's sleeve. "You can't go in there with them. What if there's a fight?"

"Exactly," her sister said grinning. "I don't plan on missin' it. Wait here by the car and beep if you see the constable." She turned and followed the others inside. They disappeared behind a green door and the parking lot was suddenly silent.

Maureen frowned. They were a bunch of imbecilic morons. People didn't win bars in card games. This sort of nonsense was exactly why her father grumbled every time Rosemarie mentioned going out with Liam Cloony. The man was a child who had somehow evaded the war and accomplished absolutely nothing while the others did their time. Yet, Rosemarie adored him.

She'd once told Maureen, *"When I'm good and ready I'll decide it's time for Liam to step up and be a man, and when I do, you can bet your arse his shenanigans will be over. Two things you should understand about life, Maureen. There's divine intervention and then there's the guarantee of really good sex. I'm not God, but I'm certainly no slouch in bed. Liam will do fine."*

Apparently, sex was why men got married, according to her sisters. Maureen wasn't so sure. Her father had always said a man was incomplete without a wife but once married, he was finished. Her mother was an easy woman, nurturing and always busy. Deep down she believed her father loved her mother very much, but they hardly showed affection. Maureen didn't want that sort of love. She craved a love that was fierce and far too passionate to keep inside. She wanted a love that held fast with bonds too strong to weaken over time.

The doors of the pub burst open and she jumped back a step as two drunkards stumbled out, one wearing a torn shirt, the other walking with a bit of a limp. A ruckus of clattering dishes and shouts sounded and silenced as the doors again closed. Dear lord, they were truly fighting in there.

Glancing at the two men hobbling to their car, she debated. It was illegal for her to enter the bar, but her sisters were in there. "For the love of Christ," she muttered, tossing the keys onto the front seat of the Falcon.

She pressed through the green door. Having never entered a pub before, she wasn't sure what to expect, but certain this was not the norm. As though everything were moving in slow motion or under water, Van Morrison's *Into the Mystic* played deafeningly from a large jukebox in the corner as bodies slammed into tables, knocking over chairs and glasses shattered. The stench of spilt lager tickled her nose.

Something hurled through the air and the shrill echo of her sister's scream caught her attention. Whipping around just in time to duck an oncoming bottle, she gasped and squatted low behind a fallen table.

Her sisters were perched on a pool table, Rosemarie cheering Liam on as he rolled across the floor with Caleb O'Malley. Colleen was shooting off her mouth at some poor bastard that made a grab for her leg and got a good taste of her shoe—the penny of her loafer likely lodged in his throat by now.

"Cops!" someone yelled and the shouting got louder as everyone scramble for the doors.

It was absolute mayhem. Maureen couldn't do more than stare as bloodied men punched with one hand and helped their opponent up with the other as the law came to take them all away. Perhaps it was the lingering taste of war that left them with such a thirst for violence. Perhaps it was simply men being boys.

Van Morrison continued to croon as the pub bore ransacked markings of a true brawl. Though everyone was angry, they were smiling—bunch of drunken, sodden lots. Didn't they know their bar was being commandeered?

A firm hand closed over her arm and she gasped, prepared to defend herself, but unsure how.

Dark blue eyes held her as his grip tightened. "Come along, lassie, before the constable hauls you away for drinkin' underage."

Breathless, she whispered, "But my sisters—"

"They'll be fine. Liam and Paulie will see to them."

She shouldn't have gone with him, but those eyes of his seemed to cast a spell on her. Over the slap of flesh and the splintering wood, she somehow made out Van Morrison's poetic words of running into the mystic and rocking a gypsy soul and suddenly she was standing, racing through the riffraff and out of O'Malley's—holding none other than Frank McCullough's strong hand.

His fingers swallowed hers as he pulled her close. The heat of his broad chest burned into her shoulders as he guided her out the door. His large palm rested heavily on her lower back and for those few seconds she had no fear of any danger.

Sirens whined in the distance. "My truck's this way," he called as he hauled her toward the back of the lot.

It was an old black Chevy, desperate for a good washing. He beat her to the passenger handle and popped it open. Not giving her a chance to climb inside, her feet left the ground as he quickly deposited her inside the truck and shut the door.

As he opened his door the sirens seemed closer. "We have to move."

The truck roared to life and she breathed in the sweet scent of his clothing, memorizing it, before the fumes of diesel stole the fresh air. There was no chance for talk during the bumpy ride through town. She was too stunned to speak anyway. Soon he was hauling her down an unpaved road she never visited before.

Her mind returned to her sisters, assuming the police were now at the scene asking questions. "Do you think anyone will be arrested?"

"You're not to worry about Rose and Colleen. The police will assume they're innocent on the fact that they're ladies."

She chuckled. "I don't know that Colleen fits that title."

He grinned and disarmed her with a quick glance, those fiery blue eyes burning into her soul. "I believe you're right, but the constable doesn't know her the way we do."

"You know my sister?" It struck her as odd that Colleen would know this man and never mention him. He was far more handsome than Liam or Paulie. Perhaps that was the issue, his attractiveness put him out of reach and therefore not a suitable conquest.

"Aye. I'd be remiss not to know the lassie my best friend plans to wed."

"Paulie's going to marry Colleen?" she nearly barked.

He chuckled, the sound deep and throaty. "If she'll have his sorry arse."

Although her father would be disappointed, there was no doubt in her mind that Colleen would eagerly agree to be Paulie's wife. "When?"

Frank tsked. "Now, what kind of friend would I be if I told you that? If you're anything like your sisters, I'm certain you can't keep a secret for shit."

Her belly tightened and rolled as they took another road she didn't recognize. Something about him was undoing all sorts of neatly kept knots inside of her and making her feel loose and giddy as though she were a feather blowing in the wind.

The question in her mind became too significant to discard. "Do you have a girl—a lassie?"

"No."

His simple answer warned her it was a subject he didn't care to delve into, so she let it drop, sparing only a small wish that she were a bit older. He was perhaps the most handsome man she'd set eyes on, not counting the lads in catalogues and such.

She rarely considered boys. They were childish and unappealing. However, she was only seventeen and far too young to set her sights on a man. Perhaps it was a result of having older sisters and hanging with their older friends that left her with a taste for maturity.

Either way, she'd figured—since Elvis had gotten fat and

no longer appealed to her—that she'd worry about meeting a husband once she came of age. Her eighteenth birthday was soon and now that she met Frank McCullough that made her anxious to age faster, as if she could somehow catch up to him.

Straightening her shoulders, she sucked in her tummy and lifted her chest. Casually, she used the fingers of her left hand to wriggle her skirt a bit above the knee and waited for him to take notice.

He pulled into an empty, unpaved lot marked only by a chain link fence. "We'll wait here for a while until things settle. Then I'll take you back to your sisters."

She looked around seeing nothing but trees and the long run of fence. "Is this private property?" No point in running from the cops only to be arrested for trespassing.

"Yes, but not to worry. It's McCullough property."

"You own this?"

He nodded.

"What is it?"

He studied her for a moment. "How old are you, Maureen?"

It seemed imperative that she form her answer in a mature manner. No seventeen and eleven months type response would do. "I'll be eighteen in July."

He grunted and nodded. "This is my family's lumberyard."

"You work here?" she asked, recalling what her sister knew of him.

"Have since I've been a boy. My dad hasn't been well since the war. With so many men drafted he came back to a mess of issues and needed someone to help him run things." He glanced at her. "You don't want to hear about this."

On the contrary, she was enthralled by the fact that he was speaking to her at all. "No, go on."

He shifted, dragging his thick forearm over the wheel and facing her. It made her feel very important. "My dad enrolled in the military when I was ten, thinking we'd win in no time and he'd return a hero—*if* he ever made it to combat at all. I grew up in the yard, delivering thermoses to my dad and uncles and running their lunches out to them when my mum had it ready. Soon enough they had me climbing trees and marking acres, because there was such a shortage of able men. When my dad deployed for Vietnam my uncles still let me work and as I got older the work got a little more demanding."

"Do you like it?"

"Aye. I love being outside and I like doing something for my family. My mother looked to me as the man of the house since I was merely a boy. I liked that too."

There was pride in his tone, something she respected and filed away as another appealing quality. If anything, Frank McCullough was a capable fellow—no, *man.* He'd been a man far before the law would label him as such, and that was beyond attractive.

"When my father returned he was sick."

"Was he hurt in the war?" So many soldiers had returned home missing limbs and wearing scars.

Frank tapped his head. "Aye. The war hurt his mind. It isn't right for a man to spend so many years staging battles and watching death. As resilient as the human soul is, some scars are permanent. At first I thought he just needed time to acclimate himself to society again." His head shook slowly. "But he'll never be the same. There's a rage inside of him too great to burn out in this lifetime."

"I'm sorry." Once again she suffered her immaturity. Her

inability to come up with comforting words left her with a sense of great inadequacy.

His head tilted, setting a dark strand of hair just to the side of his sharp eyebrow. His lashes were so thick she had the urge to run her fingers over them. "You don't have any brother's, do you?"

It was becoming difficult to concentrate on his words, but she desperately wanted to keep their dialogue going. "No. The O'Leahey's are cursed with girls." She laughed. "My poor father was bald before I was even born."

His smile was tight, his eyes creasing affectionately as if something she'd said pleased him. "You're a bonny lass, Maureen O'Leahey. I think I'm rather grateful your dad had nothing but girls."

Her breath caught as she stared at him, unsure if she'd imagined his words or if he'd actually said them. "How old are you, Frank?"

"Twenty-five."

And there it was. Lowering her gaze, she casually shifted her skirt back over her knee and folded her hands on her lap.

Though his was clearly American, his slang reminded her so much of her mother. Words like lass and bonny were familiar and soothing, having heard them since she was a child.

"Things have probably settled by now," he said, turning to face the wheel again.

Disappointment weighed heavy in her chest as the truck started and they silently drove back to town. It was foolish to think a man like Frank McCullough would take interest in a young girl like her. She'd be wise to not think of him in terms of attraction anymore.

When they reached the pub, Colleen grinned and met

them at the truck. "I was wondering where you two got off to."

"I didn't want your little sister getting hassled by the police."

Maureen grimaced at the use of the word "little". "Where's Rosemarie?"

"Inside. Cleaning up."

"What the bloody hell is she cleaning up for? Did the constable tell her she had to?"

Colleen grinned. "Now, what kind of woman would she be to not help Liam straighten up their new bar?"

"What? Caleb actually gave it to him?"

"What choice did he have? The man was indebted to Liam for nearly fifteen grand."

"But the bar has to be worth far more than that," she argued and Colleen shrugged, clearly tapped out of her knowledge on the subject.

"There's likely a mortgage to be paid. I'm sure Caleb's debts are to more than just Liam Cloony."

Unbelievable.

"It's closed now if you want to go in," Colleen said. "I'm waitin' on Paulie. Tell him to move his arse, will ya?"

She and Frank entered the bar, but he no longer held her hand or pressed his palm to the small of her back. He held the door for her, which she now found irritating and misleading. Their shoes crunched over broken glass.

"Watch your step, love." His words provoked a sigh, but she stifled the moon-eyed response she also sensed coming. This one was too charming for his own good and she was a damn fool to think it had anything to do with her.

The place was in shambles. "I'm not sure it's worth a cent now," she mumbled.

"They'll have it clean in no time," Frank answered.

Paulie stood in the center of the rubble. "Did you see the way I took out that one bastard with the arms the size of tree trunks and the big barrel chest? Ah, he was no match for me—"

"Paulie," Frank called. "Your woman's in the back growing impatient with waitin' on your arse."

That fast, Paulie's regaling tales of the brawl ceased and he was out the door like a well-trained pup. She shook her head at the control Colleen had over that poor man.

Rosemarie yelled from the back. "We'll be replacin' those pool tables too. And this bar will be needin' a fresh coat of lacquer. Are you listening, Liam? I won't be moving in until this pub is right and proper, you remember that. Oh, there you are, Maureen," she smiled. "Grab a broom in the back and start sweepin'. We've got lot's to do and the mortgage is due by the fifteenth. No time to spare and every minute those doors are closed we're losing money."

She stared, dumbfounded. Frank returned with two brooms and handed her one. She swept, in awe of what they were doing and what it signified. It was a lot to process.

"Are you really going to move in with Liam, Rosemarie?" she asked quietly as she swept alongside her sister.

She grinned. "I'm ready. I want to have babies, Maureen. Could you imagine, us having our own sweet babies someday?"

"But you're not married." Their father would never allow it.

Rosemarie's smile was the sort that spoke of many secrets and warm affections shared between her and the man that held her heart. "Liam asked Father for his permission last month and he said we'd have his blessing if Liam could provide a home for us and find a way to make a decent living."

She wasn't sure about the bar being decent, as it was won in a poker match, nor was she clear on how this amounted to a home. "Will you live with his family?"

"No, silly. We'll live here. There's an apartment upstairs. It's nothing special, but we can stay there and save for a house. Down the line, maybe you or Colleen could live there if you need to. Since we own the deed there's no rent."

Part of her was jealous and thrilled for the sudden turn her sister's life was taking, but a greater part felt left behind. It was only a matter of time before Colleen moved out of the house as well. She wanted to be happy for her sisters, but it was tricky embracing such emotions when she was terrified for herself. Her parents were not the greatest company to those that didn't get a kick out of the nightly news or *Gunsmoke*.

By the time the damage was cleaned up it was dark. There was much to still be repaired, but for the most part the bar seemed a heap nicer than when she'd first seen it. Frank had disappeared sometime while she was cleaning and it hurt that he hadn't said goodbye. Her disappointment was again inappropriate, for obvious reasons.

It was getting late and Rosemarie seemed reluctant to leave when Liam was so devotedly inspecting his new enterprise. Begging for the keys, Maureen took the Falcon home alone, something she imagined doing a lot in the future.

When she got home the house was dark, her parents each sleeping on their chairs in the den. She quietly locked the door and went to her room at the corner of the first floor. Three twin beds. What would she do with all that empty space when the time came? She didn't want to think about it, but her mind wouldn't let her focus on much else.

She considered the friends she'd be graduating with in two weeks and measured their appeal in matters of amusement, suitability as a spouse, and even potential company for summer gallivanting. Did teenagers gallivant after they graduated or did summer become just another season?

Several of her classmates were scheduled for June weddings. While they'd been planning prom, others had been picking bridesmaids and bouquets. The future was indeed daunting. The only skill beyond homemaking that Maureen possessed was an ability to type forty words per minute. She'd likely spend the next year wasting away in some dingy office with a sad excuse for a window.

Before she fell asleep, she thought about the bluest sky her memory could conjure, comparing it in all its many facets and tones to the depths of Frank McCullough's eyes. Though the sky could blush vibrant shades of pink and darken deeper than sapphires, she decided his eyes were the victors when it came to exquisiteness, and she wondered when she'd be able to see them again.

CHAPTER 2

"It seems I'm always saving you, Maureen O'Leahey."

Maureen blinked as her skin heated under the June heat. She was a liar. Her skin had been just fine in the heat until Frank McCullough pulled his truck behind her broken down Ford. Now it burned with a fiery blush that likely left her redder than a tomato. "I hit a pothole and the whole tire burst."

Frank swaggered close to the rim and examined the damage. "You got a spare?"

"Maybe in the back." She hated driving and before Rosemarie moved out this was her sister's car.

Frank opened the trunk. "Nope. You in a rush?"

It had been so long since she'd seen him, yet a day didn't go by that he didn't cross her mind. Obsessive was an understatement.

"I'm supposed to be at practice in five minutes."

"Practice?"

"For graduation. It's tomorrow."

"Congratulations." He grinned, but his eyes told a different story. "I can get you a spare and have it fixed in no time, but if you don't want to miss practice you better let me take you."

For some reason her mind automatically started calculating how many days until she became a legal adult. Too bad every time she was in his presence her mind turned to mush and simple addition became a feat even she could not manage. "Yes."

"Yes?" he smirked, as though he found her breathless answer amusing. "Get your purse." She never knew what to expect from him. Though he seemed a man of few words, she hung on every one and never got disheartened in what he had to say.

She grabbed her purse and rolled up the windows. He waited by the opened passenger door and a thrill raced up her spine at the anticipation of him again lifting her into the cab of his truck. He didn't disappoint and this time she was prepared enough to savor the delicious grip of his hands around her waist.

Though she hadn't exerted herself, when the door closed she was out of breath. He climbed in beside her and she found his familiar scent pleasing in too many ways. Her chest lifted as she drew in a deep breath, attempting to commit the unique fragrance to memory. Breathless and dizzied by his nearness, she shut her eyes and silently sighed as a jolt of excitement danced through her belly.

He drove toward the high school. "You shouldn't be driving without a spare."

"Blame Colleen. For all I know the idjit made a tire swing out of it."

He chuckled. "Are you excited to graduate?"

She shrugged. "I guess."

"What will you do?"

Good question. "I don't know. I suppose I should have an idea by now."

"Well, think of what you like and do that."

Her lips pursed. "That's a little difficult." Regretfully, they were already nearing the school.

Once he parked at the field, he turned and faced her. She sensed his expectation for her to face him, but didn't have the courage to look into those blue eyes again. "What is it you want, Maureen?" he whispered, and suddenly she felt as if he were asking about more than her choice of career.

She shrugged, no longer caring about arriving to practice on time. "I want to be loved."

"Aye."

Slowly, with trembling courage, she faced him, wondering if Frank could somehow know loneliness as well as she. "Have you ever loved a woman?"

He nodded. "I loved my mother, but that's not the same as what you're speaking of."

"No." Where was his mother? He only spoke of her in past tense.

"I think, when she passed, she took a bit of my heart."

Her lips parted. "I didn't know...I thought she was alive..." her words stupidly abandoned her.

"It's fine. The funeral was a few months ago and I'm... coping. My father on the other hand..."

Her hand instinctively went to his arm, her nature insisting she bring him some level of comfort. "I'm so sorry for your loss, Frank."

He nodded and stared at her hand. "You have pretty fingers."

Her heart fluttered and something deep in her belly tightened. However, when she looked at her bitten down fingernails, she self-consciously curled them into her palm. "They're plain. I try to grow my nails, but I'm always breaking them."

He glanced out the windshield where many students gathered on the field as the teachers tried to assemble them in some sort of order. "Do you not love someone, Maureen? Is there not a lad you had your heart set on?"

Her hand slid away. "No. They're all spoken for or too childish to court a girl like me."

When he stayed quiet she glanced at his face and found him studying her again, a slight smile curling his full lips.

"What is it?"

"I'm wondering if you're more like Rosemarie, determined and stubborn, or more like Colleen, fearless and wild."

"Perhaps I'm neither. Perhaps I'm just Maureen."

"Aye."

She didn't want to be like either sister. Not to him. She wanted him to see *her*, the real her. Perhaps when he found the real Maureen, he could introduce them, because she was still trying to figure the girl out.

"You better go."

"My car—"

"I'll see if I can get my hands on a spare, maybe find a tree swing with the right shape." He laughed. "Then I'll meet you back here."

"O-okay." If he was late she could always get a ride home with someone else, but she hoped Frank was a man of his word and the only person driving her today.

He came around the truck and opened her door. Though he didn't pick her up, he did offer her a hand. When she took it, heat traveled up her arm and her heart raced. Licking her dry lips, she stared at the ground. He didn't wear shoes like most men his age. On the contrary, he wore rugged boots that had been well worn with hard work.

"I'll be back within the hour, love. Don't fret. We'll fix the car."

Love. As the endearment met her ears a thirst took hold of her like nothing she'd ever experienced before. She wanted to kiss him, to feel his hands on her hips, in her hair, on her body. She was trembling with desire for this man and unsure how her longing had raveled so far out of control when she'd decided not to be attracted to him.

"Maureen."

Winded, she looked into his eyes, but could not manage a single word.

"Go to practice," he instructed, and she nodded.

The truck pulled away as she stepped onto the field. She'd been so out of it she left her purse on the seat, which was fine. It insured she'd have to see him again.

"Who was that?" Rhoda Greiner asked, balancing on her toes as she peered over the fence and watched Frank's truck disappear in the distance.

Maureen frowned. "Lean over much farther and all that tissue you so painstakingly shape your bosoms with is gonna litter the field. Put your eyes back in your head and mind your own business."

She wasn't sure who was more shocked, her or all the girls now staring at her. Dear God, where had those words come from?

Frank wasn't hers. Rhoda had as much right to look at him as anyone else, yet the thought made her see red. She protectively wanted him to herself, knowing she didn't hold a candle to the other girl's beauty.

Maureen was cursed with copper curls and more freckles than any person could count in a lifetime. Though her green eyes were pretty, they were overpowered by her fussy Irish skin, and therefore the last thing anyone noticed about her—like two pretty stars in a botched painting of sky.

Too many times she'd wished to be exotically brunette or seductively blond. There were the Hepburn's and the Monroe's, among the sort of women men fancied. She was still waiting for the trend-setting redhead to shift the way of the world, but none had shown up. Apparently Lucille Ball gave redheads a comedic reputation, but Maureen was usually too shy to come up with anything funny.

Like most girls uncomfortable in their own skin, she depended on a hardy dose of sarcasm and great sense of humor to get her through the day, but that only worked around her sisters. Other people filled her with doubt and most people assumed she was the quiet O'Leahey. She had plenty to say, but no one beside her sisters to listen, and they were leaving her.

Practice was a necessary bore, instructing them when they should stand and when they should sit. By the time it was over and she felt like a well-trained pedigree, her anticipation to see Frank had nearly turned crippling.

Several people left to attend a party. School was officially over, the classes and final exams now concluded. It seemed only one ceremony separated her from the rest of the world and that thought was terrifying.

As drivers peeled out of the field parking lot shouting and honking with long awaited joy, Maureen's heart sank. She didn't see Frank's black truck. Glancing back, she spotted Rhoda and several of the girl's strolling off the field. Embarrassment had her stepping into the shadows.

"Hiding from someone?" His voice was deep and unmistakable, rattling her heart like thunder in her chest.

Her breath caught as a smile crept over her lips. He came back. "I didn't see your truck."

He sucked in his lower lip as if tasting something there and her attention was drawn to his strong shadowed jaw. "That's because I drove your car here. Couldn't have you riding off on a new tire without testing it out first."

His courtesy, thoughtfulness, and masculine charm were too much to digest. Most women didn't care for that sort of coddling, finding it patronizing and chauvinistic. Maureen, on the other hand, found it seductive and sexy as hell. "T—thank you."

They slowly strolled toward the Ford. "Did you want to grab something to eat? I know a small diner outside of town we could hit."

Was he suggesting they leave town because their age difference or was she reading too much into things and he simply liked the food? "Sure, but I'll treat, since you fixed my tire."

"Not on your life," he said, opening the passenger door.

It struck her as odd that he'd drive her car. She was prepared to object, but as Rhoda spotted them and gaped she simply smiled and slid into the passenger seat.

"This is a nice car."

"Thanks. It was my dad's, then Colleen's, then Rose-marie's."

"And now it's yours," he said, smiling softly at her.

She worried what his intentions were. Perhaps he was just a nice guy and this was all part of who he was. She decided dinner would be the perfect time to get to know him better.

When they reached the diner he again held the door and she bet he would have pulled out her chair if they hadn't sat on stools at the counter. "Are you going to be Paulie's best man?" she asked, suddenly curious.

He placed the menu on the counter and turned to her. "Aye. And you…"

"I'm Colleen's maid of honor, though it should really be Rosemarie. She's paying for everything."

"It works out well that your family has the pub now, since you seem to be hosting weddings every five weeks."

Rosemarie's wedding was small, with only family. Colleen's on the other hand was going to be large. Of course hers would be at the same Catholic Church her sister and parents got married in, but this time the guests would fill every pew. Colleen always wanted a big party and now she was getting one.

"I don't know if the pub can hold all of Colleen and Paulie's guests."

"There's always a way. Don't forget there's a large back room too, and the lot's big enough for tents and tables."

True.

The waitress took their order and Frank sipped his soda. "So, apart from wanting love, what else is it you're after, Maureen?"

Every time he spoke her name her thoughts scattered like the dust of a dandelion. "I want a home to take care of, a family to care for."

"So you want children then?"

"I imagine having a family would be nice," she agreed, not wanting to sound too eager or mistakenly presumptuous.

"Aye. I think you'd make a fine mother, Maureen O'Leahey."

She laughed. "How is that when you hardly know me?"

He studied her for a long beat. "You're gentle. Kind. You got a spirit inside of you lookin' to get out and that red hair of yours tells me it's burnin' hot. Your green eyes tell me there's a touch of wild to your soul and a temper no wise man should challenge. But you're loving. I see it in the way you always consider others before yourself, wonderin' if your sisters are okay and doing whatever you can to lend a hand. I think you help others so much it's a good reason why your nails never grow."

She glanced at her unkempt fingers and curled her hands into fists, hiding the short nails. His words shocked her. He'd seen so much in such a short time, which told her she wasn't mistaken and he had been watching her indeed. "That's a lot of assumption, Frank McCullough."

"Am I wrong? Tell me I've misread you and I'll gladly apologize, but I don't think I have, love."

She swallowed, something heavy weighing on her shoulders, countering the abundant lust she was already shouldering for this man. "No, you're pretty spot on."

The waitress delivered their food, but he made no move to eat. She was starving and his steady, *accurate* appraisal was making her edgy. "Stop starin' and start eatin' before your food goes cold, ya jackass."

He chuckled, seemingly pleased at her insult and turned to eat.

After finishing the first half of his burger he asked, "How many kids do you want, love?"

His question caught her off guard, as they'd settled into a comfortable silence. She wiped her mouth and considered the question. It was hard to say, being that she didn't have a man willing to wed her. "I suppose as many as the Lord grants me."

"Are you Catholic?"

"Oh, yes, born and raised. I've never missed a mass on Sunday."

"Is it the big church on Main Street your family belongs to?"

"Yes. My father's very active there."

He nodded and continued eating. The meal was nearly finished when she recalled she was supposed to be finding out about *him*. He was a tricky bugger, turning the tables on her the way he had.

"Why do you not have a girlfriend, Frank?"

He shrugged. "I'm busy with work. Paulie's going to take on a job at the yard, which will help a great deal, but until then I have no time to date."

She frowned. "But Paulie's splitting the mortgage on O'Malley's with Rosemarie and Liam." And Paulie had time to date.

"Aye, and he'll pay that mortgage with his earnings at the yard. Liam will tend bar while your sisters waitress and if ever Paulie needs to do more, the opportunities there."

Again, she felt forgotten. "I wonder where I fit in."

His head tipped to the left. "Do you want to work, Maureen? I figured you were the kind of woman that would prefer to stay at home, keeping house and family."

He hadn't made the job sound condescending. On the contrary, his tone held a great deal of respect for homemakers. "Was your mother a homemaker?"

"For the majority of her life. When times got tough she'd do side work here and there, sometimes she filled in at the office if they were between secretaries at the lumberyard."

She decided on honesty. "I think it would be lovely to be a wife and mother, devoting all my time to a family and taking care of a deserving husband."

"I suppose finding a man deserving enough is what's slowing you down."

It was finding a man at all, but she didn't possess the

courage to admit that. "Aye." He smiled, noting the way she mimicked his common accent.

"O'Leahey. That's quite Irish."

"My mum's right off the boat. My dad traveled here from Dublin. He doesn't have quite the accent, but my mum has a thick one."

"Aye. My grandparents spoke mostly Gaelic, but my grandfather on my mother's side was rumored to be a Scott. I never met him, so we aren't sure, but it seems my McCullough blood prefers Celtic dialect. The words are pretty, like you, lassie."

Her chest lifted as she glanced at the counter, her face heating as her mouth hid a smirk. "And your parents?"

"My mother's English was clear unless she was angry. My father..." He shook his head. "It's been a while since I've heard his voice without a whiskey accent. It's hard to recall how he spoke before the war."

Imagining Frank so estranged from his father yet living under the same roof seemed unfathomable. Though she was not overly friendly with her parents, they spoke to each other every day, her mother more than her father. The longer she thought about her parents, the more she realized how her mother had been approaching her more.

Perhaps, now that Rosemarie was gone and Colleen was hardly ever home, the house seemed lonely to her too. Or maybe it was more an attempt to finally build a friendship with her youngest daughter.

"What has you thinkin' so hard, love?"

"My mum. I suppose we are friends."

He nodded. "I considered my mother one of my dearest friends in the end. It gets easier as we get older. Don't be afraid to let her in."

Perhaps he was right. "Do you want children, Frank?"

"Aye. A great deal of them."

She laughed. "Well, yes, from my understanding it's the man that has the difficult job in making that happen," she joked.

"From your understanding? Are you not sure, wee lass?"

Her cheeks burned as her lips pursed. She glanced at her plate, her belly now full. "I've never…"

"Ah," he answered quietly. "I forget you're still young."

"Young, but not stupid."

He frowned and his easy posture shifted. "Never said you were. What is it you mean by that?"

She needed to draw a line before her heart got any more wrapped up in this man. "It means that while I'm smart enough to know a tomato is a fruit, I'm wise enough to know it doesn't belong in fruit salad."

"Are you calling me a tomato, Maureen O'Leahey?"

"No, I'm the bloody tomato."

"So I'm the fruit salad?"

"Yes. No. Oh, for Christ's sake it was a metaphor!" Frustrated, she stood and looked for her purse.

He stood as well, his height intimidating and appealing all at once. "Well then perhaps you best start talkin' in plain English so I know what it is you're tryin' to say, love."

"Where the bloody hell is my purse?"

He caught her arm and tossed a few dollars on the counter. "It's in the truck and I told you you're not paying for dinner. Now, tell me what it is you meant."

Breathing roughly, her face pinched as she met his hard gaze. "All I meant was that you're seven years older than me and I'm still in high school. I've never seen two people more unsuited, so I don't see a point to wastin' our breath about family and such. It's a bunch of bullshit, is what it is, and I don't need you danglin' some carrot that ain't real in front of my face so you can get your jollies off by getting some sad teenager to drool over unlikely possibilities."

She'd lost track of her words and he stared at her, his expression unreadable. "Do you often reference vegetables when making a point?"

"What?"

He shrugged. "Carrots, tomatoes…"

"I told you, tomatoes are fruit. Were you even listening to me?"

"Aye. I was listening. But now I'm wondering what tomatoes and strawberries would taste like."

Men—of all ages—were idiots. Rolling her eyes, she huffed and left.

"Maureen, wait a minute," he laughed, telling the waitress to keep the change.

Every word made her sound more like a child and she wanted to stop talking.

"Hey," he called as he met her by the car.

She reached for the handle of the driver side door, but it was locked. As it snapped back she broke another nail and grimaced, letting out a profane curse. "Give me the damn keys."

He grabbed her shoulders and squeezed, his arm banding across her upper chest as the heat of his front pressed into her back. Sucking in a hard breath she trembled, not used to having a man so close.

"You curse too much," he whispered, his hands following her arms down to her wrists. He gently turned her so her back was against the car door. Lifting her hand, he unfolded her fist and kissed her fingers. "I had high hopes for that nail."

She'd never met anyone like him, so able to see into her mediocre life and make sense of all the trivial nonsense. He continued to hold her fingers against his lips, his warm breath sending chills up her arm. Her heart thundered and she wondered if he could feel her pulse through the steady beating in her fingertips pressing into his soft lips.

"I told you before and I'll tell you again, you're a bonny lass, Maureen O'Leahey."

Her chest rose as her dress suddenly felt tight. "What do you want?" she whispered, far beyond her comfort zone.

A beat of laughter escaped his throat as his eyes drilled into hers, the moonlight turning the deep sapphire into silver. "You."

She stepped back, but made it only an inch as the car blocked her way. He released her fingers and the soft jangle of metal filled the air as he produced her keys. Ushering her aside, he led her to the passenger door once more and strangely, she allowed him.

He wanted her.

What did that mean? Sex? He wanted sex? Or was it more than that? They were little more than strangers connected only by family and friends. Could it be possible that the emotions he provoked in her she also stirred in him? Perhaps her lust wasn't one-sided at all. Maybe it was chemistry.

Not a word was spoken as they drove from the diner to where he'd left his truck. When he pulled to the shoulder of the road, there were no other cars and she wondered how late it was. He put the car in park and faced her. She stared out the windshield at the dark taillights of his truck.

"When's that birthday of yours, love?"

She frowned. "July twenty-fifth. Why?" Was he planning on getting her a present?

He nodded, making a masculine sound in his throat. "I'd like to get my lips on you before then, lassie."

Appalled, she turned and scowled at him. "And that is

how you ask? I'd like a lot of things, Frank, mostly, to meet a man who knows how to ask a woman for favors. And if that is why you're waitin' for my birthday you can just forget it. I'm saving myself for marriage."

Every trace of cockiness fled his face as her words sank in. *Oh Christ.* She wasn't necessarily saving shit, but it pissed her off that he'd assume the calendar was all that was holding him up from gettin' into her knickers.

"I wasn't… I hadn't meant to insinuate—"

"Don't try backtracking now. I know what you meant." It was like her mouth had disconnected from her brain and there was no stopping her words.

Like a runaway train, she'd unleashed on him. "You think I have nothin' better to do than wait around so you can legally take my virginity? You can think again, Mr. McCullough. I have standards and they aren't the sort that crumble for some blue eyed, silver-tongued Irishman wantin' to put his lips on me. I'll be expectin' a gentleman, next time I see you, if your lips will be getting' anywhere near me—"

His mouth was suddenly crushing hers as he pulled her halfway across the seat and cut off her words. She'd never been kissed before, at least not like that. His hand cupped the back of her head as his mouth slanted and his tongue pressed deep, teasing and awakening parts of her she'd rather ignore. Her eyes held wide as his other hand fit around her thigh and massaged through the fabric of her skirt.

"You talk entirely too much, Maureen O'Leahey," he whispered against her lips. "I'm thinkin' it's high time a man shut you up in a way you found acceptable."

He kissed her again and her chest lifted, her nipples tightening as heat pulled in her stomach and a strange pressure set her insides on fire.

"No," she mumbled as his hand slowly rubbed higher on

her thigh. Pulling back as that hand steadily crept to a place she strongly considered off limits to others, she did the first thing she could manage and smacked him across the jaw.

The sharp slap left the car in dark silence. Quietly, he chuckled. "You really are something."

"I told you," she said, out of breath. "You'll need to be a gentleman to get your lips on me. Buyin' me dinner doesn't prove shit."

The side of his mouth kicked up in a half-smirk. "You sure got a mouth on you, woman."

She liked being called woman, considering she was only seventeen. "And wouldn't you like to see all the things it can do."

His half-smirk turned into a full smile as he laughed. "Well, look at you. You're tongues as sharp as mine is silver. You better be gettin' home before real trouble finds you. Tomorrow's a big day."

That was right. Tomorrow she was graduating. Funny how such a monumental achievement paled in comparison to being kissed by Frank McCullough.

"Good night, love," he said, cracking open the door.

"Frank?" He stilled and she took a second to process her sudden insecurities.

He paused, still facing the door. "Yes, Maureen?"

"The kiss… did I do it okay?"

His head tilted as he again faced her. "Have you not been kissed before?"

"Never like that," she whispered, her fingers tracing where his mouth had been.

He slid back inside the car and turned to the windshield, pulling his lower lip in for a taste. A quiet chuckle escaped, but he didn't seem amused. "You're that innocent then?"

"Never mind," she immediately said, wishing she'd never opened her mouth—for anything.

"No, it's fine. I shouldn't have assumed…" he shook his head. "A gentleman indeed." He laughed. "I'm sorry I came on so strong, love, but when I'm around you, I lose sight of right and wrong and all I can tell is that I want you."

Her eyes widened as she choked on her words. "Me?" That couldn't be right.

His gaze turned on her, his eyes appearing almost pained. "Aye, you. I think you're bonny, smart, funny, and I think about you naked every day."

"Frank!"

"Sorry, but it's true. Your curves enchant me."

Was that how men and women spoke to one another? "I've never been naked in front of anyone but my mum and my sisters."

A smirk pulled the corner of his mouth tight. "We could remedy that."

She smacked his arm. "Don't be a pig."

"I have a healthy appetite for beautiful women, love. There's nothin' wrong with that."

"Aye, well if your wantin' this woman you'll lose your taste for all others, do you understand?"

"Aye."

They were silent for several minutes. She fidgeted as she waited for him to say more, but he didn't. Finally, she broke the silence. "What does this mean, Frank? People will talk if they see us together."

"It means I like you."

"Like me? Why?"

He shrugged and pointed to his chest. "It's here, in the way my chest gets tight at just the sight of you and I want to hold you fast, but never feel like we have enough time."

"Oh." That was rather sweet and more poetic than she'd expected. "Are you saying we're…"

"I want you to be mine for more than a minute."

Lots of things were longer than minutes but still quite short. "Are you askin' to date me? I'm not trying to be thick headed, but I've never much dated and…"

"Aye. I'm wantin' you to be mine, Maureen O'Leahy. Mine and only mine."

Liquid heat swirled in her belly as her veins pulsed with excitement. "I can't let my parents know."

"It's no one's business."

Insecurity made it difficult to look in his direction. She didn't want to say the wrong thing and sound foolish. "I…I never much dated," she repeated.

"Me neither."

She laughed, still finding that hard to believe. A thought occurred to her and she frowned. "I'll not have you hitting on other girls if you want to be with me."

"I wouldn't dream of it."

His gentle tone retrieved a bit of her courage. "And I'm not easy. I'm not promising you a thing, if you get what I mean."

"Aye. It'll keep."

Shooting him a sidelong glance, she snickered. "You seem certain I'm keepin' it for you."

"You are," he said with palpable cockiness.

Her mouth gaped at his surety. "There's something wrong with you."

"To be sure, but I speak the truth. I'll have you, Maureen O'Leahey, make no mistake of that. I'll be a gentleman for you, as you're deserving of such, but make no mistake, I'm a man and I will not deny what I want no matter how long you deny me from gettin' it."

"Me? Am I the 'it'? I don't think I like that term, Frank."

"There are other terms. Would you like me to whisper them to you?"

She rolled her eyes, disguising her intrigue. "No." *I'll ask Colleen what the other words are.*

After a long moment, he asked, "Did you not like my kisses?"

Her body burned, the heat of his touch still warming her blood. "It was fine."

He laughed. "Pretty indifferent for a girl that's not done much kissing in her life."

She shrugged. She could be cocky too. Truth be told, she had to stop the kiss because the moment his lips touched her, her mind short circuited and she wanted to rip her clothes off and do all sorts of inappropriate things to him.

His arm slowly reached across the distance separating them, cupping her jaw as he dragged a thumb over her lower lip. Her breath trembled as she stared at him intensely watching the journey of his finger. The glass was beginning to fog. "Let me kiss you again, Maureen."

"O-okay." She should have said no, but what was the point? Nothing could be better for her in that moment than feeling his lips on hers once more. She was sure of it.

"Come here, love."

He pulled her hand and she scooted closer. Gently brushing the hair over her shoulder, he leaned close. Her spine elongated as his breath skated over her jaw and his lips pressed to the side of her throat. His palm glided down her back igniting a fire in her bones. Chills chased over her shoulders and under her clothes. Soft kisses traveled to her ear and down her jaw until his mouth slowly found hers.

Her lashes drifted close as her breathing accelerated. She

swallowed, parting her lips on a silent gasp as his mouth delicately closed over hers.

This time she was prepared—sort of. She waited for his mouth to open and when it did, she slowly teased her tongue with his and he groaned long and low, which she interpreted as him liking what she was doing. He pulled her closer, her body pressing warmly to his. Her lips closed over his, kissing gently in a rhythm that seemed right.

"That's it. Kiss me back, love." As he whispered, his lips still against hers, her flesh seemed to come alive.

Her heart raced as she lifted her hands and slid her fingers through his soft hair. How did anyone manage to have hair that silky? Rising to her knees, she crawled onto the seat and crept closer as he deepened the kiss. His hand slid lower, startling her as it cradled her behind, but then he slowly massaged and she pleasantly hummed into the kiss, lost once more.

The car became stuffy and a cramp was developing in her leg. She pulled away and looked around. People made out in cars all the time. There had to be a trick to it. "Should I lie down? Or should we go to the back?"

He frowned. "No."

"Oh." Self-conscious, she returned to the seat and fiddled with her hands as she glanced at her lap. Her dress was wrinkled and her stockings were slipping. She'd have to stop somewhere to fix her appearance before returning home, in the off chance that her father was still awake.

"You're a dangerous lass, Maureen."

"Why?"

"Because you make me forget myself. In about three minutes I'm going to leave and you're going to go home, as innocent as you came."

She frowned. "Why three minutes?"

"Because I can't quite stand at the moment."

She glanced at his lap and quickly looked away. "Oh." Averting her face, she smirked, feeling more powerful than Wonder Woman in that moment.

"You're rather pleased with yourself."

Glancing over her shoulder, she smirked. "Rightly so. Look at the mess you're in."

"Wench."

She sent him a promising look. "We don't have to stop you know."

Arching a brow, he asked, "To what point? Eventually we'll have to stop. I'd rather take it slow and pull back before I've lost total control."

"Are you saying a man can't stop if pushed too far?"

"No. I'll always stop for you, love. No matter what. I'm simply saying the closer we get the more painful stopping can be."

"You're in pain?" She didn't know men could feel pain from being denied.

"Not quite, but my body doesn't understand why we stopped kissing."

"So let's kiss some more."

His head tipped back as he laughed. "You're going to be the death of me. What happened to all those standards you barked at me ten minutes ago?"

"That was before I realized how fun kissing can be."

"My kisses," he pointed out. "Only my kisses. You wouldn't enjoy any other man's kiss."

She giggled. "You're a possessive thing."

"You bet your arse I am, woman. Remember that."

A sharp thrill raced up her spine as his gaze turned territorial. She smiled. "I will, so long as you remember I'm the same."

"I will." He glanced at his watch and frowned. "It's getting late. What time's your ceremony tomorrow?"

"Four."

"I'll be waitin' for you at the edge of the field where the big sycamore grows."

Stunned he intended to attend her graduation, she smiled. "Okay."

He leaned forward and brushed his lips lightly across hers. "Good night, love."

"Good night—" She wanted to call him something sweet like love or dear, but lacked the courage.

He climbed out of the car and she immediately missed him, despite still being able to see him. The tail lights of his truck lit and he returned to her door, carrying her purse.

Sliding behind the wheel, she rolled down the window. "You'll be needin' this I assume."

She took the bag. "Thanks. And thank you for fixing my tire."

He cupped her jaw, his fingers chasing over her chin and teasing the slight bow of her lips. "Any time. Drive safe."

As he pulled away he took it slow, as if waiting for her to safely follow. He kept with her until she turned at the light in town. She watched as his lights worked up the mountain in the distance where he'd driven her the day they met. She didn't know anyone lived up there, but now she was curious, curious about all things Frank McCullough.

CHAPTER 3

Frank waited for the crowd to break up as he leaned on the trunk of the sycamore tree. It had been years since he'd been on that field.

He'd stood through close to a dozen speeches and nearly six hundred names just to watch her get her diploma. Though all the women wore the same emerald gowns, Maureen wore it best. Her fiery red hair a sharp contrast to the dark green, her eyes vibrant under the green brim of her cap.

He was smitten. Typically he'd be ashamed at having such a reaction to a woman, but no one seemed to notice. His best friends, who would typically break his stones for such nonsense, were dealing with the same—all three of them under the spell of an O'Leahey woman.

Poor Liam was buried with the undertaking of O'Malley's, but Frank didn't have sympathy to spare for the man. No, all his pity went strictly to Paulie who was facing a life of matrimony to Maureen's sister Colleen. He loved the girl, but wouldn't marry her for a million dollars.

Maureen was different from her sisters, sweet yet feisty. She turned him on with just a smile and a quick flash of those sharp jade eyes. Aye, he'd definitely had his fair share of fantasies about her, but he needed to cool it until she was legal. Unsure if she was telling the truth about saving her virtue for her husband, he might be facing a longer sentence than what he was geared up for, yet he wanted her too much to walk away now.

It pleased him that she was the marrying type. So many woman foaming at the mouth these days to join the work force, he'd lost hope for finding a lass that shared his somewhat dated values. But Maureen was different and stunningly beautiful to boot. When he looked at her he saw life—a life he definitely wanted to grab hold of with both hands, knowing she could take a good squeeze.

Cap gone, the flash of copper hair was easy to spot. He grinned and fluffed the blooms in the bouquet that had wilted in the heat. The closer she came the faster his heart beat until finally her emerald eyes met his and she smiled.

Turning to the woman next to her, she excused herself and slowly walked to him, her gown flowing in the subtle breeze. She took his breath away faster than he could get it back. He wondered if he'd ever breathe right in the presence of Maureen O'Leahey.

"You came!" Her face wore a touch of rose from the sun that day.

"Aye. I brought these for you." He held out the flowers and her eyes went wide.

Slowly, she took the blooms. Her copper lashes lowered as she breathed in the soft fragrance. Her gaze returned to his and she grinned softly. "You're a sweet man, Frank McCullough."

"It's an important day for you."

"Maureen." Her expression turned apprehensive as her father called from about twenty paces away.

"You should probably return to your family," he suggested.

She hesitated, glancing over her shoulder at her mother and father. "Wait here."

Skipping off, he watched as she waved her hands, expressing each word she spoke as she likely asked permission to leave with friends. He knew there would be issues with a man seven years her senior gifting her with flowers and compliments, but perhaps the right thing to do was to act honorably and be upfront with his intentions.

Clearing his throat, he strode to where she spoke to her parents. "Pardon. I wanted to introduce myself. I'm Frank McCullough."

"Oh, I know who you are, lad," her father said, eyes shrinking with scorn. "What I don't know is what you think you're doing with my youngest daughter."

"Shamus," her mother gently scolded. "He's Colleen's friend. I'm sure his intensions are good." Her accent was thick, traces of Maureen's voice stretched over broken syllables and throaty elocutions.

"Quiet, Mary. How old are you, son?"

"I'm twenty-five—"

"And my daughter is seventeen. You keep away from her, understand?"

Stepping back, regretting he'd made the mistake of approaching her parents, he glanced apologetically at Maureen. Her brow creased and her face flushed. He'd expect to see a sheen of tears in a typical woman's eyes, but none were in hers. Those wild sage eyes darkened to emerald as she scowled furiously at her father.

"Say your goodbyes, Maureen. We'll see you at the car."

Mr. and Mrs. O'Leahey walked off and Maureen stared after them.

"I'm sorry," he said, hoping she wasn't too upset with his interference. "I only meant—"

She quickly turned. "I'll meet you here in two hours. By then everyone will be gone."

"But your father said—"

"Are you going to fight for me or not, Frank McCullough?"

"I don't want to fight your father, Maureen. There are ways around this. Perhaps if I speak to him again—"

She waved away his words. "The man is as stubborn as a mule. If he gave Rosemarie her blessing to marry a man that stole from my mother's family—"

"What? Liam doesn't steal."

She grinned, cheeky and full of secrets. "Did he not tell you then? My mother is first an O'Malley. That bar belonged to her cousins."

He laughed. "I didn't know. But now it's her daughter's, so perhaps Liam's actions were not that criminal after all."

"My point is, my relatives were livid, but my parents still allowed Liam and Rosemarie to wed. All you're askin' for is a date. He'll have to accept that."

But he was asking for much more than a date and her father likely knew that. Gently, he clasped her chin in his fingertips. "You're a force to be reckoned with, Maureen."

She laughed. "There'll be no reckoning with me once I get something in my head. My mum says I'm difficult."

"Aye." And he wanted to take her, with all her stubborn difficulties and turn her soft like he had before. She was a temptation he had no comparison for. "I'll see you in two hours, love."

She nodded and bustled away, flowers fisted in her hand, gown flaring behind her like a queen.

"FRANK…" her breathy sigh met his ears as he struggled to slow down.

The inside of the truck was hidden behind steamed glass and her plush little body cushioned him. Her mouth tasted of sweet cherries and her hair smelled of lemongrass. Her skin was soft ivory and she was wearing far too many clothes.

As her thighs bracketed his hips, his body rocked over hers. His pants were about to burst. He needed more. Anything. Sliding his hand up her calf and over her knee, he found the top of her stocking and glided his finger across the soft flesh there. She sighed and pulled back, her lashes slightly lifting.

"Your skin is so soft."

"No one has ever touched me there," she whispered.

"No one?" Could she truly be that virtuous?

Her head shook. Only a few inches and he could be inside of her. Honor battled with selfish lust and he—painfully—forced his hand out from under her skirt and sat up.

"What's wrong?" she asked, her hair a tumble of red waves against his leather seats.

His body was on fire. "You undo me, Maureen. I have to remind myself how innocent you are."

"I didn't mind what you were doing."

He swallowed. "I minded. It's easy to get carried away."

She shifted and fixed her clothes as she sat up. Folding her hands on her lap, they silently stared anywhere but at each other for several minutes.

"Do you want me to go?" she asked quietly.

No. He wanted her to stay. "Perhaps you should."

Her brow creased. "Is it because of what my father said?"

"No, love. It's because of what *you* said. I aim to respect your wishes regarding your virtue."

"What if I wasn't a virgin?"

He laughed. "Well, then this conversation wouldn't be happening."

"So let's remedy that."

"Maureen!"

"What? It seems stupid to worry about such a thing that eventually won't exist. You're the first man I've liked, Frank. You can have my virginity. The way I see it, it's really just in the way."

She was out of her mind. "What about saving it for your husband?" Just yesterday she'd chastised him—*slapped him*—insisting she was saving herself.

She rolled her eyes and waved a hand. "You were being cheeky. Of course I wouldn't give you anything then."

He'd never met a woman like her. "And now?"

"Well...now you're being sweet and I rather like your hands on me."

His body shamelessly reacted to her words as his mind

begged his arousal to quell. "I'll not rush things with us, Maureen. It isn't right," he decided.

She huffed. Crossing her arms over her voluptuous chest, she threw her back into the seat. "Fine." A few minutes later she asked, "Do you think it hurts? The girl…it's supposed to hurt her."

Christ, she'd be the death of him. "I hear the first time for a woman can be uncomfortable, but it gets better."

"I'd like to get to the gettin' better part."

He laughed. "You're not familiar with the term playing hard to get, are you, love?"

"Oh, I'm not easy. I'm actually quite selective. You happen to appeal to me. That can change at any moment though, so watch yourself."

He chuckled and pinched her side, causing her to squeak and jump. "I think it's you that needs watchin'."

"It was nice that you tried to speak to my father today, Frank, even if it didn't go the way you wanted. I think someday he'll appreciate that."

He could only hope. "You look like your mother."

"I do. But I get my freckles from my father."

"I wonder if your children will be a clan of redheads with hot tempers."

She smiled softly. "I think a brood of blue eyed devils could be quite dashing."

Warmth spread in his chest as he imagined his own sons, perhaps a few daughters as well. "I think you'd make a fine wife, Maureen."

"You've not tasted my cookin' yet."

"There's lots to taste, but my gut tells me it will all be to my liking."

As their eyes met a thousand wishful thoughts seemed to

pass between them. What was it about her that was so unlike every other woman? He loved her fiery spirit balanced by her nurturing nature. To him, she was a perfect mix of all things feminine.

"How about a picnic tomorrow."

"Don't you have work?" she asked.

"After work. Do you think you could cook something for me, love?"

"What do you like?"

It had been so long since he'd had a home cooked meal made with love. "You decide. I trust your judgment."

She laughed. "Not a very wise thing to do, but I'll bring you something good."

HE DROVE her to a secluded section of the mountain where they wouldn't be disturbed. It was possibly a foolish move on his part, but he did it anyway. She'd packed a wicker basket that smelled sensational and carried a tartan blanket in her arm.

He spread the blanket so half was in the shade of a tall

maple and half was in the late sun. Maureen was indeed a gifted chef. As she unloaded Tupperware, steam rose from savory cuts of turkey, fluffy stuffing, and hand whipped mashed potatoes. Everything tasted even better than it smelled.

He ate until he was stuffed and Maureen seemed to take great pleasure in every bite he enjoyed. "You're an amazing cook, love."

"I'm glad you enjoyed it."

"Every bite." Lying on his back, he reached for her hand. His fingers gently toyed with hers and her head tilted.

"Why is it, when you touch me, I can barely think of anything else?" she asked.

"I feel the same. I don't know."

"Is it…did you find it was that way with other girls?"

"No. No other woman has done to me what you do, Maureen O'Leahey. You're one of a kind."

Her mouth curved sweetly as a blush stole over her freckled cheeks. "You just like my food."

"Your food, your smile, your smart mouth, your fine arse—"

She smacked his shoulder.

"It is a fine arse, love. You can't deny it."

He laughed when she glanced over her shoulder at her bum. "I see nothing remarkable about it. My thighs are thicker than tree trunks and my hips are too wide."

He frowned. "Your thighs are as they should be and your hips will be a blessing if you ever get that big family you want. Don't put yourself down, lass. It steals your beauty faster than any physical flaw ever could. You're lovely as you are. Don't ever question that."

"Even with this hair?"

"Especially with that hair." He watched her for a moment and suspected she was swiftly degrading every beautiful part of herself. Why did every woman have to nitpick? "That's enough," he said rolling her to her back and kissing her. "I'll not have you pouting on such a lovely day."

She smiled as his mouth teased hers. "That's a sure way to chase away my thoughts."

"Then every time I see you look a little sad I have to lay a kiss on your lips."

"Promise?"

"Aye. Promise." He kissed her long and deep and soon enough his body was fully engaged and wanting her more than ever.

Breathing heavily, he eased back as her fingers pulled at the tiny buttons at her chest. Her dress was the deep red of marigolds with tiny yellow flowers. The entire front was made of a line of buttons from her chest to her ankles. "What are you doing, Maureen?"

"Did you not want to see me?" she asked, a bit of worry clouding her eyes.

He swallowed. "I want to see you very much, love, but we should—"

"Then I'll show you." Her fingers continued down the line of buttons, not stopping until she was past her ribs.

He didn't blink and though every objection rested on his tongue, not a single word was spoken. Sitting back on his knees he waited, but she didn't move to part her dress.

"You do the rest."

His throat was bone dry. "The buttons?" had she meant for him to unbutton the entire outfit?

She nodded. "If you like."

In a trance, his hands slowly unclasped each button, his mind bargaining and promising he'd eventually stop before things spun wildly out of control. Little flashes of alabaster skin peeked through the red material as his breathing turned labored.

As he reached the last button he slowly swallowed. She'd kicked off her shoes and her toes were covered by stockings shades darker than her true pigment. He would not touch her—penetrate, he corrected, he would not penetrate her. Licking his lips, he parted the dress and unveiled her body.

Long, curvaceous legs, tapered at the ankle, plush at the thigh, were trapped in plain white garters. He admired her lower belly, concealed by all that women insisted to wear under their clothing, the shape of her full hips nipping into a trim waist. Pacing his breath, his gaze lifted to her breasts.

Full, ripe, and mouthwatering, they filled the slight fabric of her brassiere. Satin covered her nipples, but by the way she was breathing he could see the press of each tip through the material. Her breasts lifted as she quietly watched him, looking up at him with her hair spread over the tartan, shades of fire and gold spun within.

"You are lovely, Maureen."

"Do you want to see more?"

"No," he rasped. "I desperately want to know your body as well as I know my own, but that's for another day. I'm quite content to just look at you now."

"And what about you? I've never seen a man's body."

He arched a brow, liking her innocence. "Never?"

"Well, I've seen my little cousins when they were babies, but I'm thinkin' a man is quite different."

"Quite."

She lifted her shoulders, balancing on the backs of her elbows and causing her breasts to fill out more of the satin. "So shall we have a look at ya?"

"You'll be the death of me, Maureen O'Leahey."

"I haven't killed you yet." She arched a brow. "Come along then, let's get to some of those buttons."

"I'm afraid not. Not today at least."

She pouted. "Why?"

"Because with you lookin' the way you do, if my clothes come off I'll be sendin' you home with a souvenir in your belly." The warning did not have the effect he hoped. "What the bloody hell are you smilin' about? Do you want a baby now?"

Her grin grew as she brushed a hand over her flat belly. "It would be nice. I don't think waitin' several years will make me any better of a mum."

And oddly, he agreed with her. She'd make a fine mother. "My first born won't be a bastard. If you want my children you'll be takin' my name first."

"Are you offering, Frank McCullough?"

Was he? It seemed a mere thread, spun of fantasy and hope, separating where they were from reality. What stopped them from moving onward, marrying, and starting a family? "Aren't you afraid to marry someone you hardly know?"

She shrugged. "I'd think marriage would make you get to know someone better than any number of dates ever could. I'm willing to bet people date for years and still marry someone they never truly met. Every honeymoon ends."

"And you'd risk that?"

"With a man like you? Well, I think the odds are in my favor. I'm no peach."

Ah, but he bet she was as sweet as one. "Every peach can be a little tart at spots."

She laughed. "Are you calling me a tart then?"

"I'm calling you beautiful. Sexy. Lovelier than any sunset and brighter than any star." If anyone heard him spouting such sap he'd never live it down, but she had him under some sort of incantation.

"Now you can't say things like that and not kiss me—"

Kiss her he did, long and passionately. The heat of her bare flesh scorched him through his clothing. Everything inside of him wanted to run off with her and never come back. He'd never suffered such greed, such longing to possess another person. His mouth ripped away from hers as they panted.

Her head fell back and her fingers delicately toyed with his hair. "I'll marry you, Frank McCullough, if you asked me to that is."

His heart thundered so hard behind his ribs it nearly knocked him out. Slowly, he caressed the swell of her breast and she inhaled, filling his hand with soft, feminine flesh. "Christ, Maureen. You make it hard for a man to do right."

"If you gave me your word I'd let you have me now."

He shook his head. "No."

Her face lowered. "Oh."

He tipped her chin upward. "You listen to me, Maureen O'Leahey. I'd make you a McCullough tomorrow if I could, but your father would never have it."

"In a month, his opinion won't matter."

He shook his head. "You're a good girl. Your father's opinion of you will always matter."

"Yes, but it's my life and I'm the one who has to live it. I'm falling in love with you, Frank, and I don't know how to stop."

The world stilled as her words sank into his soul. That's what this was. Love. "I'm falling in love with you too."

She shifted, sitting on her knees, uncaring that her dress gaped wide. "Let's get married. I know it's soon, but who cares. Plenty of girls my age get married. What good would it do to wait?"

Suddenly everything was moving way too fast. He couldn't breathe and his fingers began to tingle. Standing, he paced. "You have to slow down, Maureen. We're rushing things. You only met me a few weeks ago." He wouldn't be panicking if such a large part of him weren't so eager to agree with her. That wasn't the responsible thing to do and he should know better.

"Wait for what? All my life people have told me to prepare for what comes after high school." She swung out her arms. "Well, here I am! What the bloody hell good am I? Sure, I can type and answer a telephone, but I'd rather put a pistol in my mouth than sign up for a life sentence of fetching coffee and having orders barked at me by someone I don't love."

"But you'd sign up to a lifetime of cooking and keeping house, changing diapers and mending clothes?"

"Yes, because those things would be *mine*. It would be a labor of love. What do I own if I'm only doing menial tasks for someone else?"

"You don't know if you'll feel that way in ten years. Women are different now. They want to work."

"And what happens in five years when I still feel the same and I've wasted time waiting for an unwanted epiphany. I know what I'm good at, Frank. I don't have many skills, but I know how to love and my mum taught me that's all you need to know to be a good wife and mother."

He stared at her, not completely trusting her certainty. She was young, too young to decide her life it seemed, yet he'd not changed much since graduating either. Maybe she was right. "Do you also know how to bake?"

She laughed. "I can bake a cake that will bring you to your knees."

He chuckled. "I bet you can."

She glanced down at her gaping dress and sighed. Shaking her head, she began fastening the long line of buttons. "I don't want to marry you anyway."

"*What?*" She'd changed her mind? After all that?

"What the hell good is a man that can't make up his mind? I need another indecisive person in my life like I need a third tit."

"Well maybe you'll be needin' an extra tit since you're in such a rush to run off and start having babies! For cryin' out loud, Maureen! I said we needed to slow down. Is it always all or nothing with you?"

She paused as if to consider this. "Yes."

He dragged his palm over his face and growled. "I'll bloody marry you!"

She stood. "Oh, forget it now. Any man that wants me, knows it. I can't have you hemming and hawing about, deciding it will only work if the weathers just right and my father's in an agreeable mood. We'll be waitin' 'til we're gray that way. I don't have time for that shit."

She snapped the last of her buttons and fisted her hands on her hips. "You can take the leftovers home, but I want my Tupperware back."

He gaped at her as she stood like an admiral about to go to battle over some plastic dishes. "You're crazy."

"It's top of the line Tupperware."

"I don't give a rat's ass about the damn dishes! I think you're certifiably insane."

She shrugged. "Maybe." She bent to fold the blanket. "This will need to be washed."

His shoulders swelled with each heavy breath as he watched her fold the silly blanket with a palpable air of indifference. He wanted to throttle her. She had him all over the map. One moment she was an enchantress and the next she was the most infuriating woman he'd ever stumbled across.

How could any woman be that stubborn, that rigid and decidedly set on something? She packed up the basket and shoved it in his direction, her face averted. "Here." She sniffled.

He took the basket and frowned. "Look at me."

"I don't want to look at you right now."

Dropping the basket to the grass, he reached her in half a step and turned her face. There, trembling above her copper lashes, was a wall of unshed tears. "You're upset."

She shook him off. "Don't be ridiculous. Upset over what? You?" She laughed. "I don't think so."

He grabbed her arm and pulled her close, not letting her escape this time. "You have tears in your eyes. Why?"

"Pollen."

"Liar."

"It's true. The air here is for shit."

"I've never heard a woman curse as much as you."

"Well, no one's stopping you from covering your fuckin' ears if you find my language so offensive too."

"Too? What else did I find offensive?" he asked, genuinely curious.

She laughed without humor. "Oh, please. I saw the way you looked at me, like some...*whore*." Her voice cracked and his heart pinched. "You make me practically beg for you to touch me, but you've touched other women."

Releasing her arm he stepped back and scowled. "I did not call you a whore, Maureen, nor did I look at you like one. You mistake respect for judgment. If you had as much respect for yourself as I do, we wouldn't be havin' this argument—"

The slap came out of nowhere. "Saying I have no self-respect is no different than calling me a whore, Frank!"

He caught her wrist and growled. "Now that's the second time you slapped me and I'm warning you now it'll be the last."

"Oh, so you're suddenly going to find manners?"

His nostrils flared as he let out a harsh breath. "You're eager for something you know nothin' about, girl."

Her arm tugged, but he wouldn't let her go. "Get your hand off me before I plant the heel of my shoe right in your crotch."

He was as equally turned on as he was furious, but something told him to heed her warning. He let her go and stepped back. "You need—"

"Shut up."

He turned, sensing he'd truly wounded her with his words, but unsure what exactly had pushed her past her limit. He didn't mind her in a temper, but the hurt he saw on her face now disarmed him. "I was going to say—"

"I'll meet you at the truck." She turned and bustled away.

Staring at the heavens he opened his hands in a pleading gesture. "She's a lunatic, isn't she? You sent me a faulty model." Grumbling, he marched after her. "Maureen."

She was already sitting in the truck, her head bowed low, clearly upset.

Refusing to let her leave angry, he opened her door. "Why are you ignoring me?"

"Leave me alone." She sniffled.

"Maureen." He grabbed her hand but she pulled her arm away as if his touch scalded her. "What the hell's gotten into you?"

Hard green eyes turned on him. "You called me 'girl' and accused me of being a naïve fool. I might mistake respect for judgment, but you mistake trust for desperation. I've never been like this with anyone else, Frank. How dare you make me feel foolish or tawdry for wantin' to be closer to someone I trust. Well, now maybe I am the fool."

His anger gave way as he thought about the harshness of his words. "I'm sorry. I didn't mean to make you feel foolish."

"It doesn't matter."

"It does to me, Maureen. I want you to trust me. I want you to feel free to ask me about anything, including intimacy, but I also want you to trust me that I'll not lose control. I turned you down because I don't want to do anything you'll regret."

"You called me 'girl'."

"You are a girl."

Her eyes met his. "But you said it as if I were less than you."

"No." He shook his head. "I said it because you were getting the better of me and I was frustrated. That's all. It was a foolish choice of words and I'll not use it again if it upsets you."

She nodded. "Thank you."

It seemed wrong, too easy to love her so fast and so much. Like a salesman presenting the answer to every prayer, it seemed only right to be skeptical. They barely knew each other, yet...he wanted her forever and his mind seemed set on that. How was that possible? "You frighten me, Maureen. I don't think it's right to fall in love this fast."

"Paulie's going to be your partner. He's your best friend and in a couple weeks he'll be my brother-in-law. I don't think there's a way we'll be escapin' each other."

"But that doesn't mean we have to get married."

"No, it doesn't. But I'll be wantin' to see you naked sooner or later and I'm not sure I know how to deal with such a chaste man."

He scoffed. Chaste? No. Shaking his head, he said, "Women don't typically voice their sexual appetites the way you do, Maureen. I don't know what to say when you say stuff like that."

"Oh, but it's okay for you to be sayin' you want to put your lips all over me?"

"I'm a man. It's different."

"That's another thing, Frank. I may be the sort of woman that wants to stay at home and raise a family, but I refuse to live by some double standard. If you want to reference my breasts, you bet your arse I'll be talkin' about your cock."

"Where on earth did you come from?" He'd thought Colleen was the crazy one. Clearly he was wrong.

"Center County."

It was getting dark and he was on the verge of losing his mind. "What is it you want from me, Maureen? I don't have the strength to fight with you and I'd never forgive myself if one of those tears fell."

"I told you, it's allergies."

"Just be straight with me."

She was silent for a long moment, some subtle insecurities showing through her impenetrable façade. Quietly, she confessed, "I like feeling wanted by you."

"Is there any question that I want you? I've made my feelings clear on the subject."

"You don't say a lot, Frank. I could talk a preacher to death, but you're quieter than a church mouse sometimes. I'm not always sure what you're thinking."

"Ah, well, mostly I'm thinkin' how beautiful you are. Sometimes I'm counting the different shades of red running through your hair. Other times I'm thinkin' how crazy it is that I've fallen for you this fast. And every now and then I'm thinkin' how quickly you could make me lose control."

"But you never lose control. You're always there, fixing my flat tire or rescuing me from the law."

"I can't help that you're a calamity," he teased and she smiled.

"I am that."

"Let's not fight then. Never doubt that I want you, Maureen. I do. But a little temperance never hurt anyone. We have the rest of our lives to make love. No sense in rushing into it, when everything's still so new to you."

"I suppose your right. I'm just afraid I'll wake up one day and you'll be gone."

"Where would I go?"

She shrugged. "Everyone's leaving these days."

Tipping her chin up he met her stare. "I promise you, I'm not going anywhere. Tell me you believe that."

She studied him for a long moment. "Is it too much to ask that you put it in writing?"

He laughed. She always surprised him and he knew, with her there would never be a dull moment. "Come along then."

Leading her out of the truck and back to the tree they'd picnicked under, he pulled out his knife. Choosing an area where the bark was somewhat smooth, he chiseled out their initials.

M.O. + F.M.
 Forever

"WILL THAT SUFFICE?"

She smiled. "It will. Thank you." She leaned up and placed a kiss on his cheek.

God help him if he ever broke his promise. He was pretty sure she'd win in any fight. "I'll take you home now, love."

"Okay."

And just like that she was content again. He was coming to realize dealing with Maureen was like dealing with a hot ember. Sometimes it looked mistakably cool, but one little jab and it was red hot again. He'd keep that in mind, because the woman certainly knew how to scold. He could only imagine how hot she'd burn in his bed.

CHAPTER 4

On the morning of July twentieth Maureen awoke with a sick feeling in her stomach she couldn't shake. Her breakfast didn't sit well and she turned down lunch. She'd helped her mother around the house all day, waiting for Frank to finish at the lumberyard, but no matter what she did, her stomach remained in knots.

"Do you want some ginger tea, dearie?" her mum asked.

"No. I'm not nauseous. I don't know what it is. Tension maybe, but God knows what I have to be tense about."

"He does and soon enough he'll tell you. You're guts likely givin' you a wee warnin', dearie."

Her mother had always claimed to have a bit of a third eye, believing that most women possessed some sort of psychic instinct. Maureen was more likely to believe she suffered from gas. But then she heard the sirens.

Center County was spread over a large bit of land, but its population was small. When sirens rung, chances were you knew the person they were headin' for. She quickly called her sisters to make sure everything was fine and then decided to take a ride. It was only natural to be curious when something happened in such a small community.

She heard the sirens for a while, but then they silenced. She couldn't locate where they were coming from. Every street she drove down showed no signs of distress. Normally, she wouldn't care so much, but there seemed to be at least three sirens and one was an ambulance.

Giving up, she pulled into the lot at O'Malley's and found her sister inside. She hadn't told Rosemarie or Colleen much about her and Frank, but thought now might be a good time. She had plenty of questions and the longer they dated the closer they came to crossing certain lines. Married or not, she was having sex with that man.

"Hey, Maureen. Did you ever find out what the sirens were for?" Rosemarie asked as she took inventory behind the bar.

"No. I drove all over town, but couldn't find where they were coming from. I need one of those scanners."

"The last thing you need is a way to interfere with the police. I'm sure we'll hear about it sooner or later. I just hope no one was hurt. I thought I heard an ambulance."

"Me too."

Rosemarie shrugged. "So how are things?"

"Wonderful, I guess."

She laughed. "You guess things are wonderful? Shouldn't you be sure before you upgrade from a general 'things are good'?"

"Can I have a soda?"

"Sure." She filled a glass from the tap. "Have you been spending much time with Frank?"

"Some. He works a lot. I'm stuck home with Mum all day. Maybe I should try to find work, because who knows how long I'll be waitin' to get married and take care of a house of my own."

"Please. I can't listen to any more bitching about mothers. You should hear what Colleen's putting up with. Paulie's mother is a critical nightmare. If she keeps it up she may move back home."

Colleen was now practically living with Paulie at his mother's. They called her Italian Mary. "But the wedding's in a week."

Rosemarie shrugged. "A mother-in-law can make a bride rethink a wedding."

Maureen frowned. Colleen would never leave Paulie. "Where's Liam?"

"He's in the back going over some bills. Things will be a lot easier once Colleen and Paulie are married and on the mortgage with us. You know, you could be a partner too. Maybe Frank would like that."

"What the hell's Frank got to do with it? He's not my husband."

Her sister shook her head. "You're so impatient. I'll tell you I've known Frank McCullough all my life and I've never seen him take an interest in a girl like he's taken to you. But I've also seen him struggle to keep up with you. You don't have a filter, Maureen. Frank's quiet. He hardly ever says more than two words. Getting him to say the right words is gonna take some time and forcing him is only going to make him clam up more."

"I'm not forcing him to do anything. He's the one with it in his head that we have to be married to sleep together."

"I think that's sweet."

"Says the woman having sex regularly."

Rosemarie arched a brow and pursed her lips. "You're not even eighteen yet. Calm your burnin' loins, woman. Jesus."

Maureen grumbled, crossing her legs. Burning loins indeed. That was probably why her stomach was in knots.

The door suddenly burst open, startling both of them as Paulie rushed in. "Where's Liam?"

"In the back. What's wrong?" Rosemarie immediately came out from behind the bar.

"It's Frank. Liam!"

"Frank?" Maureen slid off her stool and followed Paulie to the back. "What about Frank?" *Was there an accident at the lumberyard? The sirens.*

Her stomach tightened and she felt the blood rush from her face as Paulie, again, shouted for Liam. Unable to stay quiet another second, she screamed, *"What the hell happened to Frank?"*

Everyone stilled, their panic-stricken eyes set on Paulie's pallid face. He swallowed and rasped. "His father shot himself. He's dead. Frank found him this afternoon."

Rosemarie gasped and Liam cursed. Maureen grabbed onto the back of a chair as her knees gave out. Why? Why did this happen? He'd only just lost his mother. Should she go to him? She didn't know what help she'd be. What did someone say in a situation like this?

Oh, God.

"We have to go, Liam. He's all by himself at the house."

She didn't even know where his house was, only that it was somewhere up on that mountain. Liam stood and kissed Rosemarie. Maureen was still deciding if she should join them as they left. Too late. They were gone.

"Maureen? Maureen, are you okay?"

Her sister's voice pricked at the fog filling her mind, but she was too lost in worry to answer. A small glass was shoved in her face. "Here, drink this."

Whatever it was it smelled like gasoline and tasted like

fire. She coughed as it burned through her esophagus. *"Are you trying to fuckin' kill me? What the hell is that piss?"*

"Are you okay?" Her sister asked, pure concern in her eyes.

The knots in her stomach traveled upward forming a terrible lump in her throat that grew into something painful. She gasped and a sob slipped out. "He only just buried his mother."

"Oh, honey." Rosemarie pulled her into her arms and held her tight. "He's a strong man. He'll get through this."

Restless, she shouldered her sister off. "I don't know what to do. Do I go to him? Should I call him? I don't have anything to wear to a funeral. I don't even know where he lives!" she cried, losing more control of her emotions with every frantic word.

"Shh… we'll figure it out." Her sister nudged her into a chair and slid her another shot. "Drink that."

"I don't want it."

"Trust me. You do."

She tipped back the shot, this time finding the flavor a bit more tolerable, the burn slightly pleasant. "What should I do, Rosemarie? Tell me what grown women do in situations like this."

"Well," her sister started, pouring a shot for herself. "I suppose we cook. He'll be drinkin', that's for sure. Liam said he had a hell of a time after his mother died. We might as well make some casseroles to sop up all the booze."

Her only condolence was that he was closer to his mother than his father. Perhaps this wouldn't hurt him as much.

She loved both her parents, but losing her mum would destroy her. Strange, that after all her father had done for his family her heart still belonged to the woman that nurtured them on a regular basis. Mothers always got the most love. Maybe that was why she wanted to be one so badly.

She sat with Rosemarie until late that night, making grocery lists for recipes they'd be making. Colleen showed up a little after seven, but even she was not her usual upbeat self. Liam called the bar around nine, but the only report Rosemarie got was that Frank was "not well." When asked if he thought it might help for Maureen to go to him, he said no.

It hurt, more than Maureen would ever let the others know. She refused to make this tragedy about herself, yet knowing he wanted his friends and not her, broke a part of her heart.

Frank didn't have any brothers or sisters. He only had his friends. Maureen couldn't imagine her life without her sisters and perhaps there would be a time when she'd want them over Frank. It was moments like this that she realized what Frank had been trying to say. She didn't have the life experience to understand certain things yet.

It wasn't her fault. Experience would come. Moments like this were all part of becoming an adult. Realizing not every bit of adulthood would be free and fun gave her pause and she finally saw the value in a little patience.

Her mother always told her God would someday punish her with a child sharing all her sins. Maureen didn't believe such nonsense. On the other hand, if that was true she'd likely mother the most impetuous girl Center County's ever known. She shuddered at the thought. Maybe God would let her practice on some easy children before giving her the difficult ones. Either way, she'd love them all.

The following day her mother helped her prepare one recipe after another. They worked in silence, Maureen's worry taking her words away and hiding them far from her voice. Typically, she wasn't a quiet girl, but nothing seemed worth saying on a day like today.

As they wrapped up the dishes her mother quietly asked, "Do you love this boy, Maureen?"

She folded the foil over a dish of chicken casserole. "How do you know when it's love?"

"I suppose you just do. I think it's when you can't stomach the thought of a life without that person, but it might be different for everyone, dearie."

Maureen used a marker to label the casserole. "Then yes. I love him very much."

"You know, your father will come around once you turn eighteen."

"I don't see what kind of difference six days will make."

It would be a busy week. Rosemarie called that morning to say the funeral, a small closed casket affair, would be Friday morning. Colleen and Liam's wedding was Saturday. And Sunday was her eighteenth birthday. Who knew if Frank would even be in the mood to celebrate?

"That should do it. You'll need a truck to deliver all this stuff," her mother announced, jarring up the last of the gravy.

"Thank you for helping me prepare all this, Mum."

Her mother smiled. "Of course, dearie. That's what family does. Do you want me to help you load it into the Ford?"

"No. I'm going to call Paulie first to see if he thinks it's a good idea for me to drop it off."

"Why wouldn't it be? You're his lassie. I'm sure he'd be relieved to see you—especially bearing dinner."

She swallowed. "Okay."

She didn't have the nerve to ask for directions, afraid if one of the guys found out she was going there they'd talk her out of it. Rather, she drove to where he'd carved their initials in the tree and then sort of let herself get lost from there.

Several times she'd decided to give up, but she was too confused to get off the damn mountain. She couldn't quit if she wanted to.

Just as it was getting dark she spotted a one-story house in the distance, small and in need of new siding. As she drove closer, she spotted Frank's truck and relief stretched inside of her.

She parked beside his truck and used a kerchief to blot some of the sweat off her nose. Though the sun was setting it was still humid.

Deciding to leave the food in the car until she was sure he was home, she took the steps and knocked. The doorbell didn't seem to be working and the steps were rickety. Lace curtains bluffed in the windows, likely chosen by his mother, but much of the male upkeep seemed overlooked.

She knocked again.

When he didn't answer, she called through the open window on the porch. "Frank?"

"What are you doing here?"

Startled, she gasped and turned to find him standing by her car. "I…wanted to see how you were doing."

"I just hosed my father's blood off the shed. How do you think I'm doing?"

Her stomach shifted and her eyes rolled back. Suddenly queasy, she reached for the railing only it shifted unstably. Trembling, she folded her arms over her stomach. "Oh."

"Yeah. You should go."

He was being so short with her. "I brought you some food."

"I'm not hungry."

"It's casseroles. You can freeze them for later. My mum and I spent all day making them. They're going to spoil if we don't move them to the Frigidaire."

"Why are you doing this?"

She frowned. "What…" Hurt he'd think she had some motive other than checking on him, she said, "What do you mean? I want to."

He shook his head. "Don't you see, Maureen? The men in my family aren't well. My mum, I swear she died of a broken heart. It didn't matter how much I loved her. Her husband didn't."

"Your dad wasn't well, Frank. And I'm sorry for that, but you're not him."

"Time will tell. I can give you all the sons in the world, but they'll never make up for a husband that ignores you."

He was hurt and lashing out. She didn't want to drop to his level, but at the same time, his words were cruel and got her Irish up. "Have you been drinking?"

"I've had a few."

"Bottles or glasses."

"All of the above."

Frustrated, she pressed her fists into her hips. "Well, if you'll help me unload the food I'll leave you to it."

She marched past him and unlocked the trunk. Three boxes of casseroles filled the area. She reached for the lightest one holding mostly gravies and sides. "Will you grab the big one? I'll get the door."

The crease in his brow smoothed. "You made all this for me?"

It was silly, but all she could think to do. "A man's gotta eat."

He nodded and picked up the largest box. The second she opened the door her nose twitched with the urge to sneeze. It seemed their house hadn't been dusted since his mother passed. She followed him to the kitchen.

The home was nice, but small. Actually, it wasn't nice at

all. She didn't know how to label it, but it felt vacant, hollow, as if it were once a home but somehow lost its soul. The dining room table was covered with paperwork. "Are you working on something?"

"This is all my dad's stuff. Turns out he had a bit of a gambling problem. I'm trying to straighten a few things out, locate a couple deeds and such."

She sensed his tension and wondered if his father's bad habits affected the lumber business. Frank had been running things for a while, but everything was in his father's name. Strange that he'd choose today of all days to go through such paperwork, but maybe he was desperate for a distraction. "Can I help?"

"No."

Her shoulders drooped with his fast rejection. She'd honestly wanted to do whatever she could to make this easier on him, but he didn't seem to want her assistance at all. "I'm sorry about your dad, Frank."

He nodded once and remained silent.

He didn't want her there. "I'll get the last box and then I'll go."

"It's heavy. I'll get it."

"You're sure?"

He shot her a look and left her alone in the dusty dining room. Maybe she could clean it up for him. She'd be lying if she denied being a little freaked out by the dusty clutter. His father shot himself right in the backyard. But so long as she didn't look back there, she saw no harm in being there.

Without invitation, she opened the fridge. A pizza box and a six-pack of beer were all that filled the shelves. This would never do.

She removed the box, gagging when she saw the gray cheese and carried it out front. Frank frowned at her as she tossed it on the porch. "You're pizza's growing fur," she called, turning back to the kitchen before he could stop her.

When he placed the last box on the counter she was done wiping out the fridge. The icebox really should be thawed and cleaned properly, but they needed to get those casseroles into the chilled air.

Once she had the food put away, she used the boxes for trash and found a dishrag and soap and got to wiping down the counters. There were some charming patterns hidden under the dust and it made her miss a woman she'd never met. She bet Frank's mum was a sweet lady and they would have gotten along nicely.

He never stopped her, just watched from the corner of the room as he sipped his beer. She didn't mind so long as he stayed out of her way. She preheated the oven and pulled out a dish of cabbage and corned beef. Scrubbing the windows, she struggled to get the jammed ones open and let some fresh air in the house.

"Let me," he said as she pounded the heel of her palm on the stubborn frame. He grunted, gave it a knock, and the glass lifted.

"My hero."

He watched her, his eyes no longer scowling, but dark with something else.

"Where's your sweeper?"

He disappeared and returned a moment later, vacuum in hand.

"I'll be needin' some lemon polish too if you have it."

She got to vacuuming, spending a great deal of time on the furniture. In the hutch she found placemats and dishes, so she set the table. When the oven beeped the house was much tidier than she'd found it. "Wash up. Supper's ready."

He dutifully scrubbed his hands and sat at the kitchen table, his head bowed over his plate.

"Do you not like cabbage?"

His finger traced the eyelet pattern of the yellow placemat. "These were my mother's. I haven't seen them in a while."

"I'm sorry. I saw them and figured…" She stood, ready to carry away the plates and remove the placemats. "I wasn't thinking."

His face lifted and she stilled, finally seeing the pain he'd been hiding. "Thank you for doing this for me, Maureen. You have no idea what it means to me."

His gratitude filled her heart with warmth. Taken off guard, she was somewhat speechless. Her bottom dropped to her seat. "Well… let's eat before it gets cold."

They ate in silence. Frank had three helpings. She wasn't sure when he'd last fed himself, but she was glad to satisfy his hunger. It was the least she could do.

After supper, she washed the dishes and returned them to the hutch. She found Frank standing in the dark front yard when she was finished.

"I should be going."

His stare seemed fixated on the highest point of the mountain in the distance. Nothing but wide-open space. She wondered how much of the land actually belonged to his family. It would be lovely to have a house up there someday.

He turned but didn't step toward her. "Thank you again for the food and for cleaning. You didn't have to do that."

"It was my pleasure. If there's anything else you need…" She decided in that moment that if he asked her to stay she would.

"You should go."

Again her heart tightened, but she told herself he was

only creating distance in order to act honorably. "Goodnight, Frank."

"Goodnight."

Accepting he wouldn't change his mind, she walked to her car and stilled. Shit. "Can you tell me how to get to town?" Maybe now he'd ask her to stay, since giving directions could be tedious.

"Take this road about two miles until you see a water tower to your left. Turn right and follow that road. You'll go around a large lake until you pass a wide-open field and a small rancher. Turn left at the rancher and that will lead you to town."

"Or I could stay," she blurted, realizing she wanted to stay.

"I'm drunk, Maureen."

Disappointed, assuming if he'd been sober he would have accepted her offer, she lowered her head. "Okay. Call me if you change your mind."

"Drive safe."

She knew he wouldn't call and the next time she saw him would be at his father's funeral.

CHAPTER 5

War was a nasty thing. Maureen tried to avoid much of the post-war articles in the paper now that things were ending. She'd been born during a war and wasn't sure what happened when a country stopped fighting. How long until the repercussions truly ended? Perhaps never.

A soldier shouted a sharp order and his men shot into the air. It was expected, but Maureen couldn't help the flinch that came with the crack of each blast. Three bangs echoed through the mountains and Frank didn't blink an eye. He stood at the head of his father's casket, stone-faced, as the trumpets slowly whined the tune of *Taps*.

The solemn melody silenced and the soldiers carefully gathered the flag, making a production of folding it intricately. Birds flew overhead, cars drove in the distance, as life went on, this one laid to rest.

When the flag fit in a tight triangle, the soldier turned and handed it to Frank. He looked so lost in that moment, an orphan on his own, amongst people that loved him—yet he refused to let anyone in.

Her chest tightened as her vision blurred. The priest made a final blessing and everyone stood.

A yellow rose was passed to her and she placed it on the coffin. Frank didn't move. He simply stared at the gathering flowers holding his father's flag, his expression vacant of any emotion.

"Is there anything afterwards?" her mother whispered. "McCullough is Irish. There should be a wake, no?"

"I don't think so, Mum." It would be tacky to tell her mother that the funeral likely cost Frank more than he could afford.

"Do you want me to wait for you, dearie?"

"No, I'll find a way home."

Her mum nodded and patted her arm.

People whispered condolences and quietly returned to their cars. She glanced at Colleen and Rosemarie. Liam came to her side and whispered, "I asked him to come back to O'Malley's with us, but he won't. Maybe you could talk some sense into him, Maureen."

"Thank you, Liam. I'll see what I can do. Maybe we'll meet you down there."

He nodded and kissed her cheek. "Good luck."

Her sisters gave sad smiles and turned with the men toward the cars. The priest left with the funeral director and in the distance men waited to bury the casket. She slowly approached him.

"What the priest said was nice."

"Aye. It would've been nicer if he knew my father."

She glanced at the men by the backhoe. "Do you want to go somewhere? We can go to O'Malley's, or to a diner, or to your house, wherever you want."

He glanced at the cars snaking their way out of the cemetery. "Everyone left?"

"They didn't want to bother you, but they're only a phone call away if you want them to come back."

"No." He glanced at her, his eyes pained with denied grief. "You stayed."

"Of course I stayed. I'm your…"

His eyes met hers as his brow creased. "Neither of my parents got to meet you."

Her vision blurred as a lump formed in her throat. "I'm sorry, Frank. I'm so sorry you have to feel this grief and suffer such a loss. I wish there was a way I could take some of the pain from you, but I don't know how. I feel so unprepared for this."

"You stayed. That means something." He moved the flag under his arm and took her hand. "Will you come home with me?"

Relieved he was letting her in, she rasped, "Yes."

They walked to the car and drove to his house in silence. He was likely hungry. She hoped he'd left a casserole out to thaw otherwise dinner would be tricky. When they reached his house there were more papers on the dining room table and a sink full of dishes. He'd been eating her food and that made her happy.

He took off his suit jacket and draped it over a kitchen chair. She checked the fridge, but it was empty. Removing a casserole from the icebox, she started on the sink full of dishes.

"Don't bother with that."

"You have to eat. Once the sink's empty I'll fill it with warm water to speed up the thawing process. I can probably have you fed in a few hours," she explained, busily scrubbing what was filling the basin.

He stood behind her, his hands resting on her busy arms. "Is this what being married to you would be like?"

She smiled, warmth comforting her heart at such a fantasy. "Perhaps."

His lips pressed to her cheek. "It's nice."

The resounding truth that no one was home and this was now Frank's house, continued to play on her nerves. "Why don't you go relax while I get dinner started?"

He chuckled. "Already barking out orders like a good wife."

Normally she'd scold him for such a comment, but he was only teasing. He kissed her cheek again and a few seconds later the sound of the television kicked on. Was this what it would be like? It seemed so natural.

Once the glass dish of the casserole was soaking in warm water, she abandoned the kitchen to find Frank. He was sleeping on a chair in the den. Carol Burnett's voice echoed from the set. Maureen lowered the volume so he could rest.

She wandered through the house and stopped at the wedding picture in the hall. Frank's mother was tiny. How had she managed such an enormous son? Again, patience seemed wise where children were concerned.

Standing at the threshold of a bedroom, she noted the large bed and dated furniture. Deciding this was his father's room, she carefully shut the door.

The next bedroom was definitely Franks. The walls were orange and the carpet a hideous blend of browns. The bed was large and unmade. The furniture was nothing fancy, the largest piece dominated by a record player and speakers that were ridiculously huge.

Seeing his personal space made him seem more attainable. It showed shades of boyhood. She couldn't help but fix his bed. As she adjusted his pillows something caught her eye. Stuffed between the mattress and the wall was a magazine. She carefully pulled the book free so not to rip the pages.

When she saw the cover she gasped. A woman wearing only a string of pearls and covering her breasts with her hands bent over a bale of hay. "Well, that's no way to clean a barn." She tsked. *"Entertainment for Men,"* the cover read. Opening the magazine she gasped again as her bottom dropped to the bed.

Woman after woman posed topless. Some were even completely nude. She grumbled and snapped her tongue against her teeth. "Honestly, who plays guitar in the jungle without their knickers? Fastest way to get a tick bite." Shaking her head, she turned the page. They were all sexy in a way she was not.

"Catching up on your summer reading?"

She jumped and chucked the magazine on the other side of the bed. "You scared me. I thought you were sleeping."

"I was."

"Oh. Well…I made your bed."

"That issue's about five years old. I can't tell you the last time I looked at it."

Her cheeks heated. "Why do you still have it?"

He shrugged and picked it up off the floor, tucking it back under the pillows.

"Do you like looking at those women, Frank?"

"I'd rather look at you."

Good answer. "Well, none of them look like me so maybe you should toss that magazine in with the rubbish."

He picked it back up and dropped it into a wastepaper basket beside the bed. "Done."

"Well, good. I'm glad that's taken care of."

"Anything else?"

He was standing right in front of her, so close she found it difficult to concentrate. "N—no. I think that about handles it."

"How long until dinner?"

"The casserole has to thaw and cook still. We have at least an hour before I can put it in the oven."

"Give me your hand."

Slowly, she placed her fingers in his and he tugged her to her feet and turned her so she faced the bed. It was a big bed. Her heart raced as the heat of his body pressed into her back.

"You look very pretty today, Maureen. Is this a new dress?" His finger traced the boat neck collar.

"It's Rosemarie's."

"Mind if I take it off?"

Her chest lifted as she silently panted. "The—the zippers on the side." His hand dragged beneath her sleeve slowly raising her arm.

The sluggish pull of teeth echoed in the silent room as the zipper came loose and cool air caressed her hip. Her body trembled as his finger lifted the hem of the dress, pulling it over her shoulders and off her arms. "And this?" he asked, giving her bra strap a little tug.

She stiffly nodded and his fingers unclasped the covering. The brazier slid from her arms and her breasts hung heavily over her ribs. What if he found her lopsided or pudgy? Self-consciously, she covered her breasts.

"Do you want me to stop?"

"I don't know. I'm just a little nervous."

"There's no need to be nervous with me, love." He gently turned her shoulders and her feet shifted over the carpet, her T-strap Mary Janes awkward on the shag. "Let me see you." His fingers closed over her wrists as he gradually guided her arms away.

She couldn't look at his face so she stared at the buttons of his dress shirt.

"You're lovely." Bending close, his mouth closed over her shoulder and her nipples pulled tight as she swayed into him.

The heat of his hand cupped her, his calloused fingers slowly chafing the sensitive tip. Breath shuddered into her lungs as his grasp turned firm, possessive. His face pressed into the curve of her shoulder. "Maureen…I want you so fiercely I can't breathe."

Her trembling fingers tugged at his shirt, loosening it from his slacks. She unfastened the lowest button and then the one above as his mouth greedily kissed and sucked at her neck.

"What are your doing to me, woman?"

She fought with a stubborn button. "I'm tryin' to undress you, but your shirt's being a bastard."

He stepped back and her hands dropped to her sides. She watched as he slowly unbuttoned the rest, never taking his eyes from hers. As he parted his shirt her breath caught. "You've got so many muscles."

"I climb trees all day."

She nodded. "Aye. I think that's a fine job for a man."

He chuckled. "Do you want to take these off?" he asked, giving her garters a slight tug.

She nodded and moved to the chair in the corner of his room. Curving her leg, she unbuckled her shoe and placed it to the side, sitting its partner with it. "I've never undressed for a man before."

"And you never will again. Only me, Maureen. No one else sees you this way, understand?"

She nodded, finding that rule agreeable.

Once she had each strap undone, she slid the garter belt

over her hips and down her legs. When she stood, she was in only her panties and stockings. "All of it?"

He nodded. "If you don't object."

Thinking of the women in his magazine, she placed her foot on the seat of the chair and slowly rolled the stocking down her leg. It was sort of like being in a bathing suit, but not really. Unsure if she could go any farther on her own, she faced him, her eyes pleading. "Frank?"

He stood, understanding this was a lot for her, and waved her back toward the bed. Without words, he comforted her. His hands caressed her throat as his eyes looked into her soul. Bending to her height, he kissed her passionately and lifted her off the ground. Her legs wrapped around his hips as the room spun and he sat on the bed, holding her.

"You undo me, Maureen. Every knot inside of me tightens when you're not around and as soon as you're near all the tension unravels and goes away. How do you make that happen?"

Her arms wreathed around his broad shoulders as she kissed his rough jaw. "I don't know, but you do the same for me."

He lifted her again, this time pressing her back into the bedding. His mouth caressed hers, desperation hidden deep in the kiss. "I never felt as alone as I did this week, Maureen, and then you showed up. You take care of me even when I don't deserve it."

"Of course you deserve it, Frank." He rolled her to the bed.

"No." His head shook. "I was being a coward. I wasn't going to see you anymore, because I was scared. You make me feel so damn much I don't know what to make of all these emotions. I don't want to love another person if they're only going to leave me."

"I'm not leaving you. I already told you I'd marry you if you asked."

"But you also said you wouldn't."

She waved off his words. "That just means you ask again in five minutes once my temper settles. I'm a woman, Frank. I get pissed off easily, but I get over it."

He stared at her, his fingers brushing the hair away from her face. "Be my wife, Maureen O'Leahey. I want you in my home, my heart, my bed, and in the eyes of our children. I want you in my life—forever."

Her chest swelled, all obvious consequences shrinking into insubstantial nothingness. She smiled and whispered, "Yes. I'll marry you."

He grinned and pressed his forehead to her chest. "You make me happy, Maureen. I promise I'll be a good man to you always, love you even on your worst day so long as you promise the same to me."

"I promise."

He kissed her and laughed. "I suppose I'll need to see your father. Perhaps now that you're turning eighteen he'll be a bit more reasonable."

She wasn't a disobedient child, but enough was enough. "I'd like nothing more than to have my father walk me down the aisle of our parish church, but his blessing will not decide my fate, Frank. I want to be your wife and I will."

His grin was steady and sincere. "Remind me never to go against you, lass."

"We'll be married. You're bound to go against my wishes sooner or later. But you'll learn."

He chuckled. "Will you spend the night with me?"

She debated. Tomorrow was Colleen's wedding. Her parents couldn't very well be mad at her during such an important event. After that she'd be eighteen, her own person.

"You don't have to," he said when she took too long to answer.

"I'll stay with you."

He stared at her for a long moment. "I love you."

"I love you too, Frank." Her future husband. It was surreal, but seemed so right, so natural.

His lips closed over hers in a slow, drugging kiss. Her body awakened as he caressed her breasts and dragged his heavy fingertips over her body. His skin was so much rougher than hers, such a delicious contrast to her in size and texture.

His arousal dug into her belly as things turned heated. Her fingers massaged the thick muscles of his shoulders as her legs curled over the backs of his thighs. Her panties were in the way as much as his pants, so she reached for the buckle of his belt but he stilled her.

"No."

"I want to," she argued.

His breathing was harsh and she sensed his control slipping. "So do I, but we can wait. We can do it the right way, the way your church says."

"My church says we're only to fornicate when trying to create life."

"Then we're going to have a lot of children."

There was so much longing built up inside of her she was ready to burst. "I don't want to wait."

"Just a bit longer. We'll have a short engagement."

"How short?"

He laughed. "Let me have a word with your father again and we'll discuss it tomorrow. I haven't even given you a ring yet, Maureen. Be patient."

"I don't know how."

"Wantin' all those kids, you better learn," he teased and bit her shoulder. "Let's try to get some sleep."

"Naked sleep?"

He shook his head. "I'll keep my pants on. You can't be trusted."

She sighed, but grinned as he pulled her body close to his and tucked them under the covers. For the first time in a very long time, she felt right as she shut her eyes, his arms holding her tight. She decided to rest a bit and then let him sleep so she could get him fed—like a good wife.

"You may kiss the bride."

As Colleen and Paulie sealed their nuptials, Maureen watched Frank. He knew she was watching him, because he kept shooting her flirty winks and his lips would curl into a half-smirk. He looked very handsome in his tuxedo.

The organ cried and the newlyweds led the way out of the church. Colleen made a beautiful bride. Maureen wasn't so sure about the yellow dresses she'd insisted the bridesmaids wear, but Frank seemed to think she looked nice, so she supposed it wasn't too bad. Between the stiff lace collar, the puffy sleeves, and the frothy skirt dyed lemon yellow, Maureen felt like a cupcake.

Outside of the church the sun was beaming. They'd sure earned a nice day.

"Maureen, come take a picture with your sister," her mother called and she dutifully stood beside the bride.

Guests gathered on the church steps, tossing rice and

congratulating the couple. Maureen tried to imagine what such an event felt like as a bride, but she couldn't seem to summon the vision. She would be next, Frank standing as her handsome husband, yet the image of them standing together on these steps eluded her.

Trying to escape to a patch of shade, she slipped out of the crowd. By Paulie's car, decorated with ribbon and tin cans, she found Frank and smiled. Though they'd been together all afternoon, she'd yet had a chance to speak to him.

He tipped his head toward a nook in the stone of the church where a basement door showed and she followed him into the breezeway, her heart prancing at the chance to be close again. Stepping under the overhang, she grinned as he kissed her.

Her heart pounded as his mouth tilted over hers and his hand slipped beneath the bun of her hair. Forcing herself to pull back, she pressed a palm on his heart and amazingly felt it beating behind his breast pocket. "We're at church, Frank."

"God knew I was going to do that. We had an arrangement. I stopped obsessing over your beauty during the sermon in exchange for a kiss after the ceremony."

She arched a brow. "God agreed to that, did he?"

"Aye."

"Maureen!" She jumped at the hiss of her mother's voice. "Come out from there before Father Mark sees you—or worse, your father."

Elbowing Frank in the ribs, she quickly went to her mother. "Sorry, Mum."

"For the love of Mike, you can't go neckin' around church property. Tis' a sacred place! Christ, we'll be lucky if a bolt of lightning doesn't strike you dead by day's end," she mumbled, bustling back to the wedding party.

"We better get up there for pictures," she told Frank and he nodded.

The photographer was a snooty old bastard who acted as if he were being paid for his services in pudding rather than money. Every shot seemed an inconvenience and Maureen wasn't sure why anyone would work as a wedding photographer if they hated weddings so much.

"Just the men now," he called.

Thankfully, Colleen decided to take pictures at the church so they weren't in the heat, but despite the fans and high windows, in their fancy clothing the air was sweltering.

"Now the parents of the bride and groom." Her mother and father walked to the front of the church where Paulie and his mother waited with his new bride.

Paulie's mother was reed thin with the sharpest cheekbones Maureen had ever seen. Her shrewd eyes watched the photographer as her fingers, adorned with large ruby rings, smoothed her black hair.

The flash went off with a pop. "Now the groom and father of the bride."

"Oh no you don't," Paulie's mother snapped, waving her bedazzled finger at the photographer. "I pay you good money to take good pictures and I will not have one of me, my beautiful son, and his new family when I was not even looking." Her accent was a thick rolling rhythm of unbending Italian.

"The bride has a long list to get to—"

"And you will get every single photograph, but you will take it properly. Do it again, now."

Frank chuckled and whispered in her ear. "That's why they call her Italian Mary. No one messes with her. She'll put the *Mallocchio* on him."

Frowning over her shoulder, she asked, "The what?"

"Evil eye. Italian superstition."

"Surely Father Mark can only permit us in the church for a bit longer, ma'am," the photographer said.

"I'd do as she says, son," Father Mark grumbled from the pew and Frank chuckled again. No wonder Colleen was going crazy dealing with her new mother-in-law.

When the photographs were finally finished to Italian Mary's specifications, they traveled to O'Malley's, where the Cloony's had set up a feast. Much of the guests were already drunk from having to wait so long, but the wedding party wasted no time catching up, Colleen leading everyone in a whiskey toast after their father gave an Irish blessing.

There were far too many guests to sit comfortably anywhere, but that made it a little easier to sneak away. Frank caught her hand and pulled her to the back of the bar where they raced down the hall, laughing as they dodged Italian Mary coming out of the ladies room and quickly slipped into Liam's office.

"Are we allowed in here?"

He shut the door and stared at her with dark, lust filled eyes. "Liam won't mind."

She caught her breath as he approached, backing her against the door. "I keep wantin' to kiss you, but we keep gettin' interrupted."

She couldn't take her eyes off of him. He was so intense sometimes. "Then kiss me now."

"Oh, I intend to Maureen O'Leahey."

His lips brushed hers as she lifted to her toes, reaching for him. His tongue slowly slipped into her mouth as his hands crept down her back and over her behind. She gasped into his mouth as he squeezed her there.

His hands always knew exactly where to touch her, how

to hold her in a way that made her feel delicate and completely feminine, but never threatened. He was a giant next to her, yet always so gentle.

"I want to strip you down to your knickers and have my way with you, love."

"Okay."

He chuckled. "So hard to get."

"I want to be got."

He chuckled again and there was a sharp knock at the door.

"Frank?" It was Paulie.

"Go away."

"Colleen's dad is looking for Maureen. You better get back to the party."

His forehead pressed to hers as he whispered, "I need to speak to your dad. I don't like runnin' around hidin' like this."

She nodded. Everything would be a lot easier if they could be open about their relationship. "My mum doesn't seem to mind you."

"That helps."

When they returned to the party everyone had bellies full of food and whiskey and they were dancing to the band Colleen hired. "Perhaps now's a good time," she suggested as she spotted her father sitting alone watching the others dance.

Frank didn't look thrilled at the task. "Aye." Giving her hand a squeeze, he let her go and walked to her father.

Maureen watched as Frank's posture took on a non-threatening presence, his hands hanging humbly at his side as he begged for her father's blessing. Her chest constricted as her father's brow creased over his fiery red eyebrows. It was said she earned her stubbornness from her dad. There was no one more pigheaded than Shamus O'Leahey.

When her father stood, nearly knocking his chair to the ground she gasped. Stout and bow legged, he still assumed a threatening presence. She knew Frank failed when her father jabbed a thick finger at his chest and waved him away, ignoring his presence.

Frank's head lowered as his shoulders drooped. Maureen's teeth ground tight as she scowled at her stubborn dad. She marched toward her father's table.

"Maureen, don't," Frank said, catching her arm, but she shook him off.

She marched right to her father's side and demanded his attention. "Do I not deserve the same happiness you granted Colleen and Rosemarie?"

Her dad turned to her slowly, hardly investing an ounce of concern. "Your sister's wedding is not the time to discuss this, Maureen."

She leaned close and hissed, "Is it too much to give me your blessing? Frank is a *good* man. He's honorable and he loves me—"

"Honorable?" her father snapped. "Is he not the same man I forbid to see my underage daughter more than a month ago? What sort of honor is that, to go against my wishes? Now you're believing you're in love with him when you're too young to know the meaning of the word."

His accusation infuriated her to near tears. Tightening her lips she stood up straight and whispered, "I *do* love him, Daddy. Tomorrow I'll be an adult and your blessing won't be needed. But it was wanted. I'm sorry you couldn't understand that." Her arms shook as her voice quavered. "I love you, but I love him too and you can't get in the way of that."

"Maureen, tomorrow may be your birthday, but you still live under my roof. Now that is enough of this nonsense. I'll have no more of this discussion. That man comes near you again and I swear to St. Peter I'll aim my rifle at him. Now go see to your sister like you're supposed to be doing."

A sob worked its way up her throat, but she forced it back. She spun away and weaved through the cluster of finely dressed tables and abandoned chairs. Frank called her name, but she ignored him.

Colleen, dancing and laughing on the dance floor with her many guests, was in no need of her maid of honor. Her father had just wanted to make her feel bad.

Choking back too many emotions, she kept her head down and lips tight until she found the exit. Pushing through the heavy doors with too much force, she fisted her hands on her hips and let the door slam behind her.

Outside, the sky was dark and the air was muggy. The door opened and closed behind her as Frank slowly approached.

"I'm sorry, love. He's a stubborn man."

"He's a jackass."

His hands rested on her shoulders as she stared into the night, fuming with impotent rage. "Give it time."

Turning, she faced him, her mind reeling with a need to escape and her muscles jumping with the urge to run. "Let's run away, Frank."

"What?"

"Take me somewhere, somewhere away from here."

"Maureen, I can't—"

She grabbed his wrist and turned his watch into the moonlight. Eleven twenty-three. "I'll be an adult in less than an hour. It'll take them that long to even realize I'm gone.

Take me away, Frank. I want to go somewhere I've never been, do things I've never done, feel things I've never felt. And I want to have those things with you."

His eyes creased with concern as he silently debated.

"Please, Frank." Her vision blurred as she stared up at him. "I know what I want and I'm tired of people assumin' I'm too naïve to choose what's right for me. You're right for me, more than anything else in this world. I love you. If you love me, take me away from here."

"Aye, Maureen. I'll take you away." He kissed her quickly and took her hand.

The thick evening air chased up her skirts as they ran to his truck, her laughter ringing through the silent night. He started the truck and she grinned. Rolling the windows down, she scooted next to him on the seat as he put the truck into drive.

"This damn gown is strangling me," she announced, snapping the pearl buttons at the back of her neck with a tug and tearing away the lace gauze choking the life out of her bosom.

"You are a fearless woman, Maureen."

She laughed and threw the lace collar out the window as they raced down Main Street. "I have plenty of fears, but so long as my courage outweighs them I'll be fine. Go faster, Frank. Make it seem like we're flying."

He squeezed her hand as she rested her cheek on his shoulder. His foot pressed into the gas pedal as they sped away, flying off where no one could reach them.

"Am I makin' a mistake, Rosemarie?"

Her sister's sigh carried through the phone. "Do you love him, Maureen? I mean really love him, so much so that when you hate him with everything you have that love will survive?"

She couldn't ever imagine hating Frank, but that was just naïve. "When he drives me crazy I still want him to kiss me. Is that the same?"

"Not really, but maybe," her sister said.

Maureen looked down at the dress she'd borrowed from the innkeeper of the boathouse. "I wish you could be here, you and Colleen."

"See, dearie, your mind's already made up."

She lightly ran her fingers over the fringe of a doily sitting under a message pad. "Do you think Dad will ever forgive me?"

"You're his daughter. He'll have to." Her sister hesitated. "Maureen, do you have any questions…about tonight?"

She bit her lip as her cheeks heated. "Does it hurt?"

"Only for a pinch. Get the first time over with, then ride him like a sailor on leave."

She laughed. "I've never sailed before."

"You're a quick learner. I love you, Maureen. I think Frank's a fine man and he'll make you a fine husband."

"Thank you, Rosemarie. Truly." The innkeeper peeked her head into the office and nodded. "I have to go now. Tell Colleen for me, when you see her."

"I will. Take care, dear. Call me tomorrow."

Setting the phone in the cradle, she looked to the innkeeper.

"Your groom is waiting."

Her legs trembled as she slowly stood. She was getting married, promising her life to another person until the day she died. So help her God if he turned into a putz she'd have his balls.

She paused to glance in the mirror. Her red hair was braided around her head, baby's breath pinned in a crown. She hadn't thought to bring makeup, so her face was bare, wearing only her natural blush.

She'd cut a yellow strip of lace and used it to tie back some daisies she'd found growing on the edge of the property. They were in a small town about four hours from Center County surrounded by a large lake. Frank had discovered the town when purchasing a map from a gas station along the way. Apparently, the boathouse was a famous escape for lovers to visit and elope.

"I'm ready," she said, picking up her bouquet.

Following the innkeeper to the den, Maureen steadied her breathing, but all bets were off the moment Frank turned from the mantle and set eyes on her.

"My bride," he whispered, meeting her in the center of the room and gathering her hands. "You're as lovely as a summer rain."

She couldn't manage more than a smile, her nerves jangling like rampant church bells. The officiant, not at all related to the Catholic Church, stepped forward. "Shall we begin?"

"Aye," Frank said, holding her hand as they faced the mantle.

"Love has brought the two of you here today, but marriage is not just about saying I love you today, but having a reason to say it every day, for the rest of your lives. Frank McCullough, as you look into Maureen's eyes, I ask that you always remember how you feel today. Maureen, I ask you the same.

"May your union be blessed with countless good times, but know that there will also be stormy times, times of sadness as well as joy. May your love weather the good and the bad through all of your tomorrows."

Her fingers tightened around Frank's as she tried to imagine the two of them years from now. Would they have a family? Perhaps be blessed with a son and a daughter? Or would it be just the two of them? It was overwhelming to imagine a home that did not yet exist or faces of children she'd yet to meet.

"Frank, do you take Maureen as your wife to live together in marriage? Do you promise to love her, honor her, respect her, and keep her for better or for worse, for richer or for poorer, in sickness and in health, forsaking all others to be faithful only to her so long as you both shall live?"

His fingers squeezed. "I do."

"Maureen, with this understanding, do you take Frank to be your lawful husband to live together in marriage? Do you promise to love him, honor him, respect him, and keep him for a better or for worse, for richer or for poorer, in sickness and in health, forsaking all others to be faithful only to him so long as you both shall live?"

Staring into his deep blue eyes she whispered, "I do."

"The rings."

The innkeeper placed a box on the pedestal holding the two bands they'd selected from the display, Frank's a simple gold band, hers an Irish Claddagh.

"The ring is an unbroken, never ending circle, symbolizing your undying love for one another." He handed Frank the Claddagh. "Frank, place this ring on Maureen's left ring finger, pointing the tip of the heart toward her wrist and repeat after me."

The band slid over her knuckle and Frank repeated after the officiant, his voice low and husky with implication. "This ring, a gift for you, symbolizes my desire that you be my wife from this day forward. As this ring has no end, neither shall my love for you."

"Maureen, take this ring, place it on Frank's left ring finger and repeat after me."

Her fingers trembled as she slid the ring over Frank's thick finger. She repeated, possibly speaking quieter than she'd ever spoken. "This ring, a gift for you, symbolizes my desire that you be my husband from this day forward. As this ring has no end, neither shall my love for you."

The officiant smiled and the innkeeper sighed happily, her hands clasped at her heart. "May the raindrops fall lightly on your shelter. May the soft winds refresh your souls. May the sunshine brighten your hearts. May the burdens of the day rest lightly upon you. And may God enfold you in the mantle of His love.

"Frank and Maureen, you have consented together in holy matrimony and pledged your vows together, exchanged rings as tokens of your love and commitment to one another, and in accordance with the laws of the state of Pennsylvania, I now pronounce you husband and wife. Congratulations Mr. and Mrs. McCullough. You may seal your vows with a kiss."

Laughter nervously bubbled out of her as Frank tugged her to him. "My wife," he growled, before sealing his lips to hers.

Rising on her toes, she wreathed her arms around his neck and took a deep breath of him. She belonged to him and he belonged to her. There would be no going back. Their course had been set. As much as she feared regretting her decision, everything inside of her fell into such a state of peaceful contentment she knew they'd made the right choice.

"I love you, Maureen McCullough," he whispered against her lips.

"I love you too, Frank. I will for the rest of my days."

He growled, the sound full of pleased satisfaction. "Shall I carry you to our room?"

The innkeeper poured two complimentary glasses of champagne and stepped out of the den. She grinned. "I'm eighteen now. I can have all the champagne I want."

"There's a lot you can have now," he said suggestively, shifting behind her as she reached for a glass.

"Oh." Her eyes went wide as she felt the hard edges of his body pressing into her softer curves.

"I want to take my wife to bed."

"But it's daytime."

"The better to see you, my love."

She guzzled the champagne without making a toast. "Can we do something first? You might think it's silly, but it would mean a lot to me…"

"What is it?"

She turned to face him. "There's a Catholic church

around the corner. I'd like to stop in there for a moment, since we couldn't have our ceremony blessed by a priest." It was silly. She loved Frank and their marriage would be a good as any other, but part of her ached for that sacred blessing her sisters could claim.

"Of course." The pad of his thumb traced over her lips. "We'll walk there now."

When they reached the church she was glad to find the doors unlocked. A few candles burned, but no one appeared to be present. Genuflecting at the front pew, she knelt and faced the Virgin Mary. Frank quietly kneeled beside her as she shut her eyes and prayed.

She prayed for her family, her sisters, parents, and her new in-laws. She prayed for her father's understanding and Frank's honor. But most of all, she prayed for the strength she'd need in the years to come as she dedicated her heart and soul to being the best wife and mother she could be. When she finished, she whispered the Lord's Prayer and made the sign of the cross.

Frank claimed to be Catholic, but she assumed he'd lost his faith somewhere along the lines of losing his mother and father. She believed she could help him find it again and in time he and the church would be reunited. For now, she simply appreciated his understanding that her faith was an important part of her life and upbringing, something she intended to pass on to her own family one day.

When they returned to the inn, the minister and innkeeper were absent. As they climbed the stairs she suddenly found herself wishing for more time, despite rushing toward this very moment since meeting Frank.

"Do not be nervous, love," he whispered, kissing her softly outside of their room.

She nodded and gasped as he swept her off her feet and

into his arms, carrying her across the threshold. Lowering her to her feet, he kissed her slowly, deeply, unraveling a great deal of her tension.

She'd wished she'd had the money to purchase something sexy for their honeymoon, but aside from the cost of gas and the price of the room, minister, and rings, they barely had enough left to eat.

Stepping back, she fidgeted. "I'll need a moment to…there are things a girl must do."

He nodded. "I'll be here."

Grateful their suite had a bathroom, she shut herself inside and stared at her reflection. With a deep breath, she carefully unzipped her borrowed wedding gown and hung it on the hanger at the back of the door. Standing only in her bra and garters, she unbraided her hair, carefully collecting the sprigs of baby's breath as a keepsake.

As her red hair tumbled free, it crimped in flowing waves. She unclasped her bra and carefully stripped away her stockings. Swallowing, she stared at her nude reflection, wondering what Frank would think of her. He'd seen her breasts, but nothing more.

She exhaled slowly and shut her eyes, recalling her sisters warning to get the first time over quickly so it could be pleasant for both of them.

The door clicked as she turned the knob. Frank sat up on the bed. He'd removed his shirt, tie, and cummerbund. The sight of his wide, muscled chest stole her breath.

"Jesus, Mary, and Joseph," he rasped, eyes wide as he came to stand before her. "It's not right for a woman to be so stunning."

His hand brushed her hair behind her shoulders, exposing her breasts. "I'll be askin' that you take off your pants now, Frank."

He chuckled. "What did I do to deserve such a curious wife?"

"It must have been something mighty good, because I'm as curious as a cat right now." She reached for his pants and he quickly stepped back.

"Whoa. Love, there's a way to things. You can't just go rushin' in head first."

She frowned. "But we're married now."

"Aye, and as your husband I plan to see to it that you enjoy your first time. If you don't take your time it might hurt you."

"Oh, but Rosemarie said…"

He shook his head and cupped her jaw. "Don't mind what your sister said. Her marriage is her own, and we'll be leaving them to it, expecting the same respect and privacy towards ours."

She understood his meaning. He didn't want her sharing their personal details with her sisters, the wives of his closest friends. Having always confided in Colleen and Rosemarie, it seemed a difficult promise to keep. "Can I tell them if I liked it or not?"

He chuckled. "So long as you tell me first. I'll be ensurin' you have nothing but rave reviews to take home to them."

"And what if—"

He cut off her words with a kiss. "You talk too much, love."

Thoughts scattered, as she nodded in agreement.

He kissed her again, but without haste. Every sweep of his tongue and touch of his hands had her body pulling tighter only to go lax in a rhythm that built and built. It was as if she were being lulled into a trance, her limbs loosening and her mind turning to some unrecognizably malleable home for her thoughts.

The fierce instinct to move that fueled her waking hours changed shape into something soft and trusting. Frank lay her down on the bed, arranging her arms and legs in a way that pleased him. His mouth kissed over her hips and across her belly as it became difficult to stay still.

Her body reached for his, her hips lifting slowly into him as her fingers curled into the sheets and her toes pointed. When his mouth closed over her nipple a sharp bolt of heated pleasure knifed through her and she moaned. His lips tightened as he pulled at the tip of her breast, his tongue teasing. Where had he learned to do such things? She decided not to think about it and told herself it was those informative magazines he read.

His fingers spread over her abdomen as though holding her to the earth when everything inside of her seemed to want to fly away. His knuckle teased the soft red curls at her apex and she stiffened.

"Relax, love. I won't hurt you."

Could he make such a promise? She forced her limbs to relax as he nudged her thighs apart. His hand felt large between her legs, making her wonder how his body would fit there. His touch was soft, caressing and cajoling as he pet over her delicate folds.

How strange to be touched so intimately. Tiny quivers of pleasure raced up her spine as caresses traced over especially sensitive spots. Her body seemed to open the longer he teased her there and suddenly there was an intrusive sensation.

She stilled, breath tight in her lungs as he looked down at her. "Breath, love. It's just my fingers."

She nodded, but didn't breathe. Slipping his fingers over her sex, she shifted, growing accustomed to his gentle touch.

What he was doing felt nice, but had her nerves jangling and her body trembling.

He pressed a finger deeper and a slight mew slipped from her throat. Embarrassed, she looked away. He withdrew the digit and her relief was short lived as he pressed it back in, causing another gasped cry from her.

"It's okay, Maureen. People make noise when they make love. It turns me on to hear you."

Her breath left in a rush as he penetrated her again, her body now slick, relieving some of the friction. A breathy gasp passed her lips as he bent and kissed her shoulder, his mouth making its way over the slope of her breast to her nipple.

His thumb crested a sensitive spot and she jerked, but his weight had become heavier, blanketing her. Shutting her eyes, she tried to make sense of what he was doing, imagining how his fingers could make her feel so many things.

Her throat turned dry, every breath scratching in escape, forming a steady rhythm of moans and gasps. He fit another finger inside of her and the pressure was notable. Perspiration cooled her skin as she spread her legs to accommodate him.

Kissing down her belly, the pace of his touch increased, pumping steadily inside of her as pressure built and built. Her lungs worked like billows, some internal flame heating to a scalding burn.

Pressing her thighs wide, the soft tickle of his hair whispered over her belly as the wet glide of his tongue shocked her senses. Soft, delicate kisses rained over her sex as his fingers sunk deeper until finally she was certain the innkeeper could hear her cries.

His fingers moved steadily while his tongue, so soft over her flesh, tormented some sensitive part of her and suddenly she was arching and crying in a manner she'd never heard or seen a woman behave. Clearly, this was wrong, but she couldn't stop. Whatever he was doing to her was stronger than her force of will.

Her heart pounded as her limbs shook, her entire body rocked as though little earthquakes were dancing about her skin. Her body became possessed by something dark and divinely addicting as he climbed over her.

Every breath tasted like her first sampling of air. Though her eyes were closed, she saw so many bright colors, some she didn't have names for. Her muscles, tight yet warm, stretched as the heat of his flesh burned against her inner thighs.

Her body was loose and wanting, but as the blunt tip of his cock pressed between her folds she tensed, fears of pain jolting her back to reality. He gave her no time to panic as his hips jutted forward and he pierced her innocence.

"Mother of Christ! You son of bitch!" she shouted as an ache spread deep within her. "You fucking impaled me."

His palms and fingers framed her face as his pleading blue eyes stared into her scowling glare. "I'm sorry, love. You're so small. I tried to be gentle. It won't hurt anymore. Take a moment to adjust." His lips pressed to hers as he silently whispered, "I'm sorry."

She frowned and tried not to concentrate on the sensation of him deep inside of her. She was stuffed fuller than a Thanksgiving Turkey. "What on God's green earth did your mother feed you? You're enormous."

He laughed. "If you're tryin' to insult me, love, you've failed."

She shifted, but he was bigger than an ox and there was little she could do under the crush of his weight. "Well, do something before you suffocate me, you ox."

His eyes widened and he immediately lifted a great deal of his weight off of her. "Sorry." He kissed her and his hips lifted.

It was a lot to adjust to. As he slid in and out of her, taking much more pleasure from the act than her, she frowned and considered why she'd wanted this so much. They had to be doing something wrong.

Suddenly she was thinking of Eve, the harlot, and blaming her for all this discomfort and then, as if there had never been any pain at all, her body reacted to something deep inside.

Her head tipped back as he thrust deep and she gasped. The muscles of his chest glistened and twitched as he looked down at her. His gaze was heavy and dark with lust. She held onto his thick arms as he rocked into her, delicious friction building.

"Is it better now, love?"

She moaned. "Much."

His hips snapped forward, hard and deep as he filled her. Her back lifted, arching. "I love you, Maureen. So much I ache sometimes."

"I love you too. I know that ache."

He kissed her. Her breasts shook with each hard thrust. Her feet found footing in the bedding and she lifted her body to him, meeting him halfway. His eyes shut as his jaw unhinged, a curse escaping his parted lips. She did it again and again, drawing vicarious pleasure from his.

He reached between their bodies and touched her, a thousand volts of electricity sharpening her senses, ripping a breathless cry of pleasure from her throat. His fingers teased and strummed, rubbing rapidly as pressure built and suddenly she was falling. Falling through time, falling through space, she lost sight of who she was, knowing only in that moment that she belonged solely to this man.

He trembled looking more vulnerable than she'd ever recalled seeing him and then his body slowly collapsed onto her, but this time she did not mind his weight. On the contrary, she relished it.

"Maureen," he sighed, using her name as if it were a prayer.

Catching her breath, she ran an unsteady hand down his back, her senses slowly tripping back to her as her body thrummed with resonating pleasure. She sighed. "How often can we do that?"

He chuckled and kissed her shoulder. "Aye, you'll make a fine wife, minx."

"I have a healthy thirst for knowledge is all."

"Aye, a thirst for knowledge and a hardy appetite for fucking."

She smacked him in the back of the head. "Don't be crass. It's our wedding day. We're making love."

He eased back and smiled at her, his hair a disheveled mess. "I thought we were making babies."

She gasped. "Do you think we did?"

He shrugged and kissed her sweetly. "That depends on your body I suppose. There are ways for women to figure out when the best time to conceive is."

She smiled, her heart warming at the idea that she could soon be with child. "Let's do it again," she whispered, wanting to heighten their odds.

He let out a hardy laugh. "A man needs a chance to catch his breath, woman." He rolled to his side and his presence was immediately missed.

Leaning up on an elbow, she smiled at him, her ear

resting on her palm as she dragged a finger over his chest. "I think you're rather sexy for a husband."

He tugged a red curl. "And I was just thinking how sexy my wife is. You look good tousled and well ridden. I like your hair wild like this."

"Mmm," she hummed. "Well loved."

"Aye."

With a mischievous grin, she lifted the covers and peeked under the blankets. He tugged her hair and she turned to scowl at him. "What are you pulling my hair for?"

"You know why, nosy. Give me a moment to get some wind back in the sail, before you go appraising the worth of the mast."

"Now, Frank, I've waited all this time, having you tell me no over and over again. I want to see my husband's cock once and for all."

He shook his head and laughed. "The death of me, woman. All right. Have your way."

She pulled the sheets away and gasped. "This is what was poking me?"

He smacked her bare arse. "Wench! Touch it and we'll see who the cocky one is."

Slowly, she ran her fingers over his length and his hips lifted as his flesh stretched right before her eyes, thickening and darkening to what she then agreed was an impressive size. "Oh dear. Now I've really started something," she teased.

He brushed the hair away from her face and watched her, a gentle hook to his lips setting his face with a contented grin. "You better finish it."

She moved to lie on her back, but he caught he arm. "Where are you going, love?"

"I was going to lay back for you."

His head shook slowly. "Stay there. Use your touch or your mouth."

"My mouth?"

"Aye. If you kiss a man there he'll be your slave for life."

She arched a brow. "But I thought you already agreed to be such when you promised to marry me."

He pinched her arse and she yipped. "Cheeky, woman. Are you just going to tease me or are you going to do it?"

"I'll do it. Quit your bellyaching. I'm just deciding how to go about kissing such a thing."

She leaned close and placed a small kiss at the base where his hair made a nest. This seemed to make him harder, but not necessarily bring him any pleasure. Gently gripping his length, she kissed the tip and he drew in an audible breath.

"That's it, love, stroke me firmly."

Her hand gripped him, gliding down to the root and back up to where she'd placed another kiss. She licked the tip and he hissed.

"Did I hurt you?"

"Not at all. Close your lips around me, Maureen. Let me feel the heat of your mouth."

She leaned over him and slowly closed her mouth over the tip, kissing and gently sucking. Her hand stroked over his length and he gathered her hair. "That's it. Just like that."

His voice turned strained and when she peeked at his face, his hooded eyes were intensely set on her. She sucked harder and his chest lifted, his nostrils flaring.

"Deeper. Take me deeper, Maureen."

Sliding her lips so they fit against the curve of her fingers, she glided her mouth down with her hand and he groaned, his grip tightening in her hair.

"Mercy," he breathed, applying pressure to the back of her neck.

It was more like sucking than kissing. Regardless, whatever she was doing he obviously liked it. He guided her, keeping his hand buried in her hair and soon it was his moans filling the room.

The fingers of his other hand teased the backs of her thighs as she bobbed over him, her pace quickening. It must have been quite the sight, her bare arse high in the air as she swallowed his cock, but he seemed to like it as his hand cupped her behind and squeezed hard enough to leave an imprint.

His possessive handling unleashed some erotic part of her and suddenly she was set on her task, determined to erase his memory of any other woman that might have touched him there before.

She was steadily working him into a frenzy when he turned the tables on her, slipping his fingers over her sex and knocking her off balance. She tried to concentrate on what she was doing, but he slid his fingers into her and her body fell into a fit of convulsions with barely a warning.

Resting her face on his thigh she cried out as her body tensed and pleasure burst inside of her. Every muscle quivered as he derailed her thoughts and brought her to a rapid release.

He dragged her up his body and kissed her deeply, his hold tight around her waist. Words whispered from his lips to hers in a language she didn't understand as he rolled her to her back and filled her in one smooth thrust.

Taking him to the hilt, she arched and cried out as he rapidly drove into her. He was relentless, needy, and sexier than sin. She clung to him as he took his pleasure, thrilled to provide such a thing for him, and realizing there was quite a bit of pleasure for the woman as well.

The harder he thrust into her the more evident it was

how gentle he'd taken her the first time. She rather enjoyed his roughness.

In a final push, he buried himself deep and let out a guttural howl as his head tipped back. His body pulsed within hers. Trembling, he lowered himself so they were chest to chest and kissed her jaw. "I love you, my beautiful wife."

She panted. "I love you too." Her head rolled to her shoulder. "Can we sleep now?"

"Aye. For days."

CHAPTER 7

The closer they came to Center County the more Maureen's elation turned to something unwelcome and frightening. Guilt, heavy and unpleasant, rested on her chest as she considered how her father might react. Chances were he was already furious. She'd left her sister's wedding and not been home for three nights, but little did he know that wasn't all she'd done.

"It'll be fine, Maureen. Don't worry yourself sick. I'll talk to him."

She'd seen how her father reacted to Frank's reasoning. "Maybe we should go to your house first."

"You'll be needin' your things, love."

When he wanted to be, her husband was quite unbending. It pissed her off, but she knew he was right, and in a way, she respected him for it.

All she could imagine was packing her belongings in a suitcase that technically belonged to her parents. With every mile it became more evident how unprepared she truly was for this moment. And though she'd done the most adult thing in her life, she never felt more like a child, her haste drastically discounting her maturity.

When they reached her street she panicked. "I can't do this."

Frank pulled over beside the large oak tree that shaded her bedroom. "Would you have us lie and say we're not married then?" He took her hands in his and kissed her knuckles. "He cannot do more than be cross with you, love. I'm your husband. I'll not let him put you down. We made a choice and it was ours to make. Ours. I won't let you bear the consequence alone, Maureen—ever."

She swallowed and nodded. "Okay."

He walked to her door and helped her down from the truck. Back in her sister's bridesmaid gown, now dingy and in desperate need of laundering, she followed the path to the door. The screen door whipped open and her father stepped out, fire in his emerald eyes, as the point of his rifle aimed right at Frank. "I'll thank you to take your hands off my daughter, boy."

"Jesus Christ, Dad! Put the gun away. Mum, Daddy's drunk!"

Her mother came rushing to the porch. "Damn it, Shamus!" She glanced apologetically at Maureen and Frank. "I thought I hid the last of his guns. Put that thing down before the cops are called by the neighbors again!"

Her father, only a hop, a skip, and a teeny jump away from being labeled certifiably insane, cocked the rifle. "I warned you. For three days you run off and now look at you, coming home shamed."

"That's enough," Frank said calmly, his fingers tight around hers.

"Mary, call the police and tell them that McCullough boy is trespassing on our property. I'll ask you to leave now. Maureen, get in the house."

Breath sawed in and out of her lungs and something inside of her snapped. "No, Daddy. I'm going with Frank. I just came to get my things."

"If you choose to live as some godless jezebel, you'll do it on your own. I did not provide a life for a—"

"Enough!" Frank's eyes were dark as fury tightened his jaw. "You will not speak to my wife that way."

Her mother gasped and her father paled, the rifle now aiming at the lawn, as he looked Frank in the eye and wheezed, "What did you say?"

"You can criticize me all you like, but I'll not have you insult my wife. She's a good, god fearing woman, and you have no right to call her such filthy things."

She was speechless and incredibly attracted to her husband in that moment, but then he took his defense of her honor a bit too far.

Frank lifted his chest. "Now you apologize to her."

The gun rose again. "Are you telling me, you wed my daughter without my permission?"

"Daddy, we asked—"

"I'm not speaking to you!"

"With all due respect, sir, I asked for your permission—"

"And I didn't provide it. So you went and carried on anyway, is that right?"

"Aye," Frank said, a bit chastened.

"And where exactly did this wedding take place?"

"An inn three hours east of here."

Her father laughed but didn't smile. "Get off my property, you thief. Maureen, if you want into this house then you agree now to annul this sham of a union. A proper marriage is promised before God—a *sacrament*. I will not see what the church cannot."

"Shamus," her mother whispered, but she knew her father wouldn't bend.

Maureen glanced at her mum. "I'm sorry you couldn't be there. It would be my only wish, had I the chance to do it over again. But I swear to you, I would make the same choice twice. He's my husband and I love him."

Her mother's hands drifted to her lips, fisting her apron as she held back her tears. She and Frank turned and, glancing back, she noted her father's expression showed no regret. He was a hard man and she disappointed him. Disagreeing with his stance did nothing to negate the shame disappointing her parents always instilled in her. The last thing Maureen heard before they pulled away was her mother promising her father she'd not speak to him until he made this right.

Frank's grip on the wheel was so tight the pink of his knuckles bled to white. He wasn't upset with her, but rather, upset *for* her. Altogether it was an unfortunate situation only her father could relieve.

The joy of matrimony was short lived as the recent turn of events repressed their elation. It was a physical battle, refusing the sobs fighting to get out, but she would not cry over her marriage. She was proud to be Frank's wife and nothing would change that fact.

When they reached his house she tried not to cringe. Something just wasn't right with that home. It seemed tainted with misery as though the sun never shined where it sat. It was impossible to imagine her life there, but she was determined to make the house a home once more.

"What the hell?" Frank frowned and marched up the

rickety steps. A yellow notice was taped over the door where it met the frame. Plenty of small print filled the page, but from where she stood on the scorched brown lawn, the only words she could make out were the ones printed boldly at the bottom. *Foreclosure Notice. KEEP OUT.*

Her heart sank as Frank cursed and punched the siding. Of course the house was in such ill repair it crumbled. She flinched and tried to calm him. "I'm sure this is just some misunderstanding. If we go to the bank—"

"There's no misunderstanding. On top of skimming every profitable cent from the lumberyard, my father was lousy at honoring his debts." He shook his head and ripped the notice off the door, crumpling it in his fist.

Perhaps that was true, but his father was sick. There had to be someone they could see about that. He'd come home from the war with a broken mind, the evidence in his recent suicide. Why should Frank be held responsible for his father's inability to meet society's standards?

He laughed derisively. "This should amuse your father."

"Let me talk to my mother. She'll talk some sense into him and we can stay there until this is figured out. I'm sure if you approach the bank and explain your father's passing, they'll give you a chance to square up his debt."

"Don't you see, Maureen? They're foreclosing. That's months of payments missed. I was worried about making August's mortgage. I don't have the money to fix this amount of debt."

There had to be some way to make this right. "What about the lumberyard? Maybe you could use the property as collateral—"

"Only a portion belongs to me. The rest of the mountain belongs to the family that owns the lake. I was hoping between Paulie and I, we could buy more acres, but that was before I realized how screwed up my father's credit was and the company's finances are." He turned and paced away.

She jumped as he suddenly kicked the crooked railing. *"Fuck!"* He continued to kick the broken post, knocking it loose from the floorboards and splintering the dried wood. "No good piece of shit! You didn't take care of her! You didn't look after me! What fucking good were you?"

Her heart broke as his anger unleashed on a deaf ghost. Helplessly, she watched as he raged, destroying the porch steps and cursing his father's grave. It wasn't right for him to have to deal with the mess his father had left, not when he had been responsible since he was a young boy. Where was the justice in that?

He drove himself into a sweat. Picking up a broken rail, he beat at the column barely supporting the awning. "You were never there for any of us and you're still sticking it up our arse from the grave!"

Maureen's eyes glazed as tears for her husband blurred her vision. Her heart broke for him. How difficult it must be to be a man, when he so clearly needed to cry, but this rage was all his pride would allow. The wood snapped and he threw it to the parched lawn, slamming his hand against the column and sliding to the ground.

Once he seemed through, she slowly approached, and rested a hand on his shoulder, squatting beside him. "It's okay, Frank. We'll figure it out."

He shook his head. "I have nothing to offer you, Maureen. I was a fool."

Her heart literally stuttered in her chest, his misguided sense of defeat terrifying her. Didn't he understand her love came without condition? She didn't need fancy things or a house to proudly be his wife. She only needed his love.

"You listen to me, Frank McCullough. You have plenty to

offer me. What use do I have for some rotted old floorboards and broken windows? This is just a shelter and we can find that anywhere. It's love that makes a home and so long as you love me, I have a place to live in your heart. I'll not sit here and listen to you put yourself down. Now, if you want my hand, I'm here, waiting to help you back on your feet. But beatin' the piss out of an already hurting house isn't going to do a damn bit of good. I know you're angry with your father, and that's fine, but you don't need him and you don't need this house to have my love."

She was out of breath as she scowled at him. She didn't expect to snap at him, but it seemed the only way to get through his thick skull. She was sure the last thing he wanted was to be yelled at, but he'd gone hysterical and he'd specifically told her not to smack him again.

He looked at her, his brow creased with confusion. "Where will we live?"

"You know how to cut wood. Build us a house if that's what you need. *Or,*" she emphasized. "You could focus on clearing up this debt and, once the bank's no longer threatening to take your land, we can rent a small apartment together like Rosemarie and Liam."

"That'll take some time."

She nodded. The time it would take was regrettable, but what else was there to do? She wasn't one to give up without a fight, not on something she wanted and she'd never wanted anything as much as she desired a life with this man.

She nodded and tried to get a smile out of him. "I'm told I need to learn patience. This is just the chance to practice."

He took her hand and kissed her knuckles, his fingers cut from his outburst. "I wanted our homecoming to be different."

She tsked and examined his fingers. "Look at what you've done."

"I'm sorry I lost my temper," he whispered. "All I wanted was to be enough for you, to be able to provide the beginning you deserve."

"If every beginning were the same easy fix, life would be boring. You *are* enough, Frank. Get it through your thick head." She took a ragged breath and slowly released it. "I'll just go back to my parents' and ask if we can stay there."

He shook his head. "I can't face your father until I make this right, love. It's a man thing. If he doesn't see me as a man, capable of providing for his daughter, he'll never approve of our marriage—and it is a marriage—a sacrament. I'll make this right."

"He'll see you trying."

"I'd rather show him me succeeding."

Her heart pinched, as she understood they wouldn't be living together and her vision blurred once more. "Where will you go?

"I can stay with Paulie."

"But he's married now and they already live with his mother."

"Aye. Italian Mary will be a challenge, but at least she'll feed me well—"

"Don't you go lusting after some other woman's cookin'. I don't care how old she is. You get excited about my food and that's it, you understand me?"

"Sorry, love. It won't happen again," he quickly said. In a more serious voice he went on. "But for now I'll stay with him in his brother's old room. I'll go to the bank tomorrow and see how much my father owes. So long as I can prevent them from foreclosing and get them to agree to an extension, I think I can fix this in time."

"You'll come see me every day?"

"Yes. You can come see me too, at work."

She smiled, not having thought of that. Perhaps she could bring him lunch so he'd know her cooking was better than that of Italian Mary's. "I'll do that."

He nodded. "I best take you home now."

She didn't want to go, but he'd need to go speak to Paulie before it got too late, otherwise he'd be sleeping under the stars. "Okay."

She was disappointed he hadn't kissed her before they returned to her parents'. "Will you come in?" she asked, hoping he would and maybe try talking man to man to her father, but he hesitated at her door.

"I think, in light of everything, it would be easier on everyone if I didn't. You shouldn't have to fight with your father because he hates me."

"He doesn't hate you, Frank. He's just a stubborn old bastard who's pissed off I disobeyed his wishes. He should have given us his blessing from the beginning."

"Maybe he was wise not to. Perhaps my father's reputation preceded him and your father was only trying to protect you."

She gripped his shirt and tugged. "You are not your father, Frank."

"I hope not."

"I know you're not. And you're too smart to doubt me when I've got my mind made up." She pressed her lips to his. "Go see Paulie and send my love to my sister."

He nodded. "I love you."

There was a sadness to his eyes she feared, one that she didn't recognize. Meeting his gaze as though the connection would solidify her word, she said, "I love you too, Frank. Always."

Solemnly, she took the steps. Her head hung low like a chastised young girl. As she stepped through the door, she heard the rumble of his truck pulling away.

"Maureen?" her mother called, coming around the corner, a dishcloth twisting in her hands. "What are you doing here? I thought you wouldn't come back."

All her efforts to remain stoic crumbled under the confession to her mother. "I need a place to stay, Mum." She angrily wiped at her tears, hating how fragile they made her appear. "The bank foreclosed on Frank's house because of his father's debts and we can't stay there until everything's straightened out."

"Oh," he mother whispered sympathetically, pulling her into a hug. "Where has your groom gone, dearie?"

"He didn't want to face Daddy, not until he's made this right."

Her mother nodded. "Your father's on my shite list anyway, the idjit. How about I make us some tea and we go to your room for a chat. I'd like to hear all about your wedding, love." She looked down, her expression sad. "I'd hoped…"

"Mum?"

She shook her head and waved away her words. "I'd always imagined watching my youngest get married. There were things I'd meant to tell you, Maureen, things a girl should know before her wedding night."

"I know, Mum. I'd talked to Rosemarie—"

"So your sister's knew then?"

"Only Rose. Colleen found out after we said our vows."

"Well." She patted her arm. "I'll get that tea brewing and you go get out of this dress. The collar's ripped and will have to be mended."

She nodded and went to her room. It hurt, knowing she'd

excluded her mother from something as important as her wedding and she wished there had been another option. Deep down, she knew the option was waiting, something her impetuous heart refused to consider at the time.

She decided in that moment, so long as her mother accepted her choice, she'd include her in all future life events. It was nice knowing one of her parents cared enough to want to be included. Her father might care, but so long as he ran around like a lunatic pointing rifles at people, she didn't hold much empathy for his point of view.

"You can just leave it there and I'll see that he gets it," the secretary said as she continued on her call.

Maureen's molars locked. It wasn't the older woman's fault her boss had missed an appointment three days in a row. How was she supposed to know he had a lunch date with his *wife*? She dropped the paper sack on his desk and left.

The following day when Frank was again missing, she'd had enough. Getting in her car, she followed the dirt road up the mountain to where she'd heard saws buzzing and men shouting. Paulie and Frank sat in the back of his truck with the flap down, eating something that looked like pasta. Scowling, she put the Falcon in park and grabbed his lunch.

When she slammed the car door, Paulie looked up. "Uh… Frank?"

Her husband turned and the smirk washed off his face. "Maureen, what are you doing here?"

She threw the bagged lunch at him and he grunted as he caught it against his chest. "You invited me," she growled. "But I see you've already eaten."

"I'm gonna go check on that thing," Paulie said, making his way over to the other workers.

"I've been busy—"

"You've been a coward!"

He drew back. "What?"

"I know what you're doing, trying to be the big man, bigger than any pesky problem. Well, guess what, Frank, hiding from your issues doesn't make them any less real. And how dare you lump me in with the problems you plan to ignore. I'm your wife, or have you forgotten?"

He came close to her face and growled, "I'm not hiding from anything."

Slowly, she said, "Oh, no, I've forgotten my shovel and I seem to be sinkin' in a pile of *bullshit!*"

"Go home, Maureen," he snarled.

"And where would that be, Frank? My parents'? You do remember how to get there, don't you? It's been a while."

"Last time I was there your father aimed a rifle at my balls."

"And he might as well have shot them off. Where the hell have you been? Five days, including a solid weekend, and I haven't seen hide nor hair of you!" She poked him in the chest. "Coward."

"I've been handling things."

"Like what? Have you talked to the bank?"

"Yes," he said, surprising her.

A bit of the wind left her sails and she blinked. "Well, what did they say?" Taking back a bit of her bravado, she reminded him, "As your wife I'd expect to know these things."

"You got an awful lot of demands, woman."

Strangely, she was suddenly torn between kissing him and clobbering him. Her adrenaline was tampering with her focus, so she decided staying angry was best. "Answer the question."

His shoulders lifted and sagged. "If I come up with ten grand by September first, I can buy back the property the house is on, but they're tearing down the house and everything in it is going to auction."

Her hopes crashed as her anger turned to sympathy. "Ten *thousand?*"

"Aye," he said still glaring at her. "So while you're throwing out accusations, maybe you could take a breath and consider how far away that is for me. I'm workin' late and doing everything I can and I still know I'll never make that. I don't have time to run all the way back to the trailer to meet you for lunch. Not when it'll cost me. I'm the boss, Maureen. Every minute my back's turned, my men are workin' half as hard as they should be."

She'd not thought about overtime or any such thing. Her mind was hung up on all of his possessions going to auction. "Your things…" It was all the memories he had left.

"A man doesn't need records and old toys. It's my pride they're taking from me and I don't expect you to understand how that feels."

His accusation stung and she scowled at him. "Do not talk to me like I'm a child that doesn't understand, Frank."

"And I'll thank you not to come here making a scene, disrespecting me in front of my crew."

Her lips firmed as she held in a slew of foul expletives. He'd never been angry with her before—never truly angry—and it hurt more than she expected. She wanted to hurt him back, but also wanted to stop fighting at once. Wounded that he would not see her as a partner and rather made her feel like the enemy, she took a step back. They clearly needed a little more space.

"Oh," she whispered, her eyes narrowing. "You'll not have to worry about me comin' here again." Turning on her heel, she returned to her car and white knuckled her way back to town. Her tears were unfortunate, but her fear for what might come between them was certainly worth crying over. And so she wept the entire way home.

"HE'S BEEN WORKIN' his arse off trying to make that money, Maureen. The man's tense and he ain't livin' with his wife so the stress has to be getting' to him. He needs an outlet,"

Colleen explained, brimming with untested marital wisdom.

"Sleep with him? After he spoke to her like that? Are you out of your fuckin' mind? Don't listen to her, Maureen. You did the right thing by settin' him straight," Rosemarie argued.

Maureen grumbled into the fruity concoction her sister mixed her. "Married a day longer than me and she thinks she's got the market cornered when it comes to matrimony." Raising her voice so Colleen could hear her, she said, "You live at your bloody mother-in-law's house in Paulie's childhood bedroom. What do you know?"

"I know how to keep my husband's temper in hand." Her sister arched a brow and she and Rosemarie rolled their eyes.

"An Irishman is different from an Italian," Rosemarie pointed out. "They've got more pride than commonsense. Dangle your womanly bits in front of an Italian man and he'll sell his pride just to have a ride."

"I resent that," Colleen snapped. "My children will be half Italian."

"And ours will be Irish, what the hell difference does it make?" Maureen was growing frustrated. "He's never taken that tone with me before. I offended him and I don't know how to fix it."

He'd offended her as well, but she'd already forgiven him, having the insight to know he was scared and hurting. In the course of a week he'd lost his father and his home. Then they'd gone and gotten married. Perhaps he feared losing his wife next. But Maureen would never let that happen. She selfishly loved him too much to let him walk away.

"Did you mean what you said when you spoke to him?" Rosemarie asked.

"Yes. He stood me up. I'm pissed off."

"Then be pissed, Maureen. Do you think he's not

worryin' over your feelings the way you're sittin' here worryin' over his?"

She frowned and stared at her drink. "I don't know."

"Listen to me," Rosemarie whispered, leaning over the bar. "He loves you. He's trying to figure out a way to make a home for you so you can have a right and proper marriage. He hasn't said much to Liam, but I know he wants Daddy's approval. Like I said, it's a matter of pride."

"All that pride sounds like a hassle to me," Colleen mumbled.

"Shut your face and finish your beer, you drunk wench. I wasn't talkin' to you," Rosemarie snapped. Softening her tone, she turned back to Maureen. "Give him a few days and see if he comes around. If he doesn't, perhaps you pay him another visit. Bees with honey."

"What does that mean?"

"It means you ain't gonna get anywhere shootin' off at the mouth, full of piss and vinegar," Colleen explained.

Rosemarie rolled her eyes. "She may be drunk, but she's got it right. Fightin' with him is only goin' to make it worse. You've got to be sweet."

Maureen pouted. She wasn't so sure sweet was in her nature, but she could try.

MAUREEN FROWNED into the rearview mirror and sighed. Giving up on her appearance, she climbed out of the car and walked to the trailer. She would not go in there full of piss or vinegar.

She knocked and the secretary called for her to come in. "Hello. I was looking for Frank."

The woman, who looked to be in her late forties, sighed. "Sweetheart, he doesn't come back for lunch. I've told you time and again—"

"I—I know. This time he wasn't expecting me. Is there a way to let him know I'm here? I need to speak with him." It had been two weeks and he'd made no effort to contact her and mend their relationship. Out of tears, Maureen was terrified her marriage was over before it even began, but she couldn't let that happen.

The secretary sighed again. "I can radio one of the trucks, but he doesn't like to be disturbed unless it's an emergency. Is it an emergency?"

No. "Yes."

"Very well then."

She swiveled in her chair and picked up a microphone that resembled a joystick. "This is Ruby. I have a woman here asking to speak to Mr. McCullough. She says it's an emergency."

"You don't have to say it's an emergency," Maureen whispered, but the secretary held up a silencing finger.

"I repeat, I'm looking for Mr. McCullough—"

"This is Frank. What do you need, Ruby?"

"There's a woman here that wishes to speak to you. She says it's an emergency."

"Who is it?"

Maureen rolled her eyes. Did he have so many women calling for him?

"What's your name, hon?"

She'd had enough. "Mrs. McCullough."

The secretary's eyes widened. Her fingers covered the microphone. "As in his..."

"Wife."

Her lips parted and she quickly turned back to the radio. "She said she's your wife. I didn't know you were married, Mr. McCullough."

"Put her on and give us some privacy please."

"Yes, sir." She stood and waved Maureen behind the desk. "Hold this and press that button there when you want to speak. Don't hold it too long or he won't be able to answer. I'll be outside." She tapped her back as she slid into the seat, her eye's apologetic. "I didn't know you were his wife. I hope I wasn't rude to you."

Maureen had too much to worry about to comfort the secretary. As soon as the door to the trailer shut, she pressed the button. "Frank?"

"Maureen, what are you doing there?"

"I didn't know how to reach you. I need to talk to you."

"You could have called Paulie's."

"I have. You're never there and Colleen says you haven't

been getting home until late." She swallowed. "Where do you go?"

The radio was silent.

"Are you there?"

"I'm here." He paused. "Maureen, Ruby said it's an emergency. Is something wrong?"

Her face lowered and she shut her eyes. Without pressing the button, she whispered, "You're breaking my heart."

Silence. So much silence.

"Maureen? Are you still there?"

She pressed the button. "I'm here. There's no emergency. I just wanted to see you and say I'm sorry about everything. I don't want you to be mad at me anymore."

His voice sounded low over the speaker. "I'm not mad at you."

"Were you?"

"For a bit, but I'm more mad at myself." There was a pause. "I have to get back to work, Maureen."

Every time he said her name it only reminded her how he used to call her love. "When will I see you again, Frank. I… miss you."

"I need more time."

She nodded then realized he couldn't see her. Her thumb pressed into the microphone. "I love you."

It took so long for him to answer she worried he'd walked away without a goodbye. "I love you too."

When she left the trailer Ruby smiled at her. Before then, she hadn't known the woman had teeth. "Come back any time, hon."

Maureen rolled her eyes. People. She'd usually have a clever remark on the tip of her tongue, but nothing came as the pain in her heart consumed all her thoughts as she walked back to her car—alone and still unsure of her marriage.

FRANK FINISHED his beer and tossed the empty can in the bed of his truck. He didn't even have enough money to get drunk. What the hell was he going to do? Whether he raised the money or not, the house would be gone. When he drove by today the furniture was already being repossessed and loaded into a truck. He'd paid the one worker a hundred dollars just to let him grab a few pictures and a couple of his mother's dishes, but that was all they'd let him take.

"Shit."

He'd made a terrible mistake. Maureen deserved a husband that could take care of her. He had no doubt he'd eventually get back on his feet, but the way things were going, that was a long way off.

Usually, parents left their children a legacy. All his father left was a long line of debt. If he weren't invested in the lumberyard none of this would matter. He could sell off the company and start over somewhere else. But he'd put too many years into that company and it held too much potential, despite his father's efforts to bleed the accounts dry.

It was a good business with the capability to feed generations. Unlike his father, he'd be damned if he left his children without a legacy to depend on. McCullough Lumber was just that, and he couldn't let it go, couldn't give up on the legacy his grandfather had started, the only legacy the McCullough family had left.

He sat, drinking like he had for the past fourteen nights, frowning into the darkness over the lack of options left. A night owl caught his ear and he peered at the tree in the distance, remembering how foolish a boy he'd acted when he'd first fallen in love with his wife.

She was only Maureen O'Leahey then and her future still stood a chance of being bright. Then she'd gone and tied her name to his and look at what had happened since.

Sliding off the tailgate of his truck, he walked toward the tree, tilting his head as he squinted into the dark. His fingers dragged over the shadowed bark. There it was, their initials inscribed above the word forever. What a joke.

He wanted to save her any way he could, cut her off from his struggle and set her free to choose again. His fist closed over his shirt, tugging as the pain built in his chest.

He didn't want to let her go, but what choice did he have? He couldn't take care of her the way a husband should and he would not be his father. She deserved the love of a spouse that could afford to be present in her day-to-day life.

His jaw locked as he breathed through his impotence to make a better life for her. Marching to his truck, he grabbed his ax and returned to the tree.

I'll always love her, but love isn't enough... Forgive me, lassie. I've led you down a spoiled path.

He swung and the blade embedded in the trunk. Jerking

his arms he pulled it loose and swung again, roaring with each swing, he hacked the trunk apart, but the damn tree wouldn't fall.

Working his body into a sweat, he roared, "Fall, damn you!"

The word *forever* mocked him. He swung and chopped as wood splintered into the air and dust burned his eyes. The tree finally wobbled and he doubled his efforts, determined to remove every promise he ever made her so she could go ahead and annul this mistake he'd convinced her to make.

There was a crack as he took a final swing and shoved the trunk with his boot. Stepping back, he panted as the tree went down—the world strangely silent around him.

"No more," he whispered, turning his back on his word.

He tossed the axe in the bed of his truck and stared at the mountain in the distance. Against the dark sky it was only an inky silhouette. Most wouldn't even know it was there. How could something so obvious be overlooked? He thought as his mind skipped and jumped in an angry haze of self-loathing. It didn't matter anyway.

Climbing behind the wheel of his truck, he grit his teeth and turned the key. Time to face the piper.

As he drove to her house, he thought about her stubborn nature. Her father was right and they should have listened to him. It would be difficult to explain that to her and she'd likely put up a fight, probably slap him once or twice too. Maybe if she hated him the task would be easier and she'd move on faster, eventually seeing this is for her own good.

His gut swirled uncomfortably at the thought of her moving on and he gripped the wheel so tight he was surprised it didn't bend. When he reached her house he decided to go right to her father. She was right. He was a coward, because no matter how he tried, he didn't have the guts to tell her it was over.

Climbing out of the car, he took the walkway, his steps slow and reluctant.

"Psst… Frank? Is that you?" Bushes swished in the distance and he frowned as Maureen let out a short yelp.

He frowned into the darkness and hissed, "Maureen?" What the hell was she doing?

"Bloody Christ," she cursed. A moment later she came around the corner, a twig stuck in her hair and a smudge of dirt on her cheek. She smiled and whispered, "You came!"

She was in a nightgown. "Where the hell are you coming from, woman?"

"What? Oh. I climbed out the window. My parents are sleeping. I didn't want you to wake them. I've been waiting for you. I hoped you'd come."

Guilt knifed through him. How many nights had she waited, hoping he'd show only to be disappointed? She loved him too much, more than he'd ever deserve. "I need to speak to your father."

She frowned. "Why? Did something happen with the bank?"

This was harder than he expected. He tried to stay focused. "No. Can you wake him for me?"

Scowling now, she stepped back. "What's going on?"

"I…Christ." He couldn't do this. "I'll come back tomorrow."

"The hell you will." She grabbed his arm. "I've waited weeks to see you. Come with me. We'll go out back. I have to talk to you."

Reluctantly, he let her tug him around the back of the house where a picnic table sat. She shoved him onto the bench and slid beside him. Her lips pressed to his neck and his body instantly reacted. "Don't you want to kiss your wife?"

God he did, but he couldn't, not when he'd come here to end their marriage. He swallowed, as her hand cupped his jaw and turned his face. The moment her mouth found his he was a goner.

His lips sealed to hers, as heat filled his lungs and desire exploded inside of him. God, he'd missed her taste. He missed everything about her, her scent, the feel of her hair in his fingers, the touch of her body to his. He wanted to strip her down and take her then and there.

He ripped his mouth away. "We have to stop."

"I know, but I can't help it. I miss you so much."

He carefully removed her arms from around his neck. "Maureen, we need to talk."

"I know we do. I've got wonderful news."

"I—wait, what news?" Maybe her father had come around and agreed to let them rent a room of the house until things straightened out.

She smiled and her chin quivered. Taking his hand, she rubbed his fingers as if she were nervous and found the action soothing. "Frank…I'm pregnant."

Every muscle in his face went numb. "What?"

He'd mistaken her excitement for nervousness. She squeezed his hand and repeated. "I'm pregnant. I can't be sure, but my cycle is almost nineteen days late. I'm never late. I plan to see the doctor to be certain, but I wanted to tell you first."

"Pregnant?"

"Isn't it wonderful?" She tugged his hand and flattened his palm onto her belly. "Our child."

"You're pregnant?"

"I was surprised too. My mum says it isn't often so easy,

though I can't imagine people object to trying at such a thing."

He withdrew his hand. "It could just be a false alarm. We shouldn't jump ahead before you see a doctor—"

She shook her head. "I know my body. I can feel her. I'm not sure how to explain it, but I know she's in there. It's like…I know I'm not alone even when it's just me in a room. Our baby is in there, Frank."

"Her?"

She blushed. "Well, I know there's no way of knowing for sure, but she sure feels like a girl. And I've been eating a lot of strawberry ice cream, which is pink. What do you think of the name Mary, after my mum? We've gotten so close over the past weeks. I know she'd be honored to have her first grandbaby share her name."

He couldn't breathe. They were outside, yet it felt like walls were closing in on him from every angle. "Do you have anything to drink, love?"

"Do you want juice? Milk?"

"Do you have anything stronger?"

"Let me look." She kissed his cheek as she stood. When she went into the house, he stood and paced, his hand gripping the back of his neck as he tried to process her news.

Pregnant.

She was having a baby. *His* baby.

His chest lifted as his breath turned labored. Of all the turns this night could have taken, he never saw this coming. He should have been more careful, yet…

Deep satisfaction rolled through him, primal and proud. She was carrying his baby. *His.* Despite the incredible complication this caused, he couldn't help the thrill of accomplishment racing through him. Talk about a game changer.

The door opened and she slipped out quietly, carrying a bottle of some sort. "I found this—"

His mouth crashed over hers in a searing kiss. The bottle landed on the grass with a thud. He turned her, lifting her off the ground and seating her on the table.

"Oh, Frank, I thought you'd gone shy on me…"

"Never, my beautiful wife. Never. My wanting for you will always be stronger than my will, Maureen. I'm a fool for keeping away."

He quickly unclasped the buttons of her nightgown and spread it wide, his hand sneaking between their bodies and flattening on her belly. "Our baby."

She laughed and reached for his belt. "If we're quiet I bet no one will know we're back here."

He hitched up her gown and pulled her to the edge of the table. Undoing his zipper, he said, "Take off your panties."

She giggled. "I'm not wearing any."

"Christ, woman."

He clutched her under the knees and parted her thighs. His fingers went to her sex and found her wet and ready. "It's going to be fast. I've gone too long without you, love."

"You talk too much," she said, reaching for him and guiding his body into hers.

He thrust and they both gasped. His forehead pressed to her shoulder as he simply held her for a moment. Emotion suddenly overwhelmed him and no matter how deep he inhaled, he couldn't quite catch his breath.

"I'm sorry I've been ignoring you, Maureen. You were right. I was being a coward, but no more. We're going to get this right if it kills me. I promise you won't be here much longer. I'll find us a place and we'll do what we can for our baby."

She held the back of his neck and stared into his eyes as

he thrust deeply, slowly, whispering vows he intended to keep.

"You listen to me, Frank McCullough. You ever ignore me again like you have these last few weeks and I promise I won't wait. I don't ask for much, but I demand your presence in this marriage. Do you understand me?"

"Aye. Never again, love. Never again." He kissed her. "Do you forgive me?"

"I do."

The door suddenly burst open and they stilled, his heart in his mouth.

"I'm going to kill you."

"Oh shit," Maureen whispered as her father cocked the rifle. "I'll be wanting more than one child, but only one husband. Cover your goods and run as fast as you can. If anything, my father's a terrible shot."

"What about you?"

"He won't shoot me. He likes me and I'm not the one prickin' his daughter. Better go."

He kissed her. "I love you."

Hoisting up his pants, he slipped out of her and ran as fast as he could for the truck. When the first shot blasted through the air he nearly shit himself. "He's really fucking shooting!"

Panicked, he dove into the truck, his pants catching on something and tripping him as he crashed into the door. Another shot went off and Maureen shouted, "Damn it, Daddy! *Mum!*"

"Shamus, put that fuckin' gun back!"

They were all nuts. Jamming the key into the ignition, her overturned the engine and gunned it, peeling out as he rounded the corner of their street. His leg was killing him, but he didn't have time to stop.

He's almost lost his life to a madman with a shotgun, yet he suddenly laughed hysterically. Grinning so wide his cheeks hurt, he mumbled, "This is my child's lineage."

When he got to town the blood from his legs was soaking through his pants. He stopped at O'Malley's were he knew Paulie and Liam would likely be.

Hobbling into the bar, Rosemarie was the first to see him. "Jesus, what the hell happened to you?" She came racin' around the bar in a panic, Liam frowning from the back room.

"Your father."

She shoved him into a chair and tore his ripped pants wide to get a better look at the damage. "My father?"

"He took a shot at me. Three actually."

"What?" Her eyes went wide with disbelief. "Did he hit you?"

Frank laughed. The pain in his leg did nothing to quell his incredible mood. "No. I cut myself making an escape."

"Liam, get me a wet towel and some vodka. Do you know what you cut yourself on?"

"No."

She shook her head. Liam handed her the things she asked for and she uncorked the bottle of vodka. He hissed as she dumped a good amount over his thigh. The blood washed away and immediately welled back up. "You might need stitches, Frank. Maybe a tetanus shot."

That was out of the question. He took the vodka and tipped it back, stealing a long sip right from the mouth of the bottle.

Rosemarie pressed the wet towel into his leg. "Put pressure on this and keep it there until the bleeding slows. Try not to gush all over my floor."

Liam took a seat and slid him a glass, holding one for

himself. Frank filled his tumbler with some of the vodka and tipped the bottle at his friend. Liam nodded, so he topped him off.

His friend sipped slowly, studying him as he grinned and swallowed. "What were you doing that he took a shot at you?"

Frank arched a brow and Liam burst into laughter. "You're lucky he's got shitty aim."

"Aye." He turned and found Rosemarie's expression no longer friendly.

"He might not have missed if you had bigger balls."

"Honey," Liam warned, but she waved him away.

"Don't you 'honey' me. I know you agree with me."

"Agree with her about what?" Frank asked.

"Nothing," Liam said, but Rosemary, a typical O'Leahey woman, talked right over her husband.

"Your wee little balls."

He frowned. "I'm lost."

She rolled her eyes. "Where the hell have you been, Frank? You've got a wife now!"

"Honey, it's none of our business."

"Oh, shut up, Liam. She's my little sister. Of course it's my business." Her scowl returned to him.

Frank swallowed, wishing his leg would quit bleeding so he could leave. "I know I've been absent, but I plan to remedy that. I've apologized to Maureen, and we're starting fresh."

"Have you ever seen my sister cry, Frank? She only does it when her heart is truly breaking. You broke her heart, runnin' off hiding like you did."

He swallowed. "I was wrong, but I plan to make it up to her. I'm going to find a place for us to live and we're going to do this right."

"What about your dad's house?" Liam asked.

Frank shook his head. "It won't be there in a few weeks. Let the bank have that acre. I'd rather take the money I've saved and put it towards…other things."

For some reason he hesitated mentioning the pregnancy, figuring Maureen might want to tell her sister herself, but it wasn't easy. He wanted to celebrate and share the incredible news with his friends.

"All right then," Rosemarie agreed. "You owe me ten dollars for that bottle of vodka. I'll get you another towel. The bleeding should have yielded by now."

When she walked away he grinned at Liam. "They're all nuts."

"Aye," Liam agreed. "But would you have them any other way?"

"No. Their passion's unmatched."

"That it is." He raised his glass. "To love, marriage, and fathers with terrible aim."

"Salute."

CHAPTER 8

"*D*o you not feel well, love?" It was the second time he noticed her shifting and pushing around the food on her plate.

"I don't have much of an appetite today."

He chuckled. "You likely shouldn't have eaten all that watermelon."

She pouted. "What was I supposed to do? Mary wanted it."

He grinned, loving when she used their daughter's name. Lord help them if the baby turned out to be a boy. They'd have to call him Mary out of habit. "Do you want me to order you something other than the chicken?"

"No. I'd like another glass of water though."

He nodded and went to the bar. Rather than bother Rosemarie as she dealt with a customer, he refilled Maureen's glass on his own.

It had been three weeks since discovering Maureen was pregnant, making her roughly six weeks along and she was just starting to slightly show. Pregnancy agreed with his wife.

She never complained, even when he knew she wasn't always comfortable. Her complexion was glowing and her overall disposition was one of serene, maternal tranquility. She'd already made Mary several blankets and was currently working on some booties.

He returned to the table and handed her the water.

"Do you mind if we go soon? The smoke is starting to turn my stomach."

"We can go now." He helped her up.

"I'm just going to use the ladies room first."

"Take your time." He waited by the bar and when Maureen returned they left.

He'd made a habit of having dinner with her every night, though there weren't many places to go in Center County. One of these days he hoped to be invited into her home to share her family's table, but that was a long way off. Until he proved himself a capable provider, her father was nowhere near accepting of their marriage.

They were getting there. They'd looked at a few apartments, but the two bedroom ones weren't as easy to come by. The ones they found were not where he wanted his wife and child to live.

As they drove home Maureen was quiet. He reached for her hand and rubbed his thumb over her knuckles. "You feel all right, love? You're being quiet."

"I'm fine. My back's bothering me."

He frowned, knowing it must be really hurting her for her to say something. "We could go to the mountain, park under the stars and I could rub your shoulders."

"I just want to go home. Sorry."

"It's okay."

She shut her eyes and he took the turns slow. When he reached her house, he gently touched her cheek. "Love, we're here."

Her brow tightened and she hissed, her hand going to her stomach. "Frank, something's not right."

"Is it your back?"

Her eyes closed as she sucked in a jagged breath. "I don't know. I need…Get my mum. Please. Hurry."

He yanked the door open and ran to the house, not bothering to knock, "Mrs. O'Leahey!"

"What the hell do you think you're doing bursting into my house, boy?" Maureen's father snapped.

"I need your wife. It's Maureen. Something's wrong," he snapped and her father paled.

"Mary! Maureen's in trouble."

Her mother came racing through the house. "Where is she?"

"My truck. We were at dinner and she didn't feel good. Then she complained about her back hurting. Next thing I know she's doubled over in pain—"

She was gone before he could finish. When they followed her to the truck, both men timidly standing back, she turned and shouted, "Shamus, call Dr. Carol! Tell him Maureen's miscarryin' and he needs to get here right away." She turned back to Maureen and at his wife's sob, his world came shattering down.

The breath knocked from his lungs as if someone kicked him in the gut. Gasping, he reached for something that wasn't there and stumbled. Time stood still as he waited for her mother to turn around and admit she'd made a mistake, that the baby was just fine and Maureen just had indigestion.

All he could do is breathe harshly as his wife cried. "No. She'll be okay, Mum. I can't lose her."

Her mother whispered soothing words, but he saw how she trembled. "Frank…Frank, you'll need to help her into the house."

Swallowing, he rushed to the door of the truck and saw pure agony in Maureen's face. Her mouth flattened as she silently sobbed, her cheeks red and wet with tears. Her mother stepped aside. "Be gentle with her and try to keep her legs up."

He nodded and stepped closer. His arm slid under her knees and he cringed at the heat of her blood. "It's okay," he whispered, pulling her to his chest. "Everything's okay." He didn't know who he was reassuring, but it was all a lie. Everything was not okay.

She wept as he carried her through the house, her mother opening door after door. Her father stood in the corner of her room as he laid her on the bed. She curled onto her side and sobbed. "No…"

Every breath, every swallow of stale air hurt, as he struggled to find *anything* at all to say. There was nothing. Her pain was the most agonizing thing he'd ever witnessed. She'd been so happy, so content. Perhaps all was not lost…

Glancing at her legs, he shut his eyes. It wasn't good. He took her hands and kissed her knuckles. "Shhh… It's okay. It's okay."

It was obvious she was suffering, but she wouldn't move or let anyone touch her. When the doctor finally arrived, he and her father stood silently outside the door and waited for what Frank knew would break her heart.

Her mother came out first, sniffling. He stared at the door and followed her to the kitchen. "Is she okay?"

She sniffled again and filled a pot with water. "Poor thing. It just wasn't meant to be. I'll clean her up and then you can see her." She lifted the pot of water and gathered a stack of towels. "I'll ask that you stay here with her tonight." Her hand closed over his arm and squeezed. "I'm sorry for your loss."

His hands fisted at his side as she shut herself back in the bedroom. He turned away from her father and blinked hard as his vision blurred. A hand rested on his back and he shut his eyes, lacking the strength to deal with Shamus O'Leahey on a night like this.

"I'm sorry, boy. Very sorry." His hand slid away and the man walked out the front door where he stood on the porch staring into the darkness.

The doctor left and Shamus likely paid him. Why had they ever given the baby a name? Every trace of their child washed away, but she was real. She was theirs. Mary.

When he was finally welcomed back into the room, he lost the battle against his tears. Maureen rested on her side, her hands curled in her lap, and her knees drawn up to her chest. She looked so small in her blue nightdress, with her hair braided down her back.

She sniffled and he waited for her to look at him, but she didn't. Sighing, he slipped off his shoes and rounded the bed. Carefully, he climbed in behind her and gently rested his hand on her shoulder, afraid to hurt her.

She continued to cry, each whimpered sob ripping at his heart. His jaw locked as he tried to make sense of such hardship. Why her? Why did this have to happen to his wife? Hadn't they suffered enough? He'd lost his parents and his first child, all in the span of a few months. It was too much to bear and she shouldn't have to shoulder such grief.

"We'll have more, Maureen. I know that doesn't replace her, but I swear, you will have your family."

That night he didn't sleep. The following day she stayed in bed and he eventually left her in the care of her mother.

The promise he made last night, as he held his broken wife in his arms, was all he could think about as he went to find his best friend. It was a promise he intended to keep and one he intended to see to right away.

He found Paulie hauling wood on the fifty-sixth acre of the mountain. When he convinced him to take a ride, he drove him right to the tree he'd cut down weeks before. There, he confessed all that had happened the night before.

Paulie, despite his juvenile antics, was a good friend. He listened to Frank as he told him about every obstacle that got in their way since coming home and silently waited as Frank cried. Perhaps he cried for his sad wife or the child they lost. Maybe he cried for his father or the mother he barely had a chance to mourn. It didn't matter. All that matter was that the sadness inside of him found its way out so he could move forward.

"I'm going to build her a house, big enough for ten kids."

"That's a lot, Frank. What if this is a sign that she won't have an easy time of making a family?"

"No." He couldn't believe that. "She's too stubborn and used to gettin' her way. She wants a big family and I gave her my word she'll have one. I don't care if we have to run around collecting orphans, that woman was born to be a mother and a wife and I promised her I'd make it so."

His friend sighed. "Are you going to buy your dad's land back from the bank?"

"No. I'm going to take a portion of the business and build a house there. No one will buy my dad's property, stuck in the middle of owned territory. After a while the bank will lower their price and I'll buy it back, but I can wait a decade for that if I have to. I should have done this from the beginning."

"Why didn't you?"

He shrugged. "I don't know. I guess part of me was waiting for her to take back her vow, another part of me didn't want to take from the lumberyard for personal gain."

"But it's yours to take."

"Aye, but my dad took advantage of that and the business hasn't thrived in years because of his greed."

"Frank, establishing a home so you can continue to run the business is not greed. It's common sense."

He was starting to think so too. "I'll be pulling a lot of the guys off the regular runs to help out with the construction."

"Whatever you need. Just tell us when and where."

"Tomorrow, at the top of the mountain."

Paulie's eyes widened. "Do you know how difficult it will be to—"

"My heart's set on it, Paulie. It's the best place and you know it. It's what she deserves."

Paulie sighed. "All right."

"And that tree there..." He pointed to the trunk he chopped down. "I want that to go in our bedroom. It's where I carved our initials the day I started making her promises. I want her to see it and know, even if I don't get it right the first time around, I intend to keep every promise I make her." He paused, weighing the gravity of all that happened over the past few months. "I'll always keep trying for her. No matter what."

"You're a good guy, Frank. Your father embezzled the lion's share from the business, though I'm not sure you can call it that when he was the owner, but look how much you've done to bring it back. The lumberyard will be everything you wanted. So will this house. You're an impressive guy when you set your mind to something. It's time you realized that."

"Thank you." Humbly, he accepted his friends criticism

sweetened with compliments. He'd never succeed at anything if he didn't find the courage to believe in himself.

Maureen made him courageous—demanded it. She gave him cause to try and a reason to hope for more. He knew if he could make this work with her, she could be happy. Seeing her happy, made him happy too. If it took him a lifetime, he'd see to that happiness anyway he could.

MAUREEN SAT in the quiet church for hours waiting for some explanation that never came. She thought of the Bible and those that had visions of Christ. Sometimes she wondered if those visions were moments of divinity or just a case of bad fish. Why would God speak to all of them and not her? Was she not worthy of some clarification?

The fading sunlight cut across the pews as the heavy door opened. Maureen turned to see Frank wandering in, his motions telling of a practiced Christian, despite his absence at mass. Dabbing a finger in the holy water, he made the sign of the cross and quietly approached her. Genuflecting, he slid into the pew at her side.

His hand closed around hers and squeezed. What was

there to say to each other? For days, they danced around the painful incident, neither having the courage to discuss the loss. She'd been so overwhelmed with joy, so happy to receive the gift she'd been given, it was all she'd thought about for weeks. She'd forgotten how to talk or think of other things.

"I was hoping I could take you to dinner, love," he whispered.

Returning her hands to the back of the pew, she folded them as though in prayer. But her prayers were said, fallen upon what might just be a hollow room with fancy statues and pricy chalices. "I'm not very hungry."

"We have to push through this, Maureen. I know you're sad. I'm sad too. But there's no bringing her back now."

It wasn't fair. Her vision trembled under a fresh wall of unshed tears, as she said, "It hasn't changed for you, so you wouldn't understand. I *felt* her, every minute of every day she was with me. For you she was never more than recollection you often thought of, a circumstance to prepare for. For me she was already real."

His brow creased as he stared at her. "How could you say that?" he hissed. "Do you think my heart is not breakable? She was to be mine as much as she was yours."

Swallowing, a tear skittered down her cheek. "Was to be, but never will."

"Maureen," he said slowly. "I love you, but I will not let you turn this tragedy into a battle between us."

If only she could turn her anger and hurt at God, but…for the first time in her life she couldn't seem to find Him or her faith. Glancing down at her lap, she wrung her hands. "I know what you were planning."

"What are you talking about?"

She swallowed. Perhaps there was a reason her baby was

taken. "The night I told you I was with child, when you said you wanted to speak to my father. I know why you were there, Frank."

"It doesn't matter now."

"You came to break up with me."

He didn't deny it, only sat silently beside her, his unspoken agreement cutting through her heart like a rusty knife.

"I'm not as foolish as people think. Just because I try to stay positive and talk over someone wishing to give me bad news, that doesn't mean I'm unaware of what's really happening. I'm not stupid."

"I never said you were, nor did I think it, Maureen."

"I'm easy to take advantage of most days, because the last thing I want to do is fight, but sometimes somethin' takes hold of me and I have to say my piece. Most times I'm fightin' with those I love most." She took a long breath, her eyes again wet with tears. "I'll not fight you anymore, Frank."

"Maureen," he rasped.

She shook her head and sniffled. "If you want to undo what we have done, there's nothing stopping you—aside from my spent virginity, but I was never plannin' on keepin' that anyway. It was more of a pain in the arse than anything else."

He grabbed her shoulders and turned her. "You are my *wife*."

The pain in her heart remained, thickening, growing heavy, a burden she wished would go away. "We don't live together. We don't sleep under the same roof or share a bed. We have no children." Her chin quivered, but she went on. "My family does not accept our union and our vows were not made before God."

He shot to his feet and hissed, "Is that what you want?"

His hand shot out, a long finger pointing to Christ on the cross. "You want me to make a vow before God? I love you. I promise to love you on this day and every day after, for the rest of my life, for better or worse, in sickness and health. I swear it now and I'll swear it every day after if that's what it takes for you to believe me. Before this God or any other, my love and promise to you will always remain."

"Then why are you always running away?" she cried. She was so tired of hoping he'd come to her, hoping he'd run toward her instead of away from her.

"Have I been running lately? I was scared, Maureen. I have only a shadow of a memory of my parents together and happy. I don't know how to do this, but I gave you my word and I'm trying my best."

"I do not want a man to love me because his honor dictates that he should!"

He staggered back a step as if she'd struck him. Quietly, he whispered, "Well, I promised my honor and respect and I'll not take them back because you suddenly find them offensive measures of affection. But know this, Maureen McCullough, you are my wife and I love you with every breath and beat of my heart. You are a part of my soul and losing you would be the worst death I could imagine. I may not always have something to say, but when somethin' needs sayin' I say it. I love you, not because I'm honor bound or because you will someday carry my child again—which you will. I love you because you are the best person I know on this earth and when life isn't so kind, you always are.

"You take care of me, even when I tell you not to. You're stubborn and fearless and nothing seems too much for you to handle. I could talk for days on all the reasons I love you, but I don't think I'll ever understand why such an incredible woman wastes a moment of her time loving me. You can criticize my stature, my craftsmanship, and my morals, but you cannot criticize the way I love you, because whether you feel it or not, I love you with everything I have and all that I am. Now, I'm sorry if you want an annulment—or whatever this argument is about—but I'm not giving you up. Not now, not ever." He nodded and marched out of the church.

The door closed and her heavy breathing was all she could hear. Grabbing her rosary, she quickly stuffed it in her pocket and chased after him. Her palms slapped against the heavy wood door as sunlight pierced the dim interior and she flung her body over the threshold. *"Frank! Wait!"*

He turned and scowled as she raced down the cement steps. She didn't stop until she cast her arms around his neck and hugged him tight. "I'm sorry."

His arms closed around her. His voice hoarse, he whispered, "I love you, Maureen. Doubting that is like doubting I'm alive."

"I know you love me. I love you too. I'm sorry. I just didn't want to hold you to a marriage you didn't want."

His lips pressed to her hair. "I want our marriage, love. Every day I want it more than the last. It's all I want."

She nodded, her arms tightening around him. "I want it too, but I had to be sure of your feelings."

He tipped her chin up and stared into her eyes. "Never doubt my feelings, Maureen. They're the only thing in this life I own that no one can take from me."

"I love you, Frank. I want to go home, wherever that is. I want to go there with you."

"I'm trying to get us there, love."

They ended up going to dinner at the small diner outside of town they visited the first time they went on what one might call a date. They didn't talk about Mary and tiptoeing around the subject brought about an exciting sense of unfamiliarity. It was as if they were getting to know each other all over again for the first time, only now they were a bit wiser and a touch more patient.

There was the ache that took hold every so often, the quiet reminder that her once full belly was hollow. There were no words to describe such a loss. Most people were not aware she'd had anything to lose, but for her, in those few weeks of knowing she held something precious, she'd built a thousand dreams that would never stand.

In the coming days, the battle to appear normal came a bit easier, but the ache still remained. Maureen wondered if it would always be there, silently hurting, even if she had other children to fill the void.

There would never be another Mary.

Frank was different. She wasn't sure if it was the pregnancy or the miscarriage or perhaps a culmination of both that changed him. His actions spoke of a confidence she hadn't noticed before. The hesitance that took hold of him after his father died was gone and he seemed so much more the man he was meant to be.

Deciding it was time to intertwine their lives beyond physical relations and legal contracts, she often asked about his work. Frank would light up as he spoke of funny stories about the men at work and she loved seeing him so animated.

It hadn't occurred to her how great the undertaking of McCullough Lumber was for her husband. Frank existed somewhere between rich and poor. He had no home, but always enough money to pay their way. Although he was the owner of the massive company, he still lived paycheck to paycheck, claiming it kept him honest.

She was stunned to learn how much the company was actually worth. Frank said it was valuable, but not liquid, meaning it would only equal such a large sum if he sold it whole, but he wasn't willing to do that.

It impressed her that his stubbornness came from a desire to provide a life for his children and the generations to follow. Such foresight was indeed an attractive thing.

Her father no longer made more than a grumble when Frank came to pick her up. One day he'd been changing a tire and Frank even gave him a hand, though they didn't speak to each other through the entire process, no weapons were pulled.

She and her mother would watch the two men and roll their eyes. With all her father's griping and bitching, Frank hadn't run off scared. Perhaps he'd been testing her husband. Her dad often called her his greatest pain in the arse, which was true, so maybe he was checkin' to see if her husband had the patience for such an undertaking.

She hadn't realized the house Frank grew up in was gone. The bulldozers came and erased all that once was. The day she mentioned the house and he explained it was too late, he also explained what a relief it was to see it go, too many sad memories, the last recollection of his father taking his own life.

Frank was an impressive man. He didn't show much emotion, but he felt things deeply. She understood he gave her a side of himself other's didn't know, a side she cherished and held close to her heart.

As autumn took hold and the days grew shorter, she worried where this would leave them. There would be no escaping in his truck and making love under a sky of stars, nor would there be any more picnics or lazy days by the falls.

The more he took her to the mountain the more she fell in love with all its secrets. Like a large bear, the snow would come and the land would sleep through the cold months of winter, but she wasn't ready to let it go.

Late November, just before Thanksgiving, he took her to the top of the mountain where he said a surprise waited. The wind whipped through the trees, the higher they went, and the altitude was enough to make her ears pop.

He pulled the truck between two evergreens and put it in park. She stared at the open stretch of land, seeing three young trees, obviously freshly planted amongst the natural landscape. "What is this?"

He opened the door. "Come with me."

They walked to the trees and a small stone rested in front of the center one. They were cherry blossoms, though this late in the year their flowers were gone. He held her hand as they slowly approached. When she saw the name on the stone, her legs refused to take another step.

MARY

HER HEART PINCHED as he looked at her, sadness softening his eyes. "I know I didn't hold her, but she was mine too, and I lost her. It seemed only right to do something for her."

Her throat tightened as her fingers drifted to her lips and her lashes grew heavy with tears. "Oh, Frank."

"Three trees," he said. "One for her and one for each of her parents. We can put a tree for every child we have, Maureen, and one day there may be a copse to keep her spirit company, all from our love."

Her lips trembled as her tears quickly fell. Stepping forward, she dropped to her knees and traced her fingers over their daughter's name. Her palm flattened on the rock and she prayed for God to guard her. "This is so special, Frank. I...I don't know how to tell you what this means to me."

He lowered himself beside her and took her hand. "I've written you a letter, in case you need remindin' of how I feel."

She took the letter and slowly unfolded it.

MY DARLING BRIDE,

I swear to you, God, and on all that I own, I will never stop loving you. I will not grow discontent with the mundane toils that build a life for our family. I will always take pride in providing a house for you to make a home, so long as you never stop filling it with love. I know the loss we suffered has cost you dearly, and if I could bear your pain, I would. I give you my vow, I will do every-thing in my power to fill the hollowness Mary left. Your heart will be full again, and filling your life with moments of love and happi-ness will be my greatest accomplishment. It is my vow to you. You will be happy.

Your loving husband,
Frank

SHE LOWERED the paper and shut her eyes, her emotions getting the better of her. "You promise so much, Frank." She shook her head, fearing how much she cared for this man, her love turning cumbersome and difficult to manage. She laughed. "You're turning me into a weepy disgrace."

"I just wanted you to know."

She nodded and wiped her eyes. "I know. I'll never doubt your affection again, you sweet, sweet man."

She folded the paper and lifted the stone. "I think I'll leave this here, so I know where it is, whenever I need remindin'."

"I don't tell you enough, but I love you, Maureen. I should tell you every morning and every night, so you don't forget. I'm sorry for giving you reason to worry otherwise."

She smiled. "I suppose with someone that talks as much as I do it's hard to get a chance to say what you feel."

"I could listen to you ramble for years, woman."

"Well that's good, because we got a lifetime with each other ahead of us."

He grinned and nudged her with his shoulder. "Stand up. I want to show you something else."

He helped her off her knees and took her hand. They walked past the trees, over the knoll and down a slope on the south end of the hill. He pointed. "Look there."

Her eyes landed on a sprawling field and a house in the distance. They were very high on the mountain, and the house was on the neighboring peek, looking small, but she understood the house was anything but.

The exterior was wood, logs stacked like toy blocks. Two mammoth chimneys made of stone anchored each side, but no smoke billowed from the tops. A large wrap around porch appeared to be in the process of being built. Lumber stacked here and there around the property, and a cluster of trucks parked off to the side.

"That's a big house."

"Aye."

"Do you know who lives there?" Whoever got to call that place home already earned her envy.

"No one yet. The plumbing still needs finishing and electric has to be run. Tis a wedding present for the property owner's wife."

"How lovely." Her heart fluttered at such a romantic gesture. "I hope she appreciates it." She smiled.

"Me too."

A chill raced up her back as the hairs on her nape slowly rose. Not wanting to sound foolish or imply anything that might make him self-conscious, she carefully asked, "Frank, who owns that property?"

He smiled. "You do, love. You and I. That's McCullough Mountain."

Her stomach flipped as she took a step back. "What? But… How is that possible?"

"I decided it would be wise to take a portion of the land and invest in our future. I'm tired of living without my wife." He stepped close, running his hands down her arms and lacing his fingers with her numb ones. His forehead rested on hers. "Do you think you have enough love in that young heart of yours to fill a house of that size?"

She swallowed, struggling to process a gift of such magnitude. "It's a *big* house."

"Aye."

"I still don't see how this is possible."

"I owned the land. The deed became mine when my father passed. I used the company as collateral to get a loan from the bank. Once I stopped trying to salvage my father's droppings and considered starting from scratch, in my own name, things became a bit easier. We'll have a payment for the next thirty years, but so long as trees continue to grow and McCullough Lumber continues to exist I think we'll do just fine. Now, do you like the house, love?"

She laughed. "I absolutely love it."

"You haven't seen the inside yet."

"I don't need to. Frank…it's breathtaking."

He smiled, pleased. "We should be able to move in soon, if

you don't mind roughing it for a while. Once the electric and plumbing is finished, there's nothing stopping us from staying there. As we settle in we'll get furniture and whatever appliances you like."

"All I need is a bed."

He laughed. "Minx."

"And a table, a great big one, large enough for all our family to sit and talk."

"Aye. I'll build you a table."

"And maybe a spare ice box for meats."

He nodded. "An ice box."

"And there should probably be a garage to keep the cars over winter, but something nice that matches the aesthetic style of the house. Maybe a barn or something."

He nodded again, his expression somewhat overwhelmed. "Right, well in time we'll work on—"

"And I've always fancied a tree swing where the children could play. It should be outside the kitchen window so I can watch them while I'm making supper."

"I'll plant a tree."

"Plant several. If we have boys they'll like climbing them. Maybe a weeping willow tree for shade in case they have fair skin like me."

"How about I get you a notepad and you write all this down." He turned and headed back toward the truck.

"We're just talkin'. No need to get overwhelmed. But you'll want to make sure the pantry's big. If we're going to have a lot of children we'll need space for food."

He held the door and helped her in.

"We should have our own bathroom too."

He shut the door, rounded the truck, and slid behind the wheel.

"We'll choose the paint together."

"Yes, dear."

"And a house that big comes with a lot of windows. I'll be needin' a measurement of each one with a detailed list of which room it belongs in so I can start sewing the curtains and drapes."

"Yes, dear."

"I think it would be nice to have a yellow bedroom, don't you? Or, no, perhaps a nice cornflower blue."

"Yes, dear."

THE NEWER POWER tools came with a pull start, one swift tug and the friction of the spring-loaded pawl lifts, starting an internal combustion strong enough to make a lawnmower, a chainsaw, or even a small vehicle go. Maureen's mouth was sort of like that. And building her a house was just the tug that got her motor running.

Frank didn't quite grasp all the nagging wife jokes at first. Perhaps that was because he and Maureen had yet to live as a married couple. He got them now, but they weren't so funny anymore.

Maureen was like a jar full of tornadoes, begging to be set

free. The moment he gave her purpose she stormed in and changed everything. Every day she showed up at the jobsite, arguing with plumbers and electricians. The woman didn't understand that time went into blueprints and every change cost them. She'd alter an entire room, simply because it made sense to have an outlet where she wanted to use her blender.

The men now referred to her as The Foreman, not just for this project, but the foreman of his life. Her mother was no treat either. Sure, Mrs. O'Leahey was a bit more accepting than Mr. O'Leahey, but that seemed to give her the impression she had the final say in things. If Maureen felt something should be a certain way and he disagreed, her mother was right there calling him an idjit or jackass or something worse.

And then there were her sisters. When the three of them were together there was no winning. Like three witches, they cackled and pointed fingers and whatever they wished seemed to come their way.

The only good thing about Maureen and her family getting involved was that it made the men anxious to finish the job and the work sped up. By early December the plumbing and ductwork were complete and every room had functioning outlets.

He'd assumed things would be easier now that the brunt of work was done, but that was naïve. The day the floors were being finished he'd come to check on the men only to find Maureen's Falcon haphazardly parked out front.

"Christ." He yanked his keys out of the ignition and went to find her. No one could walk on the floors for twenty-four hours once they were sealed and today was the day he wanted them done. "Maureen!"

"Frank? Get in here!"

Taking a deep breath, he walked into the room that

would be the den. Jimmy stood with a mop and bucket of lacquer in his hand. "Mr. McCullough, I tried to get started but she won't let me."

"Maureen, what's the problem?"

"The problem is I don't like that finish. It's too dark and it'll show all the dust."

"It's the finish I picked. It'll match the cabinets."

"Well I sure as shit don't recall discussing it. I never would have settled on such a dark color. You'll have to send it back."

"I can't send it back. The second floor's already been done."

"*What?*"

He sighed and sent his employee an apologetic look. "Take a walk, Jimmy."

"Yes, sir." Obviously anxious to leave, he made a quick escape.

"Maureen, you cannot come in here and interfere with the men. They have a job to do and their only doing what I told them. You come in and tell them something else and they don't know who to listen to."

"Oh, well tell them they should listen to me."

He grit his teeth. "I don't want them to listen to you. I want them to do what I tell them."

She huffed. "Fine."

"Fine?" That seemed a bit too easy.

"Yes, fine. We'll just have a gaudy house. It's fine. I'll buy throw rugs and work my fingers to the bone dusting the dirty floors so no one sees our collective filth. And when they say, *Maureen, why are you always so tired?* I'll simply explain, *because my husband didn't want to listen to me and bought the wrong finish for our floors.*"

He rolled his eyes. "For the love of Christ."

She stepped close to him and brushed her hand over his chest. "Please, Frank. A nice honey would be so much easier to care for."

He glared at her. "You are a pain in my arse, woman."

"But you love me."

"Aye," he grumbled.

And so the first floor of the house was finished in a warm honey. She didn't always get her way, but most of the time she did. She always had some far-fetched explanation to justify her methods and he never stopped finding her rationale amusing. When he did bend, she gave as well, always showing him how much she appreciated his concession. It made giving in to her an easy thing to do.

When a project was as consuming as building a house, one lost sight of time going by. There was always something left to improve and he wasn't sure any house was ever perfect or complete. It felt odd, reaching the end of construction, but, slowly, the crew returned to the field and got back to doing what they were best at—cutting lumber and logging.

The table was his contribution as were the cabinets. It was a fine table, large and sturdy, great enough to fit twenty bodies. The kitchen was the gem of the house and he knew his wife would bring it to life.

As he stared at the long farm table, he imagined children filling the benches, some dark haired like himself, others with Maureen's fiery locks, and maybe even a few with the flaxen curls of his mother. It was a good table, the sort that would last for decades.

As he took the stairs, inspecting each null post and every rung, he smirked at the top step where the floor changed from honey to dark maple. The hall was long, doors spaced evenly for all the bedrooms.

Turning left, he stood outside the master bedroom and breathed in a breath of satisfaction. He'd told her to meet him there tonight and bring dinner. It would be the first night they spent together as husband and wife in their new home. Never again would they sleep apart.

Turning the knob, the door gave and he crossed the threshold. Furniture would come. But for now they had everything they needed. An enormous bed stood against the far wall. Exposed wood made up the interior perimeters of the house. He grinned, reading their initials, just the way he carved them, above the word *forever*.

"Frank?"

"I'm in the bedroom," he called.

"Are you coming down? I brought dinner."

"I'll be there in a minute."

He sighed and took a moment to adjust the coverlet she'd made. Blue it was, with soft yellow trim. She'd done a beautiful job on the curtains and pillows. Little touches, just like his mother used to make, were slowly turning this house into a home.

Taking the stairs slowly, he sensed her presence and drew great pleasure from her nearness. Turning right at the foot of the stairs, he entered the kitchen, and stilled.

"Welcome home, my love," she said, sitting on the edge of the table in nothing but her wedding ring.

His throat was instantly dry. He smelled food, but had a hungering for something else. Slowly, he stepped to the table and dragged a finger over the milky slope of her shoulder and down to the tip of her breast. "Do you know how bonny you are, Maureen McCullough?"

Her lashes lowered as she nuzzled her cheek to his hand. "We could eat, or we could get to christening this house. It's very big, so it'll likely be a long ceremony."

"I've always been of the religious sort." He stepped between her knees and yanked her forward. "I say we christen her."

Leaning in, he sealed his lips to hers and kissed her deeply. Her body arched into his, so eager and unabashed. As he laid her back on the table, she dragged her hands over his chest and shoulders, wrapping her legs around his hips and using her heels to pull him closer.

That night they made love in the kitchen, the den, and three of the eight bedrooms. When they finally got around to having supper they were famished.

As they lay in their bed, wrapped in each other's arms, they smiled through the moonlight. "Thank you, Frank, for building us such a lovely house."

He kissed her softly. "Thank you, Maureen, for making it a home."

She reached for him under the covers and he arched a brow. "Again?"

"What can I say? We have a lot of lost time to make up for. It's normal for newlyweds to want each other all the time."

"I'll never get enough of you, love." He rolled her to her back and kissed her.

"Oh, pish. I'm sure you'll be sick of me someday. I imagine you'll want to strangle me by the time we're sixty."

"There've already been days I've wanted to strangle you, but I still love you and I still want you, same as I will then, same as I will always."

She smiled and ran a hand over his strong jaw. "My sweet husband."

"My sweet, caring, insane wife."

CHAPTER 9

"So help me God if you touch me I'll rip off your balls and shove them down your throat, you rutting swine! You did this to me!"

"How are we doing?"

Thank Christ the nurse was back. "I think she's ready."

The nurse examined his wife briefly and helped her get more comfortable.

"Thank you so much," Maureen sighed.

Sure, she's nice to everyone else.

"I think you're far enough along to move to the birthing room now. I'll let the doctor know."

Maureen nodded and as the nurse left she held out a hand to him. Reluctantly, as if it were a trap, he approached.

"Oh, Frank, can you believe the day has finally come?"

He couldn't. It seemed like just yesterday he was holding her in his arms as they said goodbye to Mary. Still too afraid to trust their blessing, he worried over the last stretch before the finish. Once he knew his wife was safe and their child was healthy, then he'd relax and celebrate. It seemed like he hadn't exhaled in nine months.

She squeezed his hand, nearly cracking some of the smaller bones as another contraction hit. It was agony, seeing her in pain. "Is it a bad one?"

Sweat beaded at her brow as she bore down and clenched her teeth. "What do you fuckin' think? I'm on a gurney, not a pleasure cruise."

He'd best stay quiet from now on.

The contraction appeared to end and her body went lax. She didn't seem to be as big as some women, which made him believe it was a girl.

He didn't like to think too far ahead on the subject, but if it were a girl, he thought the name Katherine was nice. They could call her Kate. If it were a boy, they might call him Frank, or perhaps something Irish like Braydon or Finnegan. Maureen would likely argue over the name, being that she had her own favorites. She liked Kelly and Luke and Colin for boys and Sheilagh for a girl.

The doctor returned and his gut clenched. He'd dreaded this part, knowing he'd have to let her go where he couldn't follow. Swallowing, he waited as the doctor explained some things to her. When they started to ready the gurney to wheel her to the birthing room, Maureen's emerald eyes found his. "Frank."

He stepped close and took her hand as something cool and small pressed into his palm. "I'm here, love."

A sheen of tears built at her copper lashes as her eyes changed to the shade of an Irish meadow. "I'm scared."

"It'll all be over soon, love, and we'll be three. A family."

She squeezed his hand in both of hers and brought his fingers to her lips. He bent and placed a kiss on her forehead. "I love you."

"I love you too."

Her eyes closed as she hissed and tensed, another contraction taking hold. They wheeled her away and his worry nearly paralyzed him. Staring at his fist, he opened his fingers and found what she'd placed there. Her wedding ring.

With a bracing breath, he slid the ring onto the tip of his pinky and made a fist. The next hours would be a nightmare of waiting and worry.

Her parents and sisters waited anxiously in the waiting room. "Is it bad? Did she look like she was in a lot of pain?" Rosemarie asked, her own waist thick with child.

Taking sympathy on her, he said, "She barely made a fuss."

Her sister sighed with relief. "Thank God."

The minutes ticked by slowly. Paulie and Liam showed up with cigars, but Frank couldn't relax until he knew she was okay. He paced by the window, impatiently awaiting the doctor. Mr. O'Leahey read the paper as he puffed on a pipe. Apparently after three daughters he didn't see this as a cause for alarm.

"She'll be okay, Frank."

He turned and found Colleen. She passed him a soda. "I know. I just want the waiting to be over."

She laughed. "In a year you'll be back here again. You better get used to it. Maureen's always wanted a clan to call her own."

He was beginning to rethink the whole big family thing. The stress was too much. Having a family to feed didn't worry him half as much as his wife's health being jeopardized. Maybe they'd adopt.

As the minutes ticked into hours his mind skated over images that seemed so clear, yet so vague. He imagined her growing soft with age and feeding a brood of children at their table, one by one, small heads filled the vision, but he could not make out a single face. She would be loving but rigid and he would find great contentment in watching her and their family grow.

Frank didn't need to be in the limelight. Standing in the shadow of a woman like Maureen wasn't a cold place to be. It was cozy and warm and so much more than he'd ever imagined. Being in her company meant being alive. That was his wife. She was life.

"Mr. McCullough?"

He spun and faced the door, his heart suddenly lodged in his throat. "That's me."

The doctor lowered his mask and grinned. "Congratulations. You're now the father of a healthy baby girl."

The women sighed.

"And my wife?"

"She's a little groggy, but doing well. We'll be taking her to the recovery room shortly and you'll have a chance to see her and your daughter briefly."

"Thank you. Thank you very much." He sighed and Paulie and Liam patted him on his back.

"Congratulations!"

"Oh, a sweet baby girl! How lovely!" Mrs. O'Leahey cried.

Mr. O'Leahey chuckled, a satisfied smirk curving around his pipe. "Looks like you'll be needin' your own rifle."

"Don't listen to him," Colleen said, giving him a hug.

They celebrated with cigars and waited for Maureen and his daughter to be wheeled by. He was like a kid anxiously awaiting the fire engines of a parade. When he saw the double doors open at the end of the hall he held his breath.

Four nurses, three guiding Maureen's gurney and one pushing a small bassinette came down the corridor. He smiled as he set eyes on his wife's face. She looked tired indeed, but happy.

Meeting them halfway, he went to her. "Did you see her?" she asked. "She's so lovely, Frank. What should we name her?"

He glanced at the tiny bundle, pink skin and strawberry hair. He laughed. "I'm a father."

Maureen smiled, her eyes wet with tears of joy. "And I'm a mum."

Taking her hand, he kissed her knuckles. "What do you want to call her, love?"

"You decide. I'll pick the next one."

He leaned over the bassinette. Her face was so tiny, a little nose and a sweet little mouth. Their love had brought this person into the world, given her life. "I think Katherine is a nice name. We could call her Kate."

Maureen hummed. "Kate. Like your mother? I like that very much."

He sighed, overwhelmed with pride and other emotions he didn't have names for. "You're amazing," he told her as he kissed her one last time before the nurses wheeled her away. He slid her wedding ring back on her finger. "My beautiful wife."

The days that followed were full of timid bravery, each moment a new experience. When they finally took Kate home he felt like he was stealing something, but she was indeed theirs.

Maureen took to motherhood like he knew she would. It amazed him how natural she was at parenting, knowing when their daughter needed to be rocked versus wanting to be fed.

As the weeks passed, he grew more comfortable with

fatherhood, finding it rewarding in a way nothing could compare. While the snow usually was an inconvenience for his line of work, he didn't mind it so much that winter, as it allowed him time at home to get to know his daughter.

It wasn't long before Maureen's figure returned to its original form, but there was something about her curves that enchanted him more than ever. Her thighs and hips seemed thicker, her breasts a bit fuller and soon enough he was all over her again.

Kate wasn't even four months old before they were expecting their second. While such an accomplishment did great things for his ego, it distressed his wife.

"I'll be called the trollop of Center County! Kate will have to rest on her sister or brother's head while she nurses!"

"You can't be a trollop. We're married."

"My fingers are so damn swollen soon enough my wedding band will have to come off, and then who will know I have a husband that put me in such a state. I'll be waddling up and down Main Street and people will say, *Oh, there goes that poor lass with her ginger baby and big belly. It's amazing she can get off her back long enough to get the grocery shopping done.*"

"Maureen, you're being ridiculous. Everyone knows you're my wife."

She sniffled. "Aye. I'm your fat, dumpy wife."

"Stop that." Her emotions hadn't been this out of whack with the first pregnancy. "You're beautiful."

"Oh, please. My arse looks like it exploded! You're making me fat, Frank McCullough!" she accused, standing and snatching his dinner plate right out from under him.

"Hey! I was eating that!"

"Tough. We're going on a diet starting right now." She opened the refrigerator. "I have lettuce in here somewhere."

She shifted some things around. "Who the bloody hell ate the lettuce?"

Sighing, he stood. Kate sat in her high chair happily banging her bowl with a spoon. He grinned and brushed a hand over her strawberry curls.

Coming up behind Maureen, he moved the mayonnaise and palmed the head of lettuce. "Here, love."

"Thank you." She peeled back a leaf and stuffed it in her mouth.

"Aren't you going to put dressing on it or something?"

"No." She sniffled and shoved another leaf in her mouth.

"Why are you crying?" He tried not to get frustrated.

She sniffled again. "Because this tastes like wet nothing and I really would rather eat the pudding I made for Kate earlier."

He chuckled and took the lettuce from her, wrapping it up and putting it back in the fridge. Opening the bowl of pudding, he dug a spoon out of the drawer and scooped up a big sample of the mousse. "Eat it. Your arse is as adorable as ever and you're not fat. You're pregnant."

She debated for only a second before taking the spoon and shutting her eyes in ecstasy as her lips closed over the pudding. "Thank you, dear. I don't know why I'm so emotional with this one. You should be grateful I'm not always crazy like this. Could you imagine?" She picked up the bowl and carried it to the table, happily eating her fill.

"Aye. I could imagine."

There comes a moment as parents, when one truly questions their sanity. Not because of things said, but because after so many midnight feedings, silly squabbles over who's turn it is with the ball, and which kid got to use the toy caterpillar last, no one's really sure what's right and what's wrong. Edicts are made in terms of *because I said so.*

When Colin was born, Frank's arrogance got the better of him. Colin and Kate were two of the sweetest angels, much sweeter than all the other kids he'd met. However, he now understood this was part of God's trickery. The first couple was easy and pleasant. Then, when they were least expecting it, God stepped in and proved just how clueless they really were.

"Twins?" He had to have heard her wrong.

"Yes. Twins. As in two babies," Maureen explained as if he were an infant.

"Mum! Colin keeps pulling my hair!"

"You got hands, Katie girl, pull his right back."

He shook his head. "How the hell are we going to handle two more? There's supposed to be time between them to recoup."

"Don't you give me that bollocks," his wife snapped. "What the hell do you have to worry about? It's not your body they'll be shooting out of. Good Lord, it'll be like a flume ride, babies flyin' everywhere. And then the nursing! This is your fault, you know." She pointed an accusing finger at him. "Always comin' at me with that damn cock of yours, never givin' me a chance to rest."

He gawked at her. "You're the one who say's I don't pay you enough attention!"

"Oh, now I'm the jezebel? Well, let me tell you something, Frank McCullough, after this, I'm through. Four children in a matter of five years, all under the age of four. This is what I get for marrying a pervert!"

She stormed off and he sat, dumbfounded. Twins?

Luke and Finnegan were born in the middle of the night on a Tuesday. It had been an incredibly difficult birth for Maureen, one that made her swear off pregnancy. She'd even sworn off sex for a while, but he'd talked her out of that one.

Still, she was insistent that her body needed a break and her doctor suggested she try the birth control pill. Frank agreed.

Though their lives were full and their hearts grateful, four children were a lot and the six of them could barely go anywhere in a car together, let alone enjoy things like a dinner at a fancy restaurant—not that Center County was a fancy place.

They weren't certain they were done having children, but they needed a break to catch their breath. Nobody told him the pill wasn't foolproof.

The news came early spring after a long winter. Apparently, when Maureen had been fighting a bad bug going around and the doctor prescribed her an antibiotic, the medication interfered with the pill. The two of them never saw it coming and there were no warning signs like the others.

This pregnancy was quiet. Maureen was serene and content, despite the surprise. Finding out so late left them only five months to prepare and when their fourth son was born, God apparently took mercy on their souls. Braydon was a golden haired angel that rarely cried and always smiled.

After Braydon, Maureen had fallen back in love with the idea of babies. It became a joke amongst the family as to how many children they would have. Her sisters teased her, calling her the lady that lived in a shoe with too many sons to know what to do, but Maureen wasn't bothered. She loved and adored all of her children equally, and once she had four, five didn't seem to make much of a difference. Maybe six wouldn't either.

Trying for six was more fun than all the rest for some reason. It was summer and the twins were finally potty-trained. Kate was growing up so fast and a great help with the younger ones, especially Braydon, who she adored.

Colin was growing into an inquisitive boy, someone Frank sometimes struggled to relate to. Luke and Finn on the other hand seemed determined to break the house. It amazed him how five kids all from the same parents could be so incredibly different.

The warmer months were easiest, because they got Maureen and the kids out of the house. It took about six years to get the hang of it, but he thought they finally had it down to a science.

When Maureen didn't get pregnant the moment she decided she wanted to be, she of course became frustrated. Her sisters were both pregnant and that didn't help matters. Frank did his best to get a child in her belly—a grueling task indeed—part of him was enjoying the effort it took and in no rush to hit his mark.

The more they tried the more he wanted to increase his efforts. He had her in the mornings, during the day when he stopped home for lunch, and as soon as the kids went down for bed each night. One day he even took her right against the barn while the kids played in the distance with Colleen and their cousins.

True, it took a valiant effort to get her pregnant that time, but he'd never felt like more of a man than he had that summer. Kelly McCullough, the fifth McCullough son and sixth child in all, was born with dark black hair and bright blue eyes, a mirror image of Frank.

"This one will be the death of me, Frank. Look at him. He's a carbon copy of you and I swear I've never seen an infant flirt, but this one can charm a smile out of anything with tits. The lassies will be breaking down our doors."

As it turned out, there was quite a difference between five

and six. Kelly was nothing like Braydon or any of the others. He was a daredevil, always getting into something he shouldn't and so damn cute it was nearly impossible to yell at him, but in time that would likely change and he'd have his fair share of discipline.

They'd been so busy with homework and little league and potty-training Kelly—who never kept his damn Underroos on anyway—they seemed to miss the moment Maureen's cycle should have started. But soon enough they were made aware and his beautiful wife was pregnant once more.

Again, this time was different. Maureen seemed to relish every part of it, even the unpleasant moments. One night, after the children were all asleep, he found her sitting out front on a rocker, knitting a pair of pink booties. He slipped into the chair beside her and held out his hand, palm up.

She sighed and tucked away her yarn as she dropped her hand into his and together they rocked, embracing the silence. With six children, silence was a rare and incredible thing.

She sighed. "This will likely be our last, Frank. I'm tired."

"Aye. But would you change anything, love?"

She smiled and rested her head against the back of the chair. "No."

She laughed softly. "I'm convinced if I keep making pink clothes God will give me a girl. I don't know if I can handle another son. They're breaking all my nice stuff. Luke used my good flowerpot as a football helmet today. The jackass is lucky he didn't need stitches when he was done head butting the barn. I swear he gets that from your side of the family."

"Careful what you wish for. Not every daughter is easy. Just because Kate was, doesn't mean the next one will be. We could wind up with a Colleen."

She gasped. "Bite your tongue!"

He chuckled. "They're good kids."

"Aye," she agreed. "We're truly blessed."

That summer, Maureen's father passed away suddenly and she spent a great deal of her last pregnancy crying. There was nothing to do for her grief. It was simply something she had to work through. Her mother came around more frequently, which helped with the kids and meals and such.

Frank was sad to lose the man that challenged him more than his own father had. For Maureen, the year she shared with her father as their family grew brought much joy. He was a stubborn, but good grandfather, who loved his grandchildren dearly.

It had been a very long time since Frank had seen his wife truly sad and he wanted to give her the time needed to process the loss. He regretted that a depression had deprived her of fully embracing her pregnancy, but she'd loved her father very much and losing a parent was—in his experience —a process that took years to fathom.

Sheilagh came into the world without warning. Maureen's water broke just after midnight and her contractions were so intense and so quick they'd barely made it to the hospital in time. With fiery red hair and eyes greener than Dublin fields, he knew this one would give them a devil of a time.

She had every bit of strong will her mother had and more. She was barely an infant for more than a few months. Everything about Sheilagh seemed faster than what the others had done. All she needed was to see her older siblings do something and she'd set her mind to teaching herself. The child had too much independence, but she was so clever there was no slowing her down. She walked, talked, and read earlier than any of the others had.

Once she was toddling around there was truly no stopping her. She'd practically potty-trained herself and by age two she was chasing after her older brothers, insisting they include her in their fun.

One evening, as the children caught fireflies on the front lawn, he and Maureen shared an Irish coffee, enjoying the sights and sounds of their children playing.

She sighed. "We could have another, you know."

His gaze jerked to her and he scowled. "How much damn whiskey did you put in that coffee, woman? Seven is enough."

Her lips pursed. "Fine."

His mouth opened as he stared at her. She couldn't be serious? Where the hell would they put another one? Of course, Kate was getting older—no. It was simply insane.

After twenty minutes of welcomed silence, he said, "If you truly have your heart set on another one, I suppose we could try."

She snapped her tongue against the back of her teeth and rolled her eyes. "Oh, do you now? It took you twenty minutes to make up your mind? You know how I feel about indecisiveness." She stood. "Kids! Time for bed! Go wash up and *do not* make a flood in my bathroom! Luke, wait for your sister!"

He grinned. "You're better than the toughest drill sergeant. Look at your troops go."

She smirked. "They're not my troop, Frank. They're my clan."

"Aye."

That night when they made love he was careless on purpose, knowing if they had an eighth child it would be a welcome blessing. But Sheilagh had been their last.

It seemed to happen too fast. Just yesterday, he'd been a

twenty-five year old kid, rescuing a wide-eyed girl out from a bar during a brawl as Van Morrison crooned about a gypsy souled woman and slipping into the mystic. She was his gypsy.

He'd only meant to save her from trouble, never intended to fall in love. But when she looked at him with those bright green eyes and smiled up at him, he'd never felt such a pull. He'd held her fast and never let go.

It was as though she'd cast a spell on him, and he'd let her do it all over again. He'd never imagined life could be so full, so overflowing with experience and amusement that his sides hurt almost every day from laughing. His face—over time—had creased with deep-set smile lines, proof that life was indeed happy.

Long gone was the innocent lass he'd convinced to be his wife. Motherhood had changed her, matured her. Though her hair was not as fiery as it once had been, her spirit never dulled. She never did get those nails to grow. And with every passing day, as they grew a bit older together, he loved her more than the day before.

As he sat on his favorite chair, watching the game with four of his five teenage sons as his daughters helped Maureen with dinner, he grinned. Nothing about the life they had was easy, but it was worth every bit of effort.

Contentment such as theirs could not be bought. It could only be nurtured over time with a decent sense of humor, a ton of patience and limitless unconditional love. During quiet moments like this, that didn't come so often in a house of nine, he appreciated all they'd created out of love.

The front door opened and Kelly slipped in, a guilty look on his face as he crept past the kitchen toward the stairs.

"Kelly, get in here," Frank called. Did he think he was born yesterday? "What have you done?"

His son, a wise assed sixteen-year-old now, tried for an innocent expression and failed. "Nothin', Dad. I swear."

His brothers frowned, not buying into his bullshit any more than he was. "Do you want me to get your mother?"

Kelly's eyes went wide. "No."

"What happened to your arm?" Colin asked and Frank noticed the bandage.

Kelly's hand tugged at his sleeve, but it was too late. "Did you cut yourself?"

"Not exactly."

He frowned. "Well, what the hell did you do?"

His son sighed and slowly peeled back the gauze covering his forearm to reveal a large black cross.

Frank lost the ability to blink. Quietly, he rasped, "Tell me that washes off."

"No."

Glancing up at his son, seriously questioning his intelligence he whispered, "Of all the places to get a tattoo, you picked there, where all the world can see?"

He shrugged. "I see no need to hide it from the world—"

Frank snorted. "I'm not worried about the world. I'm worried about your mother. Sweet Jesus, Kelly, she gave you a perfectly good body and you've gone and marked it up. You don't stand a chance. She's gonna beat your arse when she sees what you've done and it's your own damn fault."

The gauze quickly covered the tattoo as his brothers chuckled at his expense.

"What's that?" Sheilagh asked at from the hall as Kelly spun with an expression of sheer terror. She gasped. "Did you get a tattoo? Let me see."

"Get out of here, Devil!" Kelly snapped.

Sheilagh shrugged. "Whatever. Dinner's ready." She turned and Frank winced. The boy really was an *idjit*. The moment Sheilagh skipped into the kitchen she said, "Mum, did you tell Kelly he could get a tattoo? Because he got one."

"What! Kelly! Get your arse in here!"

Frank took pity on the boy. "Run."

Kelly took off like a bat out of hell, or, more accurately, an ill-behaved son with a lunatic Irish mother on his arse and a wooden spoon as her weapon of choice. The rest of the family took great joy in watching Kelly get it from their mother. They'd all been there a time or two before.

It didn't matter how many times she corrected them or smacked them in the back of the head for tracking mud over her honey stained floors. They all adored her. She was the glue that held their clan together, the heart and soul of their home. She was as wild as dandelions and stronger than steel when it came to matters of the heart.

He smiled softly as she marched back onto the porch, mumbling about what Kelly had done. "Can you believe what he's done, Frank? A big stupid cross, right on his arm! I gave him that arm and I don't bloody well remember giving him permission to go mark it up." She turned and yelled toward the front door, "You hear me, all of you? No one is to be markin' up the bodies that I gave you!"

She grabbed the door and he caught her arm, pulling her to his chest. She gasped and he kissed her, the anger notice-ably fading as her body went soft against his, all the tension easing from her shoulders.

She hummed, her eyes remaining closed. "What was that for?"

He nestled her ear with his nose and bit at her neck. "For being a little bit crazy and a lot sexy. I love you, woman."

She giggled. "Frank, the children."

He grunted. "Have them clean up after dinner and you

tell them we need to talk and we're not to be disturbed. I want some time with my wife."

"O-okay," she breathed.

Brushing her hair behind her ear, she holstered the wooden spoon like a dagger into the tie of her apron. He smacked her arse and watched her go. Aye, she was a fine bonny lass indeed.

PART II
NOW...

CHAPTER 10

Shoving her way through the screen door of the kitchen, the tight spring snapped shut at Sheilagh's heels and she let out an irritable growl.

"Did the sermon piss you off, lass?" Her father asked from where he knelt surrounded by tools, still trying to fix the forty-year-old oven.

"No. Mass was just fine. It's mum who has my Irish up."

He chuckled and continued to examine various hardware, determined to salvage the dated appliance. "Aye. Your mother can be frustrating." He reached for a screwdriver and mumbled, "That's why I don't keep bullets in the house."

Sheilagh scoffed. "You have no idea what she's done now, Dad. The woman is totally out of her gourd."

"Was she ever in it?" The screen door opened and snapped shut again. "How was church, love?"

Her mother plopped her oversized pocketbook on the counter. "Church was fine until your daughter rushed me out of there. I was talking with the ladies—"

"You were handing out porn!" Sheilagh snapped, her fists pinned to sides of her very thick waist.

Her mother gaped. "I beg your pardon, I certainly was not. Don't listen to her Frank. And Sheilagh, you better sit down. Your ankles are starting to swell."

She glanced toward her ankles, but couldn't see past her protruding belly. Sighing, she wobbled and sat, trying her best not to upset her sciatica. "Don't deny it. Everyone knows what that book's about."

"Literature," her mother said slowly. "I was handing out literature, dear. Don't be such a prude."

"What book was it?" her father asked.

"You know the one they're always talking about on the news," Sheilagh said. Scowling at her mother, she repeated, "It's *porn* and Mum was handing it out at church!"

His eyes went wide. "Maureen!"

"What?" She shook her head and tsked. "It's not pornography. I've seen pornography. In pornos they spit and the men are not as sexy—"

"Church, Mum! You were in church!"

She waved a hand. "And now those ladies have something worth repenting for. I'm recruiting, is what I'm doing."

The door again snapped open as Colin stepped in, his face an angry shade of red. Sheilagh sighed with relief, knowing he'd get through to her. "Have you lost your bloody mind, Mum?" He held up three copies of the book he'd confiscated. "You can't hand this out at church! She's out of control, Dad."

Her father stood and brushed off his knees. Taking a copy of the book from Colin, he fanned through the pages. A dark brow lifted.

"Colin, don't be ridiculous. I'd never hand that out during church. Mass was over and we were outside. Sit down and I'll make you some eggs. Where are Sammy and the kids?"

"They had a play date and that's not the point. Everyone knows what that book is about and now people will talk."

Her mother rolled her eyes. "Let them. I'm a good Christian and my morals will not be questioned because of my choice in literature. I've never stepped out on my marriage and I bore seven children. I'll have you know I'm familiar with sex. You think that author's the first to talk about a little slap and tickle? Pish. Your father could teach her a thing or two, but I won't let him because he's mine, not hers. He's only allowed to tickle me."

Sheilagh tossed the cookie she was eating back on the plate. "Ew."

Colin looked ready to vomit. "Mum!" He turned to their father. "Dad, you have to do something about this."

Their dad shrugged. "What can I say? I'm a stud."

"I'm gonna throw up." Sheilagh pushed up from the table. "I'm going home."

"Well, come back in a bit for breakfast. Tell the boys I said to start that casserole now. Frank, when's my oven going to be fixed? I'm down to two burners and I have a village to feed."

She walked to the door and Colin placed a gentle hand on her belly and smiled. "Tell Alec I have the papers he wanted."

"You got it."

The late April wind cut through her clothing, but the sun's heat burned into her shoulders balancing out the chill. Waddling across the field, she grinned at her beautiful home. Stone facing gave the house an aged look and Braydon had done a magnificent job making the structure look authentic, like it had always been there. Luke and Tristan's barn was an appropriate backdrop for such a farm style home.

Pushing through the split farm door, she called for her husband. "Alec?"

"In the study."

He was always in there. Most people had a den, but not her man. He had a study filled with antique books and valuable literary works of art. She found him hunched over a thick tome with his reading glasses perched on the edge of his nose. "How was church?"

She groaned. "I don't want to talk about it."

Arching a brow, he faced her. "Did something happen?"

"Suffice it to say, my mother's a lunatic."

"So just an ordinary Sunday?"

"Ha. Ha. Colin's at the big house. He says he has those papers you wanted." Being that they were all working together to plan her parents' fortieth wedding anniversary, Alec had taken it upon himself to research their honeymoon spot. He'd narrowed it to Ireland, but was trying to find the perfect town.

"Is Maureen making breakfast? I'll get them from him when we go back over there."

"Yeah. Oh, crap. I forgot to tell Tristan to start the casserole." She sighed. Eventually she'd need a crane to get up and down. As it was, she already had to be selective about the seats she chose. Once she spent an entire afternoon stuck in a beanbag chair while playing with her nephew Hunter. "Can you help me up?"

Always a gentleman, he came to her rescue. Hoisting her slowly out of the chair, she shut her eyes and rested her forehead on his chest. "Thank you."

His lips pressed to the top of her hair. "That's what I'm here for, love." His hands swept down her sides and rested on the round curve of her belly. "How's our boy?"

She smiled and hummed, soft, subtle joy blanketing her

the way it always did when she acknowledged the miracle of her condition. But it wasn't a boy. All signs pointed to girl. "She's good. Hungry."

He chuckled and kissed her head again. "I'm telling you, it's a boy. I have a sense."

"And I'm telling you it's a girl. I should know. It's my uterus she's living in."

"Why don't you grab a piece of fruit on your way over to your brothers? That should hold you over until breakfast."

"Okay." He always took such good care of her. "Give me a shove so I can start moving."

Chuckling, he turned her and lightly swatted her ass. "Go on."

Waddling through their home, down the long hallway, and into the grand kitchen, she snatched a banana. Hidden between the breakfast nook and cabinets was a door that led to the en-suite sitting room/nursery that linked their home with Luke and Tristan's. Though some might consider their situation strange, to the four of them it was a blessing.

With her and Tristan's DNA, their child would surely be as dashing as he or she would be loved. With four parents to dote over their son or daughter, a grandmother as overzealous as her mother, and countless aunts and uncles, they didn't need anyone else's approval. They had everything they needed right there, including three nurseries—one in each house and an en-suite one in the middle.

She knocked on the door leading to the guy's barn, a common understanding that though their homes were connected, they were still private residences. The door opened and Luke smiled. "Hey, Devil."

She bit her banana. "Hey. Mum said start the casserole."

"Already done," Tristan yelled from the kitchen. "It should be ready in about twenty minutes."

She entered the house and sat on Luke's recliner, winded.

"You look tired. You feelin' all right?" her brother asked.

She shut her eyes. "It's getting harder to sleep at night now that I can't lie on my belly. I never wake up fully rested."

He took the banana peel out of her hand and she heard him toss it in the trash. "Well, relax for a little bit. See if you can take a nap. We'll wake you up when we head to Mum and Dad's."

Already dozing, she mumbled. "'Kay."

AFTER BREAKFAST, Sheilagh was planning a food-induced coma for the rest of the day, but she couldn't find the energy to get back to her own couch.

"I remember feeling like that," Mallory laughed as she sat beside her on their parents' couch. "It gets better."

Sheilagh cracked an eyelid. "Really?" She thought it would only get worse as she got bigger.

"Yup. You're what, six? Seven months? Soon you'll be too horny to nap."

"What?"

Mallory laughed. "I'm telling you. During my seventh

month I drove your poor brother nuts—not that he complained. But every second the twins were down for a nap I was going down on him."

"Oh. My. God. Please stop."

She laughed. "Sorry. I forget you're his sister."

Shaking her head she tried to get the image of Finn and Mallory out of her head. "Talk about something else."

"You won't have to do the river dance in your condition."

Her eyes popped open. "The what?"

Her sister-in-law chuckled. "Finn wants all of us kids to do a river dance to a Dropkick Murphy's song as a tribute to your mom and dad."

She sat up. "Are you serious? The little kids?"

Mallory snorted. "No, us kids, your siblings and their spouses."

"That's awesome! I wanna do it!"

She laughed. "There's no way Alec, Tristan, or Luke are going to let you go jumping around in your condition."

"That's bullshit. I'm doing it." She struggled to get off the couch and failed. "Damn it. Help me up." Mallory gave her a shove and she made it to her feet. Waddling into the kitchen, she found her brothers. "How come no one told me about the dance?"

Luke did a quick scan for their mother. "Lower your voice, it's a surprise."

Cupping her hand over her mouth, she whispered, "I want to do it."

"Shei, you'll be nine months pregnant or postpartum. There's no way you'd be able to keep up," Luke said. "Sorry."

She pouted. "That's so unfair. I'm the only one that actually took Irish dance as a kid. You jackasses are going to look like a bunch of unsophisticated clowns up there."

"She has a point," Kelly agreed. "Which is why I'm still against doing it at all."

"You're doing it," Finn said. "If one of us does it we all do it."

"That's a dumb rule," Kelly argued. "Especially if Devil can't be a part of it."

Mallory, observing from the doorway, stepped into the kitchen. "Since Sheilagh actually took lessons as a kid, why doesn't she choreograph the whole thing? That way she can be a part of it."

Sheilagh clapped. "I love that idea."

"Finn, handle your wife," Kelly snapped and Ashlynn smacked him in the head.

"I think that's a great idea," Ashlynn spoke over her husband. "And so does Kelly."

"You up for it Devil?" Luke asked.

"Hell yeah, I'm up for it. When do we start practicing?"

"Colin said we can use the gym at the school. Does it matter what nights, Mallory?"

"Any night but Tuesdays and Thursdays will work. That's when the kids have practices and games scheduled."

"You'll have to figure out what to do with the kids," Sheilagh said, considering how many there now were and everyone's busy schedules, trying to get the lot of them together was going to be a nightmare.

"Why don't we ask Aunt Rose and Aunt Col to take turns coming there? They can watch the kids while we practice," Tristan suggested.

"Perfect! Tristan, you ask Aunt Rose and Kelly, you ask Aunt Col. You know you guys are their favorites. And Alec's going to need his own kilt."

"Now, hold on," he husband interrupted. "I think I would be more of an asset assisting."

Sheilagh frowned at him.

"Honestly. I'm British. There are far better uses for my skills than putting on another clan's tartan and skipping about to some Irish jig."

Silence.

Someone chuckled, but it came from the throat and she couldn't tell which of her brothers made the sound. Alec glanced at the others nervously. "I'm older than you."

Finn stood and walked his plate to the sink. "See you at practice, old chap."

Kelly, Luke, and Tristan also stood. "You've just won yourself a spot in the front, Alec. Better wax your knees, because everyone's gonna be admiring them in your new kilt."

He glanced at her, his eyes pleading.

"Alec, you may be a Devereux, but you're married to a McCullough. Bet your ass you'll be wearing our colors and prancing about." She scoffed and stood, sticking a finger out at him. "This is a family thing. No one's getting out of it, so put a smile on your British face and suck it up."

She waddled out of the kitchen, missing the days that she could march indignantly from place to place.

"Why is she so pissed off?" she heard him ask.

Her brothers laughed. "One day you'll get it."

"Get what? I'm not Irish. It just made sense that I wouldn't—"

"It doesn't matter what you are," Kelly said. "You married an Irish woman. They're all sweet psychopaths. Best to do as she says and keep your balls."

"I'd listen to him, man," Finn agreed.

She grinned, loving every single one of their dumb asses. Even Alec, who, despite their efforts, continuously refused to be Irish.

. . .

THE SCHOOL GYMNASIUM echoed with the rambunctious screams of a dozen young McCulloughs and the loud chatter of their parents. Sheilagh blew a whistle and the room silenced. Hunter, her selected assistant, covered his ears.

"Okay, maniacs, pair up with your partners and form a line—tallest to shortest."

"If it's tallest to shortest wouldn't the wives be on one end and then men on the other?"

"Don't be a pain in my ass, Kelly," she warned, and blew the whistle again because it was fun.

"Yeah," Hunter laughed. "Don't be a pain in my ass, Kelly."

"Hey," Becca called from the crowd.

Chastised, Hunter quickly apologized. "Sorry, Mom."

"Fine," Sheilagh corrected. "Line up tallest to shortest, men on this side women on that side." It was like watching a herd of stupid cows try to find a lost penny. "Haven't you people ever walked before? How hard is it to line up in order?"

"Who put her in charge?" Braydon asked.

Luke, Finn, Tristan, Alec, and Kelly all quickly shook

their heads warning him not to ask. "Don't anger it," Finn warned.

"I heard that." She blew the whistle in a warning burst. "Are we ready now?"

"Yes, Drill Sargent!" Colin yelled.

She scowled. With a sigh, knowing this was going to be a challenge, she quietly leaned to her assistant. "Hunter, can you hit play on the music?"

He nodded.

Sheilagh yelled from her chair. "You'll be dancing to this."

She frowned and did a quick double take as the music started. That wasn't the Dropkick Murphy's. From the speakers blared the recognizable beat of The Rolling Stone's *Satisfaction.*

Hunter laughed. She should have known better. The kid loved The Stones.

As Mick Jagger began to sing, so did all her siblings, falling out of formation in a display of horrifying dance skills —Finn in the lead.

"No, this is all wrong!"

"Hey! Hey! Hey!" They all shouted together with the chorus.

The little kids broke away from Aunt Rosemarie and ran over to join their parents in the sudden dance party.

Sheilagh slumped in her chair and groaned, mushing her clipboard to her face. "This is worse than when Charlie Brown tried to organize a Christmas pageant."

There was no stopping them, so she dropped the board and hoisted herself out of the chair. "If you can't beat 'em, join 'em."

Doing her best Jagger she shuffled into the melee and her brothers and sisters roared, their faces split with wide smiles as they all danced around her and rubbed her enormous belly. "I hate you all."

"Come on, Devil. Show us your pregnant Jagger jig!" Bray yelled.

They were jackasses, but she loved them.

Hunter squealed with laughter as everyone danced. Organizing the lot of them into a river dance was going to look like The Rockettes on crack. It would be best if she surrendered to the shenanigans now, rather than attempted to fight them every jig step of the way.

Come July, they'd have some sort of dance put together—likely the kind that would give Michael Flatley a coronary. But this was no longer an Irish thing. It was a McCullough thing and as far as anniversary parties went, this one was sure to break the mold.

CHAPTER 11

Thirty minutes and the woman had yet to step on to a single piece of equipment. Taking a sip of water, Mallory killed her elliptical and quickly wiped down the machine. She found her mother-in-law making friends over at the smoothie bar—or to be more accurate, instructing the girl behind the counter how to make a better milkshake.

"Maureen."

She turned and smiled. "Oh, are you done running, love? You go so fast on that little ski machine. It's as if something's chasin' you."

Mallory smiled apologetically at Jill, the woman that ran the smoothie bar. "I told Finn we'd be back before the kids woke up from their nap. I thought you wanted to work out."

"I do." Leaning over the counter she told Jill, "I'm getting remarried in three months. Well, not remarried. Same groom, different ceremony. It's our fortieth anniversary. That's the ruby anniversary, but if you ask me it should be titanium or steel. It takes a tough woman to put up with the same man's shit for four decades."

"Maureen, I'm sure Jill has stuff to do. Why don't we go try some of the machines?"

"Okay, love." She turned to Jill again. "I didn't have a wedding gown when I got married the first time. We eloped in a boathouse and I was barely eighteen. Aye, it was a different time then." She grinned. "But this time I'm having a big fancy gown made. Oh, it'll be lovely and all my sons are going to dress in tartan and my girls will be stunning and—"

"Maureen!"

"Yes, dear?"

"Come on."

"Sorry, dear. Sometimes I get to rambling."

She led her to the floor where all the machines were. "Normally, you'd walk on the treadmill for a little while to warm up, but we don't have time for that now. How about some arm exercises?"

"I'm not one for running anyway, dear. Never had to run much being as I've always had good aim. That's all a girl really needs. That and the right bullets." She laughed and Mallory couldn't help but laugh with her.

"I guess so. Okay, sit here and hold the bars. You're going to pull them down and slowly let them back up."

She did fine after the first awful clank of weights being let go too soon. As Mallory spotted her, they chatted.

"When do you think you'll be bringin' me another darling grandbaby, Mallory? Sheilagh's wee one will need a playmate."

Mallory smiled warmly. "Oh, I think you'll have to ask one of the others. Finn and I aren't quite ready yet." The truth was, they weren't having sex frequently enough to conceive a child. It wasn't that things were bad between them, just hectic.

Knowing how quickly her mind could fall into an abyss

of self-doubt, Mallory had carefully convinced herself she didn't want to be pregnant again. She, instead, focused all her efforts on being physically active, which she was reaping the benefits of at a flattering size fourteen—the smallest she'd ever been. It was strange that being skinny got her no more attention than she'd received when overweight. To her thinking, that just proved their lack of intimacy was nothing personal—at least she hoped.

They visited several different machines focused on Maureen's upper body. Mallory kept the weights below twenty-five pounds and never pushed her too hard. Though Maureen said she wanted to lose weight, Mallory had a feeling this was more about spending quality time together, which was fine. As much as she griped about her meddling in-laws, she adored them, especially Maureen.

"My arms are getting a bit tired, dear. How about something for these thunder thighs?"

"Okay." Mallory looked around. "I'll show you how to work the inner thigh machine." She led her to the contraption Finn called the gynecologist chair and adjusted the weights. "You sit like this, with the pads between your knees and slowly draw your thighs together. You try."

Maureen switched places with her and straddled the machine. "Like this? Oh! Mallory, love, this isn't for the thighs. This is a sex machine."

Her face heated. "No, Maureen, it's for the legs."

She gave her a patronizing smile and stood, patting the machine as if trying not to offend it. She whispered, "I've had seven kids, dear. My vagina's strong enough." With that she walked to another machine and started chatting with a perfect stranger who was mid-stretch.

Mallory pulled out her phone and texted Finn.

· · ·

I'M GOING to have to switch gyms.

MAUREEN REALLY LIKE the leg press, but hated the abdominal equipment. When an hour was up, she actually managed a decent sweat, but then insisted they get a milkshake at the bar.

"Well, I don't understand how there's a smoothie bar and they can't make a milkshake."

"Because smoothies are made of fruit, not ice cream. They're supposed to be healthy, Maureen."

"Hey, Mallory. Lookin' good today."

She turned and smiled at Mitch, a gym friend that sometimes spotted her while she worked out with free weights. "Hey, Mitch. Thanks. You too."

She paid for the smoothies and frowned when she noticed Maureen had fallen silent, something rare and concerning. "What's wrong?"

"N—nothing, dear. We should get back. Finnegan's probably starting to worry."

She waved off her concern. "No, I texted him. He knows we're running later than I expected."

"Still. He probably wants some time with his wife."

She was acting strange, so Mallory just nodded and drove them home.

"Do you want to know a secret to a long and happy marriage, dear?"

"Uh, sure."

"Never look at other men."

It was starting to click. "Maureen, is this because my friend at the gym gave me a compliment?"

"It's not proper to have a male friend that isn't also your husband's friend, Mallory."

"Finn knows who Mitch is. I've introduced them."

"Do you two go out with him and his wife sometimes?"

"Mitch isn't married."

"Ah, but you are."

They reached a stop light in town and Mallory turned to face her mother-in-law. "First of all, Maureen, I'd never cheat on Finn. I love him. Second of all, I find it offensive that you'd think I need a lecture on such a thing. Third, Mitch isn't into me like that. We're friends who sometimes work out together. That's it."

Clearly affronted, Maureen folded her arms across her substantial chest. "Well. I guess I misunderstood what I saw."

"I guess so."

The light turned green and she drove toward the mountain, frowning as she replayed what was said at the gym. Mitch hadn't said or done anything inappropriate. He'd merely paid her a compliment, something relevant and acceptable because their relationship revolved around improving their self-image, health, and their overall appearance. She'd worked really hard to shed the last of her baby weight and it was nice when people took notice. There was nothing inappropriate about what had happened.

By the time she dropped Maureen off at the big house the woman seemed to lay her concern to rest. When Mallory got home the kids were running around in the yard while Finn trimmed the hedges.

She climbed out of the car and the kids came to greet her. "Mom! Gianna stepped in dog poop."

She frowned at her daughter's bare feet. "Gianna, where are you shoes?"

"I lost my blip-blops."

"Well, where did you leave them? Declan, go find her flip-flops. Lachlan, go get a baby wipe to clean off your sister's foot. Gi, rub as much off as you can in the grass."

She walked over to Finn. "You let her out without shoes?"

"She had them when we came out." He kissed her. "How was the gym?"

She sighed. "Your mother…"

He chuckled. "I heard you made some friends."

"Your mother made friends with every stranger in the—wait. What? How did you hear that?"

"Mum called."

"I just dropped her off!"

He shrugged. "The woman doesn't waste time."

"You aren't kidding. What did she say?"

He chuckled. "She warned me that I'm not the only man with eyeballs around here and I should know others are checking out my hot wife."

"She did not say that!"

"I added the hot part. So, who was hitting on you?"

She threw her hands in the air. "No one." People didn't hit on her. "And thank your mother for starting trouble. She's out of her mind."

He laughed. "She didn't start trouble, Philly. I know how she is. I'm just teasing you."

She frowned. Was he that unconcerned? What if someone really had been hitting on her? He acted like it was impossible or at least nothing to worry about. The kids came barreling out of the house, one holding a pair of snow boots and the other carrying a tub of baby wipes.

Gianna already had her pants and diaper off and was running around half-naked. "Gianna, where're your pants?" Finn yelled.

"They gots duty on them!"

"Your duty or Bailey's?" Like it mattered. Shit was shit. Mallory pursed her lips. "Whose idea was it to get a dog?"

"Mine."

"And who promised to feed him and take care of him and clean up after him?"

"I'll get the poop picked up," Finn mumbled. Gianna ran by them, bare assed and in snow boots. "She looks like you when she runs."

She smacked him in the arm. "Shut up."

He grinned, that half-smirk he saved for moments of warning that promised he'd have her ass bare soon enough. Her heart skipped a beat and she swallowed. If they were going to do that she definitely needed to shower. "I'm going to clean up from the gym. Do you want anything special for dinner tonight?"

"Are you on the menu?"

Her heart raced again. "Maybe."

Stepping close, he slid his arms around her back and nudged his front to hers. "I'd like a sample." His lips dragged slowly over hers and she hummed, playfully biting at him.

"I feel you," she whispered and he gave a nudge with his hips.

"I want my wife."

"The kids are playing and I'm all gross from running."

"You're not gross. And they've been out here for a while. I told them after this we were going to watch a movie."

She sighed, wishing it was that easy. The truth was, by the time they found Gianna's pants, cleaned everyone up, got a snack prepared, and situated everyone in the living room after arguing over a movie, the moment would be over. "Tonight."

"You always say that and then when the kids finally fall asleep you're ready to pass out."

"I'll have coffee."

"Nothing like hearing my wife needs a stimulant to have sex with me."

She frowned. "Hey."

"Sorry. Okay. Tonight."

"I'm going to shower."

AS MALLORY COMBED out her hair she stared at her reflection. In only a towel she could see how narrow her shoulders had gotten. It was nice to finally be at her goal and not facing pregnancy or the holidays or anything else to throw her off track. For the first time in a very long time she felt balanced and secure in who she was. But deep down she'd have no reservation about starting over again if it meant more children with Finn.

The door opened and closed quietly as Finn stepped into their bedroom. She watched him through the mirror as he locked the door. "Where are the kids?"

"Watching *Stewart Little*."

She laughed. "That will keep the boys occupied for all of ten minutes."

"I'm not worried about the boys. I told them mommy and daddy have to talk and to keep their sister busy. She loves that movie so she'll stay put."

"And you think that's going to work?"

"I also promised them ice cream."

She laughed again. "Fine job of manipulating."

He shrugged. "It's parenting at it's finest." He stripped off his shirt and toed off his boots.

"What are you doing?"

"Having sex with my wife."

She frowned. "Finn—"

Before she could make up another excuse, he came to stand behind her and carefully loosened the towel. Reflexively, she sucked in her stomach and sat a little straighter. Her hands slowly snaked over her belly, veiling her softer parts.

"I need you, Philly." The towel fell to the floor and he brushed her damp hair over her shoulder, leaning down to kiss the sensitive curve of her shoulder.

The moment his mouth touched her, everything inside of her tightened. It never grew old, the effect he had on her. She sighed as he turned her face and his tongue stole across her lips and the kiss deepened, his hand sliding behind her ear and drawing her closer.

She twisted on the vanity chair and wrapped her hand around the back of his neck and he moaned. The soft clink of his belt buckle sounded as it came undone, followed by the slow zip of his zipper.

Fingers traced her breasts and pulled at her hardening nipples as he deepened the kiss. His hand found hers and guided it to his cock, where he held her fingers tight around his flesh, stroking slowly within his snug grip.

Her thighs clenched as pressure built. Heat coiled low in

her belly and suddenly her body was begging for his, deprived for far too long. Breaking the kiss, she grabbed his hip and turned him toward her body. Nudging his hand away, she captured his erection in her mouth and he hissed, his fingers gripping her damp hair and guiding her over his length.

As much as she wanted to relish the experience, tease and torture him with her mouth, it was only a matter of time before someone called "Mom". She worked quickly, which seemed to work just fine for him. His hips bucked as her mouth tightened and pulled over his flesh. His heavy breathing echoed through the room.

She could tell when he was close by the way his motions became jerky. With a fast tug, he ripped his cock from her mouth and planted a deep kiss on her lips. She squeaked as he lifted her off the stool and tossed her on the bed. "On your back, Philly."

She grinned as he grabbed her ankles and dragged her to the edge of the bed, wrenching her thighs apart and dragging the heat of his arousal through her folds. He thrust and they both sighed, recalling the once familiar pleasure as he sunk deep.

"We go too long without this, Mallory. I need you more than a few times a month."

She sighed, agreeing with him, but also trying not to think and ruin the moment. Her eyes closed as she focused on the satisfying weight of his body on hers, his thickness stretching her pulsing channel. "Harder, Finn."

His hips snapped forward as he quickly thrust in and out of her, the bed creaking noisily as she silenced her moans that desperately wanted to be screams. His sharp breath sawed through the air as he cupped her breasts, his mouth tightening around her nipple.

Her breasts had become so sensitive after having children and sometimes they were enough to make her come, but not in times like this. With only a few moments to spare, there would be no time to coax or stimulate any earth shattering orgasms.

Her husband had the talent to make her speak in tongues when he wanted, but anymore they were lucky to simply have sex. She was fine with the situation, or so she told herself.

He released her breasts and reared up, his hips thrusting faster. Her eyes closed as she let herself get lost for a few seconds, tasting the faint hint of an elusive orgasm they didn't have time to find. He stilled, his body pulsing inside of her as his release filled her.

His shoulders jerked as a chill chased over his skin and he grinned. "I love you."

"I love you too."

Bending down, he kissed her. "Did you come?"

"No, but that's okay."

He frowned. "No it's not. We can do more."

He reached for her and she caught his arm. "No, Finn, it's fine. The kids are going to—"

There was a knock at the door. "Momma? I'na come in." The doorknob jiggled as Gianna continued to knock.

Finn sighed. "Tonight?"

She smiled, but knew in her heart that wouldn't happen, no matter how much he wanted it to or how much coffee she had. Life always managed to get in the way. "Okay."

He kissed her and quickly climbed off the bed, finding his pants. She was handed the towel as their daughter continued to pound on the door. "Whatchya doin' in there? Do you have cookies?"

"We'll be out in a minute, princess," Finn called, buckling his belt and shoving his arms through his shirt.

She paused and stared at him, always taken aback by the surreal truth that he was hers. He caught her watching him and her cheeks heated. He was so cute with his tousled hair and five o'clock shadow. The fact that he was an amazing father only added to his appeal.

He sent her another heart-stopping grin and swaggered over to her. His palm grabbed a handful of her ass through the towel and pulled her close as his lips sealed to hers. "I'll see you tonight, Mrs. McCullough."

Despite the improbability, she let herself fall into the trap of believing they'd actually be back there in a few hours, libidos still raring to go. "It's a date."

His mouth closed over hers in a promising kiss that left her frazzled and needy. He gave her butt one last squeeze, growled, and answered the door.

Unfortunately, they never finished what they'd started. By the time they had everyone in bed and the kitchen cleaned up from dinner, it was ten o'clock. Mallory was good until about ten fifteen. She'd done as she promised and had coffee after dinner—a good thing she did—because as it turned out she was up way past her bedtime. However, that had nothing to do with her husband.

As soon as they made it to their own bed, Declan knocked on their door to inform them that Lachlan was puking. The following hours were a delightful cycle of changing bed sheets, hosing off half sleeping, grumpy Lachlan as he continued to get sick, Gianna—the reporter—waking up to see what all the hullabaloo was about, and then Declan picking up whatever bug his twin brother had. Chances were they'd all be puking by tomorrow evening.

Mallory didn't mind that their sex life had changed. That

was what parenting did to married couples. It was exhausting and rewarding and all a part of the beauty of having a family.

By Friday, Finn was the only one that escaped the stomach bug. The kids were all recovered and Mallory had only suffered a short stint of the virus, but it was enough to miss a day of work and fall behind on her weekly chores. Playing catch up only exhausted her more, which was just the way things rolled.

Finn would find time again for them sometime in the next week or so. Typically, she'd be calculating her cycle and timing conception with her summers off, but with the way things were going there wasn't a chance. As it turned out, having three children was the best birth control she'd ever used, not because they made her dislike children, but because they exhausted her and scheduling sex had a way of fizzling her natural drive.

The energy she used to apply to seducing her husband was now solely devoted to kiddie crafts, games of hide and go seek, and wrestling the kids into the tub at the end of the day.

One day she'd find her sex drive again. There was only fifteen years until Gianna went to college...so there was a light somewhere at the end of the tunnel. At least she hoped.

CHAPTER 12

Grabbing the last bag of groceries, Maureen hefted the sack of potatoes onto her hip and shut the tailgate, following Colleen into the house. "So you see, I'll be busy at the gym getting ready for my big day."

"Of course you will, dear."

"I will. I tried a bunch of fancy machines and I'm sorer than a wet nurse's nipple in a room full of newborns. That Mallory, she sure enjoys it there. And I can see why. The men, Colleen! They're all glistening with sweat and bulgin' in places I wasn't sure a man could bulge. You'd blush if you saw them skippin' about in their tight shorts, nipples all pressed against their sweat dampened tank tops."

"Jesus, Maureen, were you gawkin' the whole time you were there? Those men have to be half your age."

"My body may be old, but my eyes are just fine, Colleen. Nothing wrong with lookin'. Mallory sure does."

Her sister arched her brow. "Really? What do you mean by that?"

Unloading the groceries, Maureen pretended she wasn't

concerned when in truth the way that man spoke to her son's bride had been bothering her for days. "Oh, nothing. Just something I thought I saw."

Her sister stood and changed the filter of the coffee kettle. "Bullshit. What did you see?"

Maureen took a steak knife and cut open the netted bag of onions and dumped them into the onion bin in the corner of the kitchen. "Oh, all right." She tossed the netting away and went about making lunch for her mother who sat quietly at the table.

"Just as we were readying to leave, this man said she was lookin' fine and there was a gleam in his eye, you know the one."

Colleen frowned. "Well, Mallory is looking really good—thinner than necessary if you ask me, but she's lost all her pregnancy weight. The poor girl seems to constantly be struggling. I see her runnin' all over the place like a fugitive." She snickered. "Paulie calls her Forrest Gump."

"That's terrible."

Colleen shrugged. "So what did Mallory say back to him?"

"That's the upsetting part. She turned and smiled and said he was lookin' fine too."

"Well, you said yourself the men there are handsome."

"Aye, but Mallory...she doesn't know what she has. I can't quite explain it. We all have some demons to deal with, but that girl...she'll never see her worth. Poor thing. I know she's waitin' on Finnegan to put another baby in her belly, but she sure acts like it's the last thing she wants. She's hurtin' and that's a dangerous time to go givin' and acceptin' compliments. She's vulnerable and can't go about smiling at this man and that. *She's married!*"

"Maureen, she's madly in love with your son. You're being ridiculous."

"Am I? You said yourself she's looking wonderful and you aren't the first to take notice." She shook her head. "I told Finnegan."

"What? *Why* would you do that?" Her sister carried the plate over to their mother and quartered the sandwich. "Mum, it's time to eat," she shouted as she wrapped her fingers around a small bite.

"He should know. Shame on him for not being there when other men are paying his wife compliments."

Colleen frowned. "Wasn't he with the kids?"

"Yes, but they need to get a sitter. They have Frank, you, Rosemarie, all the kids, and me, and even Skylar and Hannah are big enough to babysit now. The two of them don't spend enough time together. I think it's an Italian thing, like she needs to do everything herself. That's just crap. What the bloody hell does she think family is for?"

"Maybe she doesn't think she needs help. Three kids aren't the same as seven."

"Mallory will never have a fourth at this rate."

"Maybe she doesn't want one."

"Pish. Finnegan wants more children. I know my boy. And she wants one too. Sammy told me. They just aren't findin' the time to make them."

Colleen chuckled. "You better keep that bit of wisdom to yourself. There's plenty of time for more. Right now, let them figure out how to be a family of five. What the hell possessed them to get a dog?"

"Finnegan said the kids wanted one."

Maureen carried an enormous bowl to the table and Colleen grabbed the sack of potatoes. They sat beside their mother and started to peel.

"Where the hell is Rosemarie? She knows we're doing this," Colleen griped.

"Stop your bitchin'. She'll be here. She can do the choppin'. My carpal tunnel can't take it anymore."

"I hear that. So what did Finnegan say?"

"He laughed at me and blew it off, but I know I struck a nerve."

"And you're proud of this?"

Maureen tossed a peeled potato into the bowl and grabbed another from the sack. She shrugged. "I love Mallory."

"No one said you didn't."

"But I really love her, Colleen. My heart breaks for her sometimes and as incredible as it is that my son loves her unconditionally, no matter if she's big, small, pregnant, or broken out in hives, he has a habit of getting a bit too comfortable with things. He did it with Erin and I worry he's doing it with Mallory."

"Erin was a twat."

"True, but Finn was her boyfriend and he wasted a great deal of their time overlooking her. He should know better than to overlook his own beautiful wife."

Her sister grabbed another potato and Maureen picked up the one she just finished, correcting the spots she'd missed. Colleen rolled her eyes. "Don't fix my work. And as far as Finn and Mallory go, you're starting trouble they don't need. Leave them be and go bother someone else."

Maureen kept her mouth shut. Her sister might be right. Maybe she was meddling, but Finnegan was a fool. Would it kill him to dote on his wife now and then? She knew better than anyone what having a large family did to romance. Her son better start paying his wife more attention, before someone else did.

"An Irishman could be as temperate as a saint, but mess with his wife and the devil will be on you," Maureen mumbled.

"I suppose that's true. I wouldn't know being married to an Italian."

The door opened and Rosemarie stepped in. "Well, it's about bloody time," Maureen greeted and scooted over so her sister could join them.

"Shut your hole. I was taking the liquor list to Kelly for the party."

"Did you order enough whiskey?"

"Do ya think my brains fell out? This ain't my first rodeo. Colleen, you're missin' half the skins."

"My potatoes are just fuckin' fine. Don't come in here late and start barkin' criticisms."

Rosemarie shook her head and grabbed a peeler from the table. "Kelly says he'll look over the order and compare it to the guest list. He knows what everyone drinks."

Maureen smiled. "Was Nate with him?"

"At the pub? For heaven's sake, no. Kelly said he was at the market with Ashlynn. He was heading there soon."

"I'm supposed to be watching the little cherub tonight, is why I was wondering. If he was with Kelly I'd fix him lunch for when he dropped him off."

Rosemarie chuckled. "And you don't feed Ashlynn?"

"She eats rabbit food. I never know what to make her."

Colleen frowned. "I don't know what you feed the rabbits this side of the mountain, but she stopped by to visit Italian Mary last night and the old woman was stuffing Ashlynn full of ziti and sausage."

"Really?" Maureen frowned. "Maybe it's just my cooking." She paused and the three of them cackled like witches. "That can't be right!"

The door opened. "Well, speak of the devil! Come here, my little cherub!" Maureen tossed the potato and peeler onto the cutting board and held out her arms as Nate barreled into them. She kissed his dark hair. "Are you going to help Mum-mum cook in the kitchen today?"

"Can we make brownies?"

"Hmm, I think we could probably do that."

Nate giggled and ran to Kelly and Ashlynn who were just making their way into the house. "We're making brownies!"

"Well, save some for us," Kelly demanded and pinched his son's dimpled grin.

Ashlynn came right over to the table and started peeling after saying a quick hello to everyone. Kelly went to his grandmother and kissed her cheek. "Hello, beautiful. How are you today?"

As usual with Kelly, Maureen's mother lit up. Maureen knew her mother didn't recognize her grandson anymore, but she was still a woman and that sort of direct attention from a flirt like Kelly would make any woman smile.

"Aren't you handsome," her mother said, gripping his cheek lightly. "We're going to the fair."

"Are you?" Kelly sent her a sidelong glance and Maureen shook her head. "That sounds wonderful. Make sure you ride the Ferris wheel."

"We did. Oh, we had a lovely time."

He smiled and gently patted her shoulder as he stood to his full height. "Here's Nate's bag, Mum. If his allergies are bothering him there's some medicine in the front pocket, but only give it to him before bed."

"Put it by the steps."

"Where's Pop-pop?" Nate yelled as he returned to the kitchen with his favorite toy truck.

"He's watching the game at Uncle Luke's. Do you want to go tell him you're here?"

"Yeah!"

"Go ahead." Nate ran out the door and Maureen watched through the window as he took the trail to Luke and Tristan's. Her heart fluttered. There weren't supposed to be favorites in families, but there was certainly something special about that little guy, perhaps because she spent so much one-on-one time with him.

Turning, she faced the others. "Do you two want something to eat? I have corn beef and some nice leftover meatloaf I could make sandwiches from."

Ashlynn hummed. "I'd love a thick slice of your meatloaf, Maureen."

She stilled, surprised. "O-okay, dearie. I'll heat you up a slice. Do you want it on some white bread with ketchup?"

"Mmm, yes, please. Oh, do you have any horseradish to give it a little kick?" She turned and stared at Ashlynn much like her sisters were gawking too.

Kelly's ass stuck out of the fridge as he rummaged around for something and Ashlynn continued to peel potatoes, only slowing when she sensed everyone gaping at her. "What?"

"Sweet Jesus, do you not realize?" Rosemarie asked.

"Realize what?"

Maureen didn't blink. She swallowed and whispered, "Are you late?"

Ashlynn frowned. "Late for what?"

"The turnip truck!" Colleen yelled. "You're actin' like you just fell off it. You're pregnant, love!"

Kelly's head banged against the top of the icebox, jostling all the jars on the door. *"What?"* He pivoted, white as a sheet and stared at his wife. "Are you?"

Ashlynn shook her head. "No. I mean…no. I'm not. I just wanted some horseradish on my meatloaf."

"You don't like my mother's meatloaf."

Maureen and her sisters gasped and Ashlynn snapped, *"Kelly!"* Eyes apologetic, she turned to Maureen. "That's not true, Maureen. I like your meatloaf. It's just heavier than what I'm used to."

Maureen swallowed again and smiled. "It's fine, dear. Colleen, heat her up a sandwich. Kelly, find her the horse-radish. I'll be right back."

Without explanation, she slipped out the back door and bustled down the porch steps toward Sheilagh's.

Frank passed her on the way. "Where you runnin' to, woman? Nate told me lunch was ready."

"Colleen's makin' it. I'll be right there. I need to get something from Sheilagh's."

"Everything okay?"

"Perfect. Ashlynn's pregnant, that's all."

"What?" Frank stilled. "Since when? Why wasn't I told?"

"I've given you seven kids, Frank. I know a thing or two about it. Don't say anything. Poor child doesn't realize it yet. Just go back to the house and act normal."

He nodded, and she rushed to Sheilagh's, hardly knocking on the front door before entering. "Sheilagh!"

"Buggering Christ!" Alec yelled in a flash of flesh as he fell behind the couch.

"Mum! What the hell are you just bursting in? We're naked!"

She quickly turned around, giving them her back. "I can see that, love. Sorry. I just needed to borrow something." She smirked, liking the fact that her daughter and son-in-law still couldn't keep their hands off each other, even in Sheilagh's condition.

Clothing rustled and Sheilagh huffed. "Go get your pants, Alec. We'll finish this later."

"I imagine after I'm done installing the deadbolt," he muttered.

"What do you want, Mum?" Sheilagh came to the entryway wrapped in a quilt.

Maureen tsked. "Oh, Sheilagh, that's your grandmother's quilt. What sort of way is it to treat such a gift—fornicating all over it in broad daylight?"

Her daughter, always a feisty one, held open the door. "Thanks for stopping by then—"

Maureen held up her hands. "Okay. Okay. Sorry. I need to borrow something from you."

"What?"

"An at home pregnancy test."

Her daughter frowned.

"It's not for me, dear," she quickly said.

Sheilagh snorted. "I should hope not. Who?"

Maureen smirked and leaned close to whisper, "Ashlynn."

"*What?* Okay, hold on. I have a few upstairs. Let me get dressed. I'm coming with you."

"I knew you'd have one I could borrow."

Sheilagh waddled up the stairs in the quilt. "A pregnancy test isn't something you borrow, Mum. You pee on it and it becomes yours."

"That makes sense." She waited by the door and turned when she heard someone coming down the steps.

"Maureen." Her son-in-law's greeting was cooler than usual.

"Alec. Sorry about bursting in. I was here on family business and in a rush. Normally, I'm much more courteous."

"Of course you are."

She frowned. "Are you being fresh?"

"Not at all, ma'am." But he *was* being fresh.

She arched a brow. "You have quite a nice little arse for a man of your age."

He stilled. "I beg your pardon?"

"Supple. I'm sure Sheilagh appreciates that."

His face flushed dark red. "I'm sure I don't know what you're talking about."

"Bet you could bounce a quarter off it if you tried. Have you ever tried such a thing?"

"Sheilagh! Your mother's waiting."

"I'm coming!" her daughter shouted.

Maureen smirked. That'll teach him to be fresh.

"I'll see you later, Maureen."

"Have fun at the lock store, dearie." The door slammed. "Bless his heart."

"Okay, got one." Sheilagh waved the test in the air as she slowly took the steps.

Her daughter was carrying so low she didn't expect her to make it to her due date. "Take your time, dear."

Sheilagh reached the bottom of the steps and let out a winded breath.

When she didn't move, Maureen asked, "Did you forget something?"

"No. I'm just trying to figure out if I have to pee. Where's Alec?"

With a contrite look, she whispered, "I might have frightened him off."

"Mum! You can't do that. Do you know how much he gave up to live here? I swore to him we weren't as crazy as we seemed."

"Well, no one told you to make such claims. Besides, he was being fresh with me."

"Fresh?"

"Yes. I didn't care for his tone so I made him uncomfortable and he stopped talking."

"You know what? I don't even want to know. Come on. I'll pee at your house."

When they returned to the big house Maureen sent a prayer of gratitude up to God, thanking him for bringing her Shei-Devil back home. It was nice having her so close and Maureen loved spending time with her, especially during her first pregnancy. She was also good for getting things done.

As soon as they stepped into the kitchen, Sheilagh interrupted everyone. "I have to pee. Ashlynn, why don't you come with me?"

"What?" Ashlynn asked, holding her sandwich.

"You know, girl talk. Come on."

"Umm…I'm eating."

Sheilagh, never one to be denied, shook her head. "No one's going to touch your food—hands off, Kelly—we'll only be a minute. I really need your help with something."

"O-okay." Ashlynn stood and slowly followed Sheilagh out of the kitchen.

Frank sent her a look that said not a single woman in their family understood the meaning of subtle. Colleen smacked Kelly's hand as he reached for his wife's sandwich.

"I'll break your fingers if you steal her food."

"Mum, can you make me more?"

Did he not know they were in the middle of something? She huffed. "Are your legs broken? Everything's on the counter."

Kelly's eyes went wide with shock, but she paid him no mind. Edging toward the steps, she looked up to the closed bathroom door.

"Do you hear anything?"

Maureen jumped as Rosemarie snuck up on her. "Nothin' yet. What do you think?"

"She's got a wee one in her belly. All that trouble before... I think it wasn't anything permanent. Knowing your Kelly, he's probably sticking her with his prick every day. Sooner or later one was going to take."

"Aye. That's what I'm thinking."

"Jesus, Mary, and Joseph, what the bloody hell is takin' so long?" Colleen barged between them and barreled up the steps. They quickly followed and huddled by the bathroom door.

"Do you hear anything?" Rosemarie whispered.

Colleen sniffed. "What the hell is that smell? Did you break wind?"

"No, I didn't bloody break wind. I was makin' egg salad this morning for Liam's lunch. The stink must be on my clothes."

"Will you two shut it! I can't hear a bloody thing over your yapping mouths," Maureen hissed. "And Rosemarie, you're full of shit. That stink isn't from egg salad. It's your arse."

Her sister harrumphed and suddenly the door opened. The three of them stepped back and admired the moldings as though just casually waiting for the bathroom. Ashlynn gasped.

"Oh, hello, dear. We were just seein' if you needed anything."

"Subtle, Mum," Sheilagh grumbled. "Calm yourselves. It was a false alarm."

She and her sisters wilted. "Tis a shame, love. I was sure with the meatloaf and the horseradish and Italian Mary's sausages that you had a wee one in there."

Ashlynn, looking a bit overwhelmed took a deep breath.

"Well, if you'll excuse me. I'd really like to finish my lunch and then we should probably be going."

The front door opened and Tristan ducked under the frame with Nate on his shoulders. Ashlynn took advantage of the distraction to make her escape.

Colleen tsked. "Poor thing. You could see how badly she wanted it for a moment."

"Aye."

Rosemarie patted her back. "They could always return to the specialist again if they wanted more."

She nodded. That was always an option, but how nice it was to hope for a moment that God alone could bless her Kelly with a child. Perhaps that was why little Nate was so special to her, because he was a miracle.

Sweat beaded on Kelly's brow as he thrust hard one last time, his wife's bare breasts were dappled in moonlight, as he filled her. They lay in a nest of blankets on the bed of his truck. Ashlynn panted, her arms falling to her sides.

His mouth closed over her shoulder and he sucked, marking her sweet ivory flesh. "I love you, Ash."

"Mmm, I love you too. That was amazing."

Still buried deep inside of her, he pulled the blankets over their shoulders and shifted his weight as he rolled them to their sides. "I'm so glad we came out here."

"Me too. I love it up here."

They were on the west side of the mountain by the falls where others rarely visited. He and Ashlynn came there often, so often that the trees held hooks for their clothesline and the rocks formed a ring for a fire pit that still held ash and soot from their last visit.

It was a private little place he and his wife enjoyed—

private but wide open. A place where they could be as loud as they wished and no one would ever find them.

"I wish it was warmer so we could swim," he whispered, brushing a wisp of her flaxen hair out of her eyes.

"Definitely too cold for swimming."

He nuzzled her shoulder and cupped her breast, teasingly wedging his body closer. "Is my wife cold? I'll have to warm her up some more. A second ago she was scalding hot."

She laughed and ran her fingers over his as he toyed with her breast. "Kelly?"

"Yeah?"

"Are you happy?"

He frowned at her. "What kind of question is that? Of course I'm happy."

"But is there something that would make you happier?"

"You mean like a blow job?"

She pinched his ass. "No. I mean something a little more meaningful than oral sex."

"Well, I think there's a lot of meaning to a good blow—"

"Kelly."

"Sorry. No. There's nothing else I want right now. I'm totally happy with our life and the way things are. Is there something you want?"

"Maybe."

"If it's oral sex I've got you covered."

She groaned. "Can you be a grown-up for a minute?"

"Sorry. Tell me what you want, sweet Ashlynn. Your wish is my command."

Her eyes searched his and the gravity of her request was evident and sobering. She licked her lips and whispered, "You already gave it to me."

His brows lifted as he searched his mind. The last thing he gave her was a hicky, but that wasn't what she was getting at. Orgasm? No, that wasn't it either. "Could you be a little more specific?"

Her fingers closed over his and slowly she dragged his hand lower. He grinned, expecting how this would end, but then his expression fell when she flattened his palm over her belly. "I'm pregnant, Kelly."

"What?" he croaked and cleared his throat. "But you said you weren't."

"Because I didn't think I was."

"But then you took a test at my mum's—"

"I lied." She bit her lip.

"Why?"

"Because they were all standing there. It wasn't really me who lied, it was your sister, but I'm glad she did. I didn't want anyone to know until you did."

Chills raced up his spine. "Are you serious? This...this is incredible."

"I know."

"Oh, my God, Ashlynn..." He kissed her. Suddenly they were both dripping with tears. His mouth pressed to hers as he laughed, trembling with shock and bursting with joy. "How did this happen?"

"Who cares? It happened. We're blessed, Kelly. It's...the moment your mother said something I rejected the suggestion, so used to having my hopes crushed, but then Sheilagh brought over the test, and I couldn't help the thrill that went through me. I've been craving really weird things lately and I've been tired and sort of foggy. The other day I was driving around for an hour before I gave up and came home, no clue where I was supposed to be. You know I only acted like that when I was carrying Nate."

"Oh my God. I'm blown away. I never thought...I always assumed it would be the same as it was with Nate, that we'd have to see the specialist again and go through all that. This is… surreal." He laughed. "I wonder if this is how everyone feels when they're surprised."

"I think it's a little bit more of a surprise for us." She giggled.

"You aren't kidding. Holy shit. Nate's going to be a big brother!"

He scooted lower, spanning her belly with his hands and pressing his lips to her tummy. "Hey, baby. I'm your daddy. We can't wait to meet you."

Her fingers combed through his hair as he pressed his ear gently to her stomach and listened. "We need to get you to the doctor's this week. I want to make sure everything's okay."

"I think everything's fine, Kel. Aside from my cravings and sudden flakiness, I feel really great. I could run a mile right now I'm so excited."

He sat up, knocking the covers off of them. "We're having a baby!" he yelled, his voice echoing over the mountain.

She laughed and he quickly covered them back up. Wrapping his body around hers, he fit his hips between her thighs and found her heat.

She moaned as he filled her. Slowly he rocked into her, making love to her under a canopy of stars, feeling like the luckiest man alive. Having another child was an incredible and unexpected gift.

As he held her, reveling in this news, Kelly considered how their lives would change. Their home was large enough, but they'd need to paint a room. It might be a girl. The thought of a daughter thrilled him and scared the shit out of him. He'd need bullets in case any boys teased her or tried to be a bit too friendly. And Nate would have to learn the key points of being a big brother, because as much as Sheilagh was a pain in his ass, Kelly always defended her.

They slept in each other's arms, whispering softly over different exciting thoughts. Names were already being put on the table. If it was a girl, they were definitely going with either Maureen or Bethany, after either of their mothers. If it was a boy, he liked Shamus after his grandfather, but Ashlynn liked Asher, from the bible, which she said stood for happiness.

They made love several times and again as the sun rose. It was a good thing his mother had Nate, because they slept well into the morning when they finally passed out. It would be near impossible, keeping up the lie in front of family, but until the doctor confirmed what they believed they weren't telling anyone.

On the way home they bought six pregnancy tests. Every single one was positive. That night they celebrated with a large pasta dinner, made with the sauce Italian Mary gave Ashlynn. His wife sure had an appetite, but that didn't bother him. If anything, it affirmed she was doing fine and the baby was healthy and growing.

Because of their history and her difficult pregnancy with Nate, the doctors got them right in for an appointment. That Friday they were flush with prenatal vitamins and deciding which room Little Bean would use. Between the two of them, it was a toss-up deciding who was more excited.

ASHLYNN SLIPPED Nate an apple slice and turned the page in the southern magazine she snatched from beside the register. "Oooh, that looks yummy. Where do you think we can buy a tub of coconut cream frosting?"

"Mum-mum knows."

Ashlynn laughed. "I bet she does." But she was not going to make the mistake of feeding her cravings in front of Kelly's mother again until they were ready to tell everyone. She dog-eared the page for later.

The market was slow and there were no new shipments to stock, which was fine since she was enjoying a lazy afternoon of sitting while Nate played at the front of the store.

"Customer," Nate called. "It's Aunt Becca and Hunter! Mom, can I play with Hunter?"

"Sure, but wait until he comes inside and says hello."

Folding the magazine and stashing it behind the counter, Ashlynn stood and smiled as Becca stepped into the market. Hunter laughed and wrung his hands as she ushered him through the automatic doors.

"Hello Hunter," she greeted.

"Hi, Hunter! Wanna play?"

Becca smiled and shook her head, her eyes telling

Ashlynn she could use a break. Ashlynn looked for something that might occupy them for a bit. "Nate, why don't you get one of the containers of sliced watermelon and bring it to me. I'll open it and then you and Hunter can sit by the front window and share it."

"Okay! Hunter, we have ducks out that window. They play in the puddles."

Hunter went to the window and paced as he spotted the ducks. His fingers twisted as he laughed. "Mom, ducks!"

"I see, bud. Sit down and have some watermelon with Nate."

Ashlynn snapped the seal and handed the tub to Nate. Once they were both happily sucking on slices of pink melon, she sighed. "Rough day?"

Becca grinned. "Ordinary day. I'm just anxious for Braydon to get back."

"How much longer is he out of town?"

"He's coming back tomorrow. The house is so quiet without him." She laughed. "I never thought I'd say that, but with the new computer Hunter's always doing something quietly and I'm stuck talking to the house plants. Hey, would you want to come over for some wine tonight? I could ask Sammy and the other girls to come too."

"Umm…" That sounded nice, but wine would be out of the question. "Sure. Are you inviting Maureen and the aunts?"

"No, I was thinking just us sisters."

"Sounds perfect."

Becca smiled. "Okay! Then I better get some grapes and cheese while I'm here."

When Ashlynn checked her out and provided ample wet naps to clean off the boys' melon stained cheeks, she asked, "Do you want me to bring anything?"

"Just yourself. Unless there's something specific you're in the mood for."

"Okay. I'll see you around seven?"

"Let's do eight, so I can get Hunter in bed."

"I'll see you then."

Apparently she was in the mood for Cajun pasta salad and salt and vinegar chips, which sounded delightful to her, but when she arrived at Becca's she got some strange looks from the others. The only one who seemed unfazed was Sheilagh, but she, of course, knew where such cravings stemmed from.

"This was a great idea," Kate said as she refilled her glass of wine.

Sheilagh frowned at her sister. "Hittin' the sauce a little heavy tonight, aren't you Kate?"

"Please. Ant's on homework duty, Skylar's watching the others, Hanna's making dinner, and I have my pregnant sister to drive me home safely. I feel like I just won the lottery. Cheers."

Ashlynn laughed when Sheilagh saluted the toast with her middle finger.

The front door opened and Mallory came in carrying an expensive bottle of vodka and a bag of limes. "Let's do this! I'm off the clock until Sammy takes me home."

Sammy came in behind her carrying a small dish. "I brought pie."

"Ooh, pie!" Ashlynn and Sheilagh said at once and Ashlynn blushed at how eager she was for the dessert. Key lime, pumpkin, coconut cream, it didn't matter. She was about to maul her sister-in-law for a slice.

"Can I get you a glass of wine, Sammy?"

"No thanks. I'm driving Philly home tonight."

"You could have one. It's early."

Sammy blushed and Kate said, "Oh. My. God. You're pregnant!"

What was with these people, did they have pregnant radars embedded in their skulls at birth? Sammy laughed, a blush stealing over her freckled cheeks and giving away her secret, and everyone cheered.

"How far along?" Sheilagh yelled, hoisting herself up to hug her sister-in-law.

"About eight weeks. I'm not supposed to tell anyone yet. Colin wanted to wait a little longer."

Ashlynn smiled as everyone's voices pitched high with excitement as they fawned over Samantha. Their children would be about the same age. She wanted so badly to tell them, but Kelly still didn't want the others to know yet.

Sensing Sheilagh's eyes on her, she turned. Her sister-in-law tipped her head as if saying 'why not tell them'? Ashlynn brushed the potato chip dust off her fingers and stood.

Everyone turned and she said, "I'm so happy for you and Colin, Sammy. It's so nice Lula and Liam will have a new baby in the house. It's also nice he or she'll have a cousin the same age." Her hand went to the front of her overalls and everyone screamed.

"You're pregnant too?" Kate gasped.

Ashlynn turned and aimed a finger at her. "Do *not* tell your mother. This is just between us girls!"

"Fine, but she's going to find out sooner or later. She can sniff a pregnancy out from a mile away."

"She already figured it out, but I lied and told her Ash wasn't pregnant," Sheilagh said with an air of cleverness.

"Oh my God," Becca said, slowly shaking her head. "I have to tell you all something." They turned and she held up her glass. "This is juice. I'm pregnant too."

"*What?*" They collectively gasped.

She nodded, a look of nervous joy on her face. "We were only trying for a few months. I didn't expect it to happen so fast. Braydon's thrilled, of course. I'm a little nervous, but so far everything's been good. I'm eleven weeks."

"This is nuts!" Sammy said, hugging Becca.

As they all congratulated each other Kate laughed. "There is no way you're hiding all this from Mum!"

Mallory stepped back, hugging her martini. "Stay the hell away from me. I don't want to catch whatever's going around. My uterus is happily vacant for the moment and I plan to keep it that way for at least a year."

Ashlynn held her smile but wanted to frown. Something in Mallory's eyes told her that wasn't entirely true.

"You don't want to have babies with us?" Becca frowned.

"Damn it, I do!" Kate slurred, tipping the last drop of wine from the bottle. "Maybe since I'm all liquored up I can take advantage of Ant tonight."

"Five is enough," Sheilagh said. "You're definitely drunk."

Kate plopped beside her sister and rested her head on her shoulder. "Mum had seven. I could have more."

"Drink your drink." Sheilagh patted her head as Kate laid her ear on her protruding belly.

The evening derailed into total baby talk. Mallory was adamant about being anti-pregnant at the moment, but by the end of the night she admitted how incredible it was that they were all going to have children at the same time—and that part of her wanted to be included in their joy. What she didn't understand was why Mallory—someone who always had an easy time conceiving—made this seem so unlikely.

Their children would all be in the same grade together. There would be so many close-knit bonds from such a phenomenon. Four pregnancies all at once.

Maureen was going to be in her glory when she found

out. Sheilagh, Colin, Kelly, Luke, and Braydon were all going to have a baby. This was one of those moments that Ashlynn adored being part of such a large, loving family. And with all this love the McCullough clan would just continue to grow larger and larger with every generation.

Her hormones got the best of her and she started to sniffle. "I love you guys."

"What?" Sammy turned and tsked. "We love you too, Ash. Don't cry."

"I'm sorry." She wiped her eyes. "I'm just so surprised by all this and it's such incredible news. I mean, first Sheilagh. How crazy is that, making a baby from Tristan's sperm and her egg?"

"I have to say, I found the act of conception a little underwhelming in the end," Sheilagh joked. "After years of fantasizing about the man, I'm now carrying his baby and he never even made me come." She shook her head and tsked. "Utterly disappointing."

They laughed. "I don't think you'd like his orgasm tactics, Shei," Kate joked and they laughed.

"Then me and Kelly," Ashlynn continued, knowing she wouldn't stop crying until she said her piece. "We went through so much trying to have Nate. This one is a total shock and we're still processing it."

Sammy smiled and squeezed her hand. "You're blessed."

"We all are. Now you and Colin and Becca and Braydon— things like this don't happen."

"Locusts," Mallory commented, obviously punch drunk at this point. "You don't see anything for years then *bam*, they're everywhere. I'm telling you, I couldn't even share a toilet seat with Finn for a while without getting pregnant."

Kate cleared her throat. "You were only pregnant twice, Mallory. I think you're being a little dramatic."

"Twins, Kate! Twins!" She pointed with her martini, taking in the entire room. "Any of you housing doubles up in there? I didn't think so. Until you do and you know what it is to have doctors pulling people out of you like they're picking up a large order at a drive through window, I don't want to hear a single word. Twins."

"Jesus, woman, don't anger it," Sheilagh mumbled to her sister as she stole the bag of chips.

After Mallory's little outburst, things sort of quieted down. Sammy took the drunkards home because Sheilagh wanted to leave early on account of being tired. Ashlynn ended up calling Kelly and telling him that she'd be home in the morning. She felt bad leaving Becca all alone and really was enjoying their time together once everyone else left.

Becca was sweet and quieter than the rest, which made her less overwhelming to Ashlynn. They stayed up until midnight discussing various fears and things they were anticipating. She told Becca the story about how Nate came to be since it happened before she was part of the family and Becca told Ashlynn all about her first marriage and the joys that trumped the fears regarding Hunter.

There was so much she hadn't considered when it came to being a parent to a child with autism. Becca was incredibly strong and Ashlynn found her to be an inspiration for all mothers.

She supposed every parent had his or her own worries to shoulder to some extent. Ashlynn hadn't realized autism ran in families, but they all loved Hunter so much, his differences didn't seem like any reason to hesitate for more children. He was a great kid, and though he could be trying at times—what child wasn't? Becca no longer let worry cloud her judgment. She was thrilled to be pregnant again and Ashlynn was thrilled for her.

Ashlynn had worries too. Nate's birth had been premature and terrifying. There really was no way to explain how it felt to have a baby and not be able to take him home from the hospital. It took a solid year for him to catch up on the percentile charts, but catching up by some statistical standard did nothing to curb their worry as parents. She wasn't sure if that sort of parental worrying ever shut off.

Holding her belly protectively, she sighed. "I'm really glad you married Braydon, Becca."

She smiled. "I'm really glad he asked. I never knew love like ours existed outside of romance novels."

"I've never read a romance novel."

Becca snorted. "That doesn't surprise me."

"Have you?"

"Not for many years. I don't really have the time. But I love a good love story."

"Maureen gave me a book she said her church group's been reading. Maybe I should read that."

Becca chuckled. "That woman. She makes you crazy, but you can't help but love her."

"She's incredible. I think their anniversary's going to be amazing."

"I'm not doing that dance now."

Ashlynn faced her. "Really? Do you think we can all get out of it?"

"I know Sammy told Colin he's on his own."

She scoffed. "Then I'm not doing it either." She laughed. "Mallory's going to be pissed."

"Might be enough to make her rethink her whole stance on pregnancy."

Ashlynn laughed. "What if no one does it once all the women all drop out?"

"No way, they're doing it. Luke's adamant they do this for their parents and Finn loves any excuse to act like a jackass."

"Well, after seeing how good Kelly looks in a kilt, I'd have to confess I'm sort of looking forward to it."

Becca chuckled. "They are some sexy Irishmen."

"You aren't kidding." Together they sighed, shutting their eyes, and imagining some of the finer qualities of the McCullough men.

CHAPTER 14

Frank, not a small man, shuffled uncomfortably from foot to foot as he and Luke waited in the tailor's dressing room.

"You all right, Dad?"

"I don't see what's wrong with my old jacket. I've worn it for all my sons' weddings. Why shouldn't it suit for my anniversary?"

His son chuckled. "Get into the spirit and stop being a baby."

Frank grumbled and folded his arms over his chest. "Seems like an awful big fuss—"

"Okay, let's have it," Luke interrupted. "You're a simple man of simple means and all this fuss isn't necessary, right? Did you ever think Mum would like seeing you in a new jacket with your plaid?"

His mouth opened and he paused. Maureen didn't care about fancy details like that. Did she? "You're mother likes me just fine as I am."

"Dad."

He huffed. "Fine. But I know your mother better than you, you little shit." His son unfolded from the petite chair he was occupying and stood at his full height. Frank rolled his eyes. "Sit your arse dawn, you moron. I could drop you like an elm if the mood struck."

There was a pregnant moment of glaring at one another, which quickly shifted and ended with them both laughing. Luke palmed his shoulder and squeezed. "Show her this is important to you and get the new jacket, Dad. She'll notice. I promise."

His son's words, although lighthearted, gave him pause. "This is *important* to me."

Luke caught his eye. "I know it is."

He shook his head. "I love your mother very much, Luke. I may not always say it or show it, but that woman is the breath of this family and my soul."

Luke's smile was slow and genuine. "You should write that into your vows."

"I have to write vows?" He twisted uncomfortably and ran a frustrated hand through his hair. "Jesus, this is getting out of hand."

"Sheilagh and Kate will help you."

That was a great idea. Maybe he could offer them a trade and they could—

"They are not writing them for you, Dad. I said help."

"Damn it."

The tailor finally appeared. He was a short man about two decades past the age of retirement and his glasses were too big for his face. "Mr. McCullough, I haven't had you in my shop in quite some time. I hear you have quite the celebration coming up."

"Yes," Frank muttered, wanting to get this over with.

"And will you be requiring a full tux?"

"Just the jacket. Mine's gotten…tight."

The tailor chuckled and grabbed a tape measurer. "Happens to the best of us. Arms out."

He endured the fitting as Luke supervised—like he needed a chaperone. As the man took his measurements, he thought about his son's words and the implication that this wasn't important to him. Of course it was. Every anniversary was important. His kids might not realize it, but Maureen did, didn't she?

When they left the tailor and returned to Luke's truck, Frank said, "Swing by Ashlynn's store. I want to grab some things."

Luke nodded and drove in that direction. When they reached the farmer's market, he felt silly and told Luke to wait in the car. Of course he didn't listen. While his son stopped to say hello to Ashlynn, Frank grabbed one of the dainty baskets by the front and went about his purpose.

Trying to be discreet, he selected some camouflaging items like grapes, a bag of peaches, and a pineapple. Finally, once the basket was getting heavy, he nonchalantly snatched a bouquet of roses and casually placed them on top.

"Oh, Frank, are these for Maureen?" Ashlynn purred as she rung his order.

His face heated. He refused to look at his son. "I know she likes the pink ones."

His daughter-in-law smirked and patted his hand. "Then she'll love these. That's very sweet of you."

"I just came for the grapes," he lied.

Her smile grew tighter as if she were trying to hide her amusement. "Of course you did."

When they reached the truck, Luke was grinning like he'd just found money. "Knock it off," Frank grumbled as he climbed inside.

Luke laughed.

As they pulled up at the big house his son still wore a stupid smirk. "Did you want me to help you carry in your bag?"

Glaring at him, Frank snapped, "I'm not a bloody invalid. Go home."

He carried the bag into the kitchen and left it on the counter. Maureen was skinning cucumbers at the table as he placed a kiss on her cheek.

"Did you have a good time with Luke, love?"

"That boy's a pain in my arse," he grumbled.

"Oh, aren't they all?" She noted the paper sack from the market. "Did you go to the market? I'd already gone."

"I just picked up a few things."

She frowned and he slipped away to the den. As he settled into his chair and picked up the remote, ready for a nice nap and some background noise, she reappeared—holding the flowers.

"What the hell is this, Francis McCullough?"

Startled she'd receive his gift with an attitude, he said, "They're flowers."

"And why are they in your bag?"

Rolling his eyes, he said, "I got them for you, woman. Thank you is usually the thing to say when a man gives you favors."

"Oh, no you don't. These roses are no favor to me. What did you do?"

He balked. "I didn't do anything—"

"The last time you bought me flowers when it wasn't Mother's Day or Easter it was because I caught you lookin' at

Georgia Spiegel's knockers. Were you lookin' at her tits again?"

He threw his hands in the air. "No! I was just doing something nice for you, you lunatic."

She glared at the flowers and back at him. "You're lying. Who were you eyein' up? Was it that new blonde woman we saw at church on Sunday? The loose looking one?"

"The new preschool teacher?"

"That's the one! That trollop."

Shaking his head, he stood. Maybe a walk was what he needed. "You're out of your mind," he mumbled.

"Where do you think you're going?"

"I'm going for a walk."

"Not without givin' me an explanation, you're not!"

He turned and faced her. With all the patience he could muster, he said, "Maureen, I was not lookin' at anyone's tits, nor was I eyeing up the new preschool teacher. We stopped by the market and Ashlynn had them on sale—"

"Liar! I was there this morning and the roses were *not* on sale. The tulips were. I know, because I said, 'Oh, how lovely your tulips are, Ashlynn', expectin' she'd offer me some on the house—gave birth to her pain in the arse husband and all —but no. She didn't make the offer. Is that what this is? Did Ashlynn feel bad about givin' her mother-in-law the old shaft?" She nodded as though that made perfect sense, her tone lightening. "I'll give her a call and thank her."

He caught her sleeve before she could get to the phone. "Ashlynn didn't say anything, you nut. *I* bought the flowers. *I* picked them out, knowing you like the pink ones. *I* paid full price. And *I* did so just because *I* wanted to do something nice for *you*! Next time I'll save myself the hassle and just bring you home a ham."

He grabbed his hat by the door and shoved it on his head.

"You wanted to do something nice for me?" she asked in a small voice.

Lord, give me strength. He let out a slow breath and gritted. "Yes."

"Why?"

Without facing her, he said, "Do I need a reason? I don't show it enough, but…I love you. That's all."

She was silent—as rare as that was. It didn't last. Quietly, she said, "That's an awful big thing to go ahead and finish with *that's all.*" She stepped closer to his back. "I love you too, you know. The flowers are lovely. Thank you."

His shoulders sagged. She was a lot of things, but never easy. "You're welcome."

"Did you want to…go upstairs?"

His head turned slowly as he glanced over his shoulder. She smiled, a smitten grin on her face as she sniffed the flowers. Turning, he placed both hands on her shoulders. "You're going to be the death of me, woman."

Her eyes turned big. "Oh, well then we better hurry." Her fingers gently brushed the graying hair at his temple. "I didn't want to tell you, but you're getting old." Her hand slipped lower, traveling over his chest and down to his pants. "But you're still as virile as ever. Let me just put these in some water."

His chest filled as he breathed her in. She carried the roses to the kitchen and took her time, humming, as she arranged them in a vase. His body hardened as he watched her. She was still as beautiful as ever.

The screen door suddenly opened and Sheilagh wobbled in. "Mum, do you have the stuff to make rice pudding?"

Maureen removed her apron. "I do, dear, but you'll have to wait. You're father and I are about to go upstairs, so if I were you, I'd go back where you came from. I'll make you pudding tonight."

Sheilagh's face paled. "Ew! What the hell is wrong with this family?"

Maureen slid her hand into his and he grinned. "Listen to your mother."

Sheilagh gagged. "You two are disgusting."

His wife tugged his arm. "Goodbye, Sheilagh."

He turned and the screen door slammed with a snap. As he followed Maureen up the stairs, he chuckled. "You just scarred our daughter."

"I made her pudding yesterday. She'll live."

He laughed. "I'm talking about the sex talk."

"Pish. How on earth does she think she got here? And how do you think she got in the condition she's in, Frank? That girl hasn't been a virgin for some time."

His smile fell. "That's enough about the kids."

She grinned wickedly and shut the door to their bedroom. "Don't go all prudish on me now. I've got an hour until I need to start dinner."

He crowded her against the door and breathed in the soft scent of her hair. "Then we'd better get cracking," he whispered, his lips teasing her neck as his hands closed over her soft curves.

"I love you, Frank."

"Mmmm." He slowly unbuttoned her dress and she caught his hand, stilling him.

Her faded green eyes were serious as she whispered, "And I know you love me. You tell me in every glance you send my way, whether you're rollin' your eyes or trying to get fed. I know you and I love you and I know you love me. You don't need flowers to tell me you do."

Closing his eyes, he breathed out a sigh of relief, pulling her into him as he hugged her close and pressed a kiss to her shoulder. "What would I do without you, love?"

She hugged him back. "You'd starve."

He chuckled and tightened his arms. "True." Laying his ear on her shoulder, holding her and enjoying the feel of her in his arms, he whispered, "I'd die of a broken heart long before starvation set in, Maureen. You may be a pain in the arse, but you're my pain and I'd be lost without you."

Her lips pressed to the back of his head. "And you're mine."

Bray sipped his beer, the sun setting low behind the trees backing up to his house as he, Colin and Kelly enjoyed the warming weather.

"This is a nice deck, Bray. Big," Colin commented, admiring the newly stained woodwork.

Kelly snorted and Bray's grin stretched wide. "Thanks, never a bad thing to be told you got a big deck," Bray said, wiggling his brows.

Colin rolled his eyes. "I'm serious. I think Sammy would like a deck this big."

Kelly couldn't resist. "I bet she would. What girl doesn't enjoy a big deck?"

"Shut up, I'm being serious," Colin said, shaking his head.

Bray took a more serious tone. "Well, if you wanted a bigger deck we could build you one, Col."

"I think we could fit it," he said.

Kelly, silently cracking up, said, "Well, it's something to think about. Sometimes the decks too big and then the girls start complaining. I should know."

"You're a child," Colin grumbled.

"He's right though," Bray agreed, hiding a smirk. "I mean, the bigger the deck the more women can fit on it, but sometimes a deck can be too big."

"And a big deck gets all the ladies to come—"

"Will you stop that!" Colin stood and tossed his beer in the recycling. "Forget I said anything." He turned and walked toward the door of the house.

"Oh, come on, Col," Kelly called. "You're a McCullough! You're entitled to a big deck!"

Braydon snorted as he tipped back his beer and the door slammed. "He's so sensitive."

Kelly's smirk showed behind the mouth of his beer. "Deck envy."

Becca came outside and Hunter took off running into the grass with a toy plane he'd just built. "Why did Colin leave? He seemed frustrated."

"He's just moping about his little deck," Kelly said, standing to toss his empty bottle. "It's hard to see someone else's big deck and not get self-conscious."

Becca stilled, her brow creasing, as she understood the play on word. "You guys are terrible."

Bray pulled her to his lap and kissed her ear. "We're gonna have to build him a deck."

She shook her head and giggled. "Sammy did mention wishing she had a bigger deck to entertain." And they all cracked up.

Kelly gave Bray a pat on the shoulder and kissed Becca's cheek. "Have a good night, you guys."

"You leavin'?" Bray asked.

Kelly shifted his belt and hiked up his pants. "Yeah. It's almost Nate's bedtime and I want to discuss decks with my wife."

Bray laughed. "Have a good night, Kel."

"You too."

When his brother's truck pulled away, Bray kissed his wife. He loved that his brothers could swing by on a moment's notice to have a beer. As always, it was good to be home.

"What was that for?" Becca asked, a bit breathless.

"You. For being awesome and moving here."

She smiled and nuzzled her nose to his neck. "You know we love it here."

"I love you." After a few minutes of enjoying his wife in his arms he nudged her off his lap and went to check on their son. "Bud, you want to see how high we can make that plane fly?"

Hunter turned and grinned. "Yeah!"

He glanced back to his wife. Her smile was soft and her eyes showed sweet adoration. Yeah, he never regretted his life. All the ups and downs brought him right to this moment and he was, without a doubt, happier than he'd ever been.

Leaping down the steps he joined Hunter and they played until the sun set, his laughter bounding into the forest, free and joyful.

. . .

THE CLOSER THEIR anniversary crept and the more people fussed over the accomplishment, the more Frank felt his age. He knew the next benchmark people would be hassling him about would be retirement, and he wasn't prepared to slow down yet.

As Tallulah sat on his lap reading him some tale about a girl named Amelia something, he considered his lineage. How lucky he was. Perhaps he didn't take enough time to sit back and appreciate all the blessings he'd been given.

"Pop, are you listening?" Lula asked, her 's's' getting caught up in her lisp.

He pulled her close and kissed her head. "I am. Amelia's going to open a lemonade stand."

Her blue eyes turned on him, her breath sweet with the chocolate Maureen had just allowed her. "Can me and you make a lemonade stand? We can call it Pop-a-Lula's Lemon's."

He chuckled. "Sure."

"When?"

"Well…" They'd been reading for quite some time. "I could see what I have in the shed."

Her eyes went wide. "You mean now?"

"Why not?"

"Mum-mum's makin' dinner."

He tousled her hair and slid her off his lap. "Then we better build up an appetite. Building a lemonade stand is a lot of work."

Her eyes danced with curious excitement. "Can I do the hammering?"

"Sure."

Taking her tiny hand in his, he led her to the kitchen where she told Maureen all about their future enterprise. "And we're gonna call it Pop-a-Lula's Lemons!"

"I wanna help!" Katie's Michael called from the table. It was always a toss-up whose kids they had on a Sunday.

"Yeah, Michael can help. We'll call it Pop-a-Lulachael's Lemons."

"Sounds good."

In the shed, Frank realized within five minutes how tedious it was to build something with little kids. After about the tenth 'what's this do?' and thirtieth 'don't touch that' he was ready to ask Maureen to bring him an aspirin, but this was what memories were made of, so he toughed it out.

As it got closer to dinner, Finn's family showed up and the twins and Gianna decided to lend a hand. The stand would now be called Pop-a-Lulachael-Declachlanna's Lemons.

The poor wood had nails hammered cockeyed over every square inch, but soon enough they had a base with two beams to fasten the big sign.

Maureen's voice rang out like a foghorn. *"Dinner!* All you

hooligans wash your hands. Girl's upstairs, boy's downstairs, and I better not find any floods in my bathrooms!"

Like a fleet of starved mini-maniacs, they ran screaming toward the house and he paused, staring at his wife, filling the doorway to their home. She lovingly touched each grandchild as they rushed by, and then slowly wandered to the shed.

"Quite the undertaking you've volunteered for," she said, admiring the numerous nails hammered superfluously across the surface.

He collected the hammers, returning each one to his tool-box. "The kids are having fun."

"I think their grandpop is having fun too."

He tightened the lid on the jar of nails and shrugged. "It's good for them to learn how to work with their hands."

Her palm pressed into his chest as she went up on her toes. "And it's good for you to show them. You're very sweet with them, Frank."

He swallowed. "I wish my father could have been there to do stuff like this with our kids."

Her smile was soft as she stared into his eyes. Any comment would only detract from his intended meaning.

The setting sun faded into shades of pink and gold, high-lighting the once vibrant red of her hair. It suddenly terrified him that she'd be alone someday.

He was feeling his years, especially the ones that put him ahead of her. "You know those boys of yours will do anything for you, Maureen. You never have to look far for a hand around here."

Her brow creased. "I know that, Frank. But I've got you."

He gently pinched her chin. "You're prettier than ever, love. Age suits you."

She shoved him. "We got a house full. Ice your balls and go wash up."

He chuckled. That was his woman, tongue sharper than a blade and a mouth as filthy as a brothel. She bustled back to the house and he yelled, "I'll be having you tonight!"

"We'll see!" she yelled back without looking.

"Yeah, we'll see," he mumbled, as he leaned down to get the last of the tools.

A sharp squeeze of pressure tightened in his chest as he stood. He frowned and rubbed at the spot. That week he'd take a trip to the hardware store for some yellow paint. Maybe some red too.

He closed the shed and paused, his back suddenly aching and his lungs short of breath.

"Dad, you coming?" Colin yelled.

"Yeah," he called, holding up a hand and gripping his elbow. He grunted as a steady ache traveled down his arm. "I'll be right there."

"Dad?"

Grimacing, he took a step and stilled. Pressure built in his shoulders as pain raced up his neck. He heard Colin shout and then the earth slammed into his knees as he went down, the pain stealing his breath and cutting out the sound of all else as the world went dark.

SHE WAS THERE, in her little dress, eyes wide as Van Morrison sung. He could never forget how much he wanted to rescue her, steal her away from that madness and have her all to himself. And then he did, as they raced down the interstate, windows low, in his old truck.

The scent of her floral perfume still freshly imprinted in his mind. She was like the rain, impossible to control, quick, and able to leave puddles as swiftly as she could bring a rainbow.

His mind skipped to another image, just after his father died. She'd brought him all that damn food and tidied up his home. He knew then he loved her more than he'd ever loved anything. What he didn't understand was why she gave her love to him in return.

He saw her body writhing under his the night they first made love, her tears as he watched her break after losing their first baby. So many tears had followed, but only a small bit as sad as they were that day.

She was happiness. His happiness, their children's happiness. Every birth, she showed her strength with only small glimpses of fear. She was so damn strong, yet he knew just how fragile she could be. And that was why he had to get through this.

The ambulance was like a rickety old amusement park ride, but he tolerated the prodding and nearness of the EMTs for her. She held his hand tight, gripping his fingers with the strength of a linebacker.

When they reached the hospital, he overheard his son's asking endless questions as he was fit with an IV of something to ease the pain, maybe something more, because he couldn't keep his eyes open.

Next he blinked and everything was calm.

"Frank?" Her voice was small.

Slowly, he turned his head on the over-bleached pillowcase, unsure when they moved him.

There she was. "Hello, love."

Her brow creased with worry as she exhaled a sigh of relief. "Oh, thank the Lord. You scared ten years off my life, you bastard." Her words were whispered, her lashes spiked with shed tears.

He squeezed her hand, which he still held. "Just keeping you on your toes." He was drowsy and a little woozy. His body felt like it was hit by a bus. "What happened, Maureen?"

She sucked in a breath and dabbed her nose with a tissue. "You had a clot in your heart. It broke up by the time we got here, but the doctors are going to put you on some blood thinners to be safe."

He frowned. Jesus. "A heart attack?"

"A little one. Just thank the good Lord you're safe and awake and here with us now."

As much as it pained him, he glanced around the room. "Where are the others?"

"They're in the waiting room. Colleen and Rosemarie took all the kids. Do you want me to go get them?"

The room wouldn't fit them. "No, just give me a few minutes."

She nodded and he saw her fighting back tears.

"Hey," he whispered, wishing he had the strength to touch her face. She glanced at him, forcing a smile that didn't reach her eyes. "I'm going to be okay, Maureen. It was just a little clot."

"I know." Her lips pursed. "I've just never been so frightened in all my life. You're sixty-five years old. This stuff isn't supposed to happen yet." Swiping away her tears she said, "You're stubborn as a mule and you eat like a beast, it's probably my fault for allowing all those second helpings."

"It's not your fault, love."

"I mean, you're fit and you walk the lumberyard every day. I never thought to put you on a diet—"

"Now wait a minute—"

"But I've been talkin' to Ashlynn and Mallory and they've given me some suggestions. Did you know they make bacon out of turkey now?"

"That sounds horrible."

"They say it's not."

"Masochists."

"Well, that's what you'll be having. I refuse to go through this again, do you hear me?" Her voice cracked. "You're my husband and I *need* you." Her chin quivered as tears build in her eyes. "I wouldn't know what to do with myself if I didn't have you. I'd drive the kids nuts, and then they'd all leave me and I'd be all alone in that big house. Why did you make such a big house? I don't want it without you, do you hear me Frank McCullough? So you had better just snap out of this and get yourself healthy before I become a basketcase of emotion and really lose my wits."

"Hey, hey, hey, easy, lass. I'm not going anywhere. I'll eat the damn turkey bacon."

"You bet your arse you will. Look at me, I'm a drippy mess."

He grinned, and found the strength to reach for her. His hand weakly cupped her jaw. "You love me."

"You know I do, you jackass."

"You love me too much, Maureen. You always have. And after all these years, I still can't figure out why?"

Pulling herself together, she sat back and composed herself, folding her arms across her chest and schooling her expression. She sighed and said, "It was your arse. I liked the way it looked in your Levis." She shrugged. "And it didn't hurt that you had your own truck."

He chuckled and winced at the remaining soreness in his chest. "Not my eyes then?"

She shrugged. "Maybe a little. Five sons have taught me not to fall for that blue-eyed charm like I once did, but I suppose that added to your appeal." She sighed, "And eventually you had your way with me."

"Oh, have you got balls."

"Aye." She grinned. "And I'm not afraid to use them, so you better not give me any lip when I tell you we'll be following the doctor's orders and you *will* be taking some time off to recuperate."

Perhaps it was whatever was pumping into his IV or perhaps it was all the sentimental thoughts he'd had lately, but for some reason she looked perfect in that moment, courageously fierce and delicate at the same time—so very Maureen.

"All right, love. You have my word. I won't fight you on it and I'll do as the doctors say."

She nodded and there was a knock at the door. Too many

McCullough's to count staring into the room.

"Well, don't all just stand there like I'm in a casket. Come on in. I'm still breathing."

They rushed into the room, stealing the air and silence as they all fawned over him. His beautiful daughters looking so much like their mother as they wept over him and kissed his cheeks. His sons were a bit more reserved with their emotions, but some hid it better than others.

Kelly approached and gripped his hand tight. "You scared us, Dad."

"I'm sorry, Kel."

His ice blue eyes shimmered as he nodded and let out a slow breath. "I'm glad you told God he was early."

"More like I begged him to let me stay. I got a lemonade stand to build."

They all started talking at once and soon enough a nurse came in and one by one they scattered, hugging and kissing each other and promising to see him tomorrow. It made him happy to see all of them like that, not a single one caught up in strife or nonsense.

When the room was again quiet, he looked at Maureen. "What are you doing all the way over there?" She came to his side and took his hand. He squeezed. "We did good, Maureen. We really did."

She smiled. "They're a great group of kids."

"I look at everything that's happened in the past years, think about all the surprises we were given. Colin's so happy as a family man and Finn has all but settled into my shoes. Sheilagh's happy and Luke's finally at peace with himself. Even Kelly's settled and Ashlynn's starting to show—"

"*What?*" She shot to her feet. "Ashlynn's pregnant?"

"I thought you knew?"

"No, I didn't bloody know! She took a test at our house

and Sheilagh said—" She paused and scowled. "*Sheilagh*. I'm going to beat that girl's arse."

"You can't get mad at Devil. She's eight months pregnant."

"And she knows that! That's why she lied. Oh! That little shit! And Ashlynn, that sneak!"

"Now, Maureen, maybe she wanted to keep the news to herself for a little—"

"But she told you!"

"Well, actually, Colin told me. He was excited about him and Sammy's news—"

"*What? What the hell is going on?*"

A nurse popped her head in. "Is everything all right?"

"Everything's fine. Maureen, keep your voice down."

"Two of my sons are having children and no one told me. I'll be calm after I get ahold of them."

"So Braydon hasn't talked to you lately."

Her eyes went wide. "Jesus, Mary, and Joseph there is going to be a reckoning."

"Calm down, love."

"Is there anyone else? So help me God, if one more person is keeping secrets from me..." She glared at him. "Kate's not pregnant, is she?"

"I should hope not."

She dropped into the chair and sulked. "Why wouldn't they tell me? And what about Mallory?"

"I haven't asked but—"

She pulled out her phone.

"What are you doing?"

"Calling your son."

"Maureen—"

She held up a silencing finger. "Hello, Finnegan. This is your mum. I have a question for you and I want an honest answer." She paused. "Because I said so. Is Mallory pregnant?" She frowned. "Okay then. I was just asking. Now, what kind of cake do you want tomorrow? You've just been promoted to my favorite child. The others are a shifty lot of liars that cannot be trusted." She nodded. "Chocolate it is. I love you too. Goodnight."

She snapped her phone shut. "There you have it. I at least have one honest child. The rest are going on my list."

He drew in a slow breath. Perhaps she was more like a storm than a soft rain. Either way, he'd weathered her conduct for forty years and he'd have it no other way.

He sighed. "You're one of a kind, Maureen McCullough. And I fear for those that lied to you. Promise you won't keep them on your list too long."

She crossed her arms and harrumphed.

CHAPTER 15

Maureen poured the liquid soap into the washer as the basin filled with water. Her patient was finally sleeping and not driving her up the damn wall—not that she was complaining. Never that.

As she checked his pockets a flash of movement drew her attention. She turned and paused. No one was there. Going back to the laundry, she—there it was again. Turning slowly, her eyes went wide as she spotted the intruder.

"Holy mother of fuck," she whispered, remaining perfectly still.

The spider—a *wolf* spider—easily the size of her hand, fingers spread, gripped the side of the drapes.

"Oh, my God," she whimpered, knowing she couldn't wake up Frank to handle the situation.

Quickly, her mind went through her options searching for the best plan of attack. She didn't typically harm insects, but this bastard was bordering on miniature dog size. It was big enough to crawl upstairs to the kitchen and get itself a cookie.

She had to be very careful not to startle the intruder. If she lost sight of it she'd have to move. There was no other option. Either she or the spider could live in the house, but not both.

With extremely slow movements, she placed Frank's jeans on the washer and backed to the corner of the base-ment where the waste paper bin sat. She'd catch the furry little fucker and run it outside.

Her heart pounded as she back-stepped little by little into the corner. Keeping her eye on the spider, she slid her foot to the right and scooted the trashcan in front of her. "Good little spider. No one's going to harm you." That might have been a lie.

The slow scrape of the small trashcan only added to her trepidation as the wooly beast suddenly began to move. "Oh, no you don't, you furry cocksucker."

Bending, she grabbed the can and dumped whatever dryer lint was inside. As she walked stealthily toward the window, she snatched an old detergent cup. The beast crawled faster, dashing behind a fold and she panicked. "Shit fucking rat farts, get back here you hairy bugger!"

Knocking the heavy material with the cup, she squeaked and winced and the climber clung to the drapes. "Drop, you nasty piece of shit! Oh, why the hell don't I have bug spray down here? This entire house is getting bombed as soon as Frank is up and about and you and all your little friends are going to get—" She whacked the drape. "—the hell—" She swatted the drape again. "Out of my house!"

With one final hit the spider fell into the bin with a *thunk* and she screamed, dropping the cup right in with it. Knowing how fast wolf spiders could crawl, she held the bin out as far as her arms would allow and ran for the back door.

"OhmyGod! OhmyGod! OhmyGod!" Doing a double take

as she fussed with the lock on the knob, she screamed again. "Not another one! Where the bloody fuck are you bastards coming from?"

The door flung open and she ran a good twenty feet to the pavement and dumped the can and banged the base, but the hairy beast wouldn't drop. In a full body sweat, she whimpered and ran back inside, abandoning the can and cup.

Racing back to the other one—thankfully not as large as his friend—she snatched up Frank's work boot and got right into killing. She brought down the boot and smacked the creepy little shit.

"Oh!" He didn't want to die, the bastard. "Die you trespassing piece of shit!" The boot came down again with a thwack and he finally crumpled. She did a partial sign of the cross and then waved off the last two parts as she huffed and caught her breath.

Panting, she leaned into the wall, eyes unblinking as she peeked at the door. "I'm going to be needing my waste basket back, damn it."

She grabbed the boot and marched out back. "Mother of God." Her steps faltered. The plastic bin had moved.

Hiking up her knickers under her dress, tightening the tie of her apron, and wiping her fallen hair out of her eyes, she studied the flipped trashcan. It was small, the kind someone would put beside a toilet, but any bug that could move something that size was simply too big and must be destroyed. She shivered and made a sound of gross disgust.

It must have had a long and gluttonous life to reach that size, so she was quite okay with ending it. Besides, she didn't want him retracing his steps and finding his way back inside.

Wiping the sweat off her lip with her sleeve, she drew in a steadying breath. "You've got this, Maureen."

She marched swiftly to the can and punted it into the grass. The spider spun on its furry legs and she could have sworn it hissed.

She screamed. *"Die!"* The boot slammed down, but the bastard still lived.

She repeatedly hit the spider with the boot, but it would not let go. "Die! Die! Die! Sweet Jesus go!" She was sweating and nearly in tears, her hair completely fallen from her bun.

Distraught, she dropped the boot and wobbled back a few steps. Of all her years living there and dealing with insects, she never saw anything remotely close to this size. When it slowly began to crawl, she screamed like a wild clansman racing down the battlefield of Falkirk. She snatched the pitchfork against the wall and charged, impaling the belly of the beast and ending it once and for all.

Like a possessed woman, she held the pitchfork to the pavement and panted. "Go with God now, you ugly bastard."

"Mum?"

She turned, still in battle mode and nearly snarled at Kelly as he came around the outside of the house.

"What are you doing?"

Pitchfork still speared to the pavement, she said, "Laundry, what the bloody hell does it look like?"

He frowned and slowly approached. Stopping a few feet away from the crushed spider, he craned his neck and shivered. "Blah. That's a big one."

"Aye and not an easy kill."

The side of his mouth hooked up as he flashed his blue eyes her way. "Quite the domestic huntress you are."

She yanked the pitchfork clean and kicked the furry corpse into the lawn with her boot. "All in a day's work. You remember that next time you're thinkin' of skimpin' on my Mother's Day flowers." Holding the tines by her shoulder now, she blew out a breath and swiped her hair away from her sweaty face. "What brings you by this time of day?"

He fidgeted, shuffling his feet and wedging his hands into his pocket. "I was hoping we could have a chat."

Her eyes narrowed. "Oh, now you're wanting to chat with me? Well, I'll have you know I found out about your little secret."

Contrite, his brow formed a small V. "I'm sorry, Mum. We just wanted to keep the news to ourselves for a while. We weren't purposely leaving you out."

"Of course you were."

"I'm sorry." Head bowed, he set his eyes on her and she sighed.

"Don't shoot those blue eyes at me, you devil. I'm immune." He continued to eye her and she huffed. "Fine. Get your arse in the house and I'll make you lunch. I've had enough nature for one day."

As they settled in at the table with lunch, Kelly eyed the den. "How's Dad?"

She sighed and sat for the first time that day. "He's a miserable patient, but he's regaining his strength every day."

"Did the doctors give the impression that this could happen again?"

Fear climbed up her spine as she repeated everything she'd been telling herself for the past two weeks. "Your father's a strong man. I've seen him overcome many difficult things in his life and he's not done living yet. So long as he starts taking better care of himself and lays off the fats and sugars, he should be fine."

Kelly nodded, but she could see his worry.

Trying to ease his mind, she brushed her hand over his. "Now, what is it that brings you by, love? I can tell you've got something big on your mind. Is it Ashlynn and the baby?"

"No, no. She's doing great."

She waited.

He let out a long breathe. "I, uh, was asked to be a part of something pretty special."

"Like a parade?"

"No, a showing."

She arched a brow and finished chewing a bite of her sandwich. "What is it you'll be showing, love?"

He reached into his back pocket and pulled out a tube. Uncapping the end, he removed a smudged sheaf of paper. "These."

Her head tipped curiously. "What do you have there?"

Sliding their plates out of the way, he slowly smoothed out the paper and her lips parted. A stunning likeness of two young boys sitting on a split rail fence showed on the page.

"Oh, Kelly…" The image was breathtaking. "That's Colin and Luke."

"Yeah."

"Where did you get this?" She couldn't get over the realism.

"I…drew it." He slid the masterpiece aside. "There's more."

She couldn't fathom that her Kelly had created such art. "That's me."

He nodded.

She knew he sometimes dabbled with charcoal, but these were extraordinary. "Kelly, love, these are amazing. I had no idea. I mean, this one of the boys, you couldn't have been more than a teenager."

"I do a lot of it from memory."

She laughed. "That's some memory. You have a gift, Kelly, a beautiful gift."

"I submitted them to a company that features independent artists and they've asked for five of my collections."

"That's wonderful!" Pride swelled in her chest.

Her son suddenly looked like a young boy again as a blush stole over his face. "I'm still in shock. They even mentioned possibly commissioning me to draw some new images. I'm considering it."

"Well, what does your heart tell you?"

His shoulders shifted as he exhaled and met her gaze. "It tells me that this is a once in a lifetime opportunity and drawing makes me happier than turning out cocktails ever could."

"Oh, Kelly…" Her brow pinched as she considered her words carefully. "I've always been so proud of you for taking on the bar, but no one is holding you there. You follow your heart. This family's big enough for someone to take over O'Malley's if you need this time to spread your wings." She smiled and squeezed his arm. "You fly up to the moon, love, and we'll all be here watching as you become a star." She chuckled. "My little Michael Angelo."

He laughed. "Maybe someone a bit more Irish. John Butler Yeats, perhaps."

She grinned. "How about Kelly McCullough, master of charcoal, rogue of his clan."

"Momma's boy to a fault."

A proud smile took over her face. "Aye." She brushed a hand over his smooth black hair. "I'm so proud of the man you've become, Kelly. I hope you know that."

"I do, Mum. I do."

"Good. Now eat your lunch. We have an infestation of spiders around here and if you leave that sandwich too long, one of them might scamper by and carry it off. They're the size of squirrels."

Maureen led the kids into the gym. "Come along, now. Declan, finger out of your nose. If I see you eat one more booger I'll assume you're too full for a milkshake."

"Ew…" Gianna cried. "You're dis-dusting, Dec."

Maureen led them to the smoothie bar. "Who wants chocolate and who wants strawberry?"

The kids yelled out their choices and she turned to the young lady behind the counter. "We'll have two strawberries and one chocolate."

"Um…" the girl glanced at the children. "We don't have chocolate." She again stared at the children. "This is a gym. We usually only serve members."

"Oh, well…" Maureen glanced around the gym, sighting Mallory at some machine with that handsome fellow hanging by her side. "Their mother's a member and so am I. I'll just get her."

"That won't be necess—"

"Yoo-hoo, Mallory!" She waved.

Mallory turned and froze her eyes going wide. The children all jumped and called, "Hi Mommy!"

The man frowned as she made an excuse and quickly walked to the smoothie bar. "Maureen, what are you doing here?"

"The children wanted milkshakes."

"Then take them to an ice cream parlor," she grit out.

"I have to say, Mallory, I don't much care for your tone." Her friend came over and Maureen eyed him suspiciously. "I don't recall your friend being so much shorter than my Finnegan."

"Maureen!" Mallory snapped. "Please take the kids back to your house."

"What about our shakes?" Gianna whined.

Letting out a frustrated sigh, Mallory turned to her friend. "Mitch, I'm sorry, I'm going to have to bail on the rest of our workout."

"It's fine. Do what you gotta do."

"Oh, he's so amicable," Maureen commented and laughed. "We're not used to such docile males in this family."

Her daughter-in-law glared at her and ushered the kids to the smoothie bar, quickly placing an order.

Maureen met the man's stare. "I'll assume you're admiring my charming grandchildren at that level and not my daughter-in-law's arse." His eyes snapped to hers. "There we go. Eyes up here like a good lad. Now, I may be old, but I know what you're doing. Mallory can deny it until she's blue in the face, but that girl's sweet as pie and doesn't know just how beautiful she truly is. I understand why you'd be attracted to her—I'm not a lesbian, mind you, but her beauty's irrefutable. However, before you encroach one more millimeter on my son's territory, I want you to know that she's a McCullough, and we don't take kindly to others poaching from us. Do you understand, young man?"

He looked like someone clocked him right in his bollocks. "Yes, ma'am."

"Good. We'll just keep this little chat between us. Enjoy your aerobics now." She turned back to the children. "I'm sorry, Mallory. I'll not be bringing them here again. I just thought it would be faster than waiting in line at the Dairy Queen."

"It's fine." Bless Mallory for lying when Maureen knew perfectly well she was cross.

"How about I keep them overnight this Friday and give you and Finnegan a little alone time?"

That seemed to lighten her mood. "Really?"

"What are grandmothers for, dearie? Of course. Go somewhere special, maybe take a trip to the city."

"Th—thanks, Maureen. I appreciate it."

She nodded. "Now, we'll leave you alone to finish your exercises. Say goodbye, my little cherubs."

The kids all kissed their mother and Mallory scanned the gym. "Where did Mitch go?"

Maureen bustled the kids toward the door. "Off to the car, dearies. Chop. Chop."

THE DAY after Maureen brought the children to the gym, Mitch had pulled her aside and suggested they grab lunch rather than finish their work out. Mallory laughed—thinking of the last time she had the chance to enjoy a social lunch with anyone that didn't color on the placemats.

"But we're working out…"

His cheeks flushed and not from the lifting they were doing. "I like you, Mallory. I think you're funny and you've gotten so pretty and I want to be more than your gym partner."

It was then she understood what he was asking and just how naïve she'd been. Worst of all, Maureen was right. She took a step back, understanding sinking in like an oily fist punching her right in the chest. Guilt filled her. "Mitch, I'm married."

"I know."

"Then why are you saying this stuff?"

"I thought…you're always here. We see each other every day…"

That wouldn't be happening anymore. She frowned, trying to grasp the fact that a body builder like Mitch could want her when the gym was crawling with Barbie type women who didn't have husbands or children.

"I love my husband." And he loved her. Finn didn't think she evolved into something pretty like Mitch so clumsily put it. He always saw her as beautiful, just as she saw him.

He frowned. "Then why are you trying to change so much for him?"

She scowled. "What? I'm not changing for him. I come here for me, because with three kids it's my only escape." She shook her head. "I run and workout, because I like the way it makes me feel. It has nothing to do with Finn. He loves me at any size. I'm his wife."

"I just thought—"

"You thought wrong." Pissed off he'd confuse their relationship and thereby threaten it, she said, "I think you need to find a new gym buddy."

"Mallory, it doesn't have to be—"

"It does. I'm sorry if I sent you any mixed signals, but my heart belongs to my husband, always has, always will. For you to even consider jeopardizing my marriage is an insult to me, my husband, and our family. I'm sorry."

She left the gym, so out of sorts she'd forgotten her favorite water bottle and didn't have the nerve to go back for it.

That Friday, when she and Finn took a trip to the city and spent the night, Mallory knew she had to tell him what happened. Her stomach knotted as she worried how her husband would react.

After a romantic dinner they returned to the hotel room. She was nervous, the intimate setting and sexual tension an almost forgotten thing between them. He plopped on the bed and reached for the remote and her heart sank. Of course he was tired and just wanted to unwind—enjoy the precious peace and quiet. She was tired too, but this was exactly why so much distance rested between them. She hated it.

But most of all, more than missing sleep or fancy clothes or her independent schedule, she missed her husband. "Finn, I need to tell you something."

FINN STILLED, as nothing about his wife's tone boded well. He placed the remote control on the pillows and sat up. "What is it?"

Mallory sighed and sat on the far corner of the bed— another bad sign. "Something happened at the gym."

He frowned. "Go on."

"You know how your mom made that big fuss about Mitch?"

He chuckled. "Yeah."

"Well…she wasn't as far off the mark as I thought."

His smile faltered. His mother, though sometimes drawn to imagined drama, warned him Mitch was trying to steal his wife. If she wasn't off her mark then… Blood roared in his ears as he scowled and sat up. His entire world flashing before his eyes as fear fisted his heart.

Quietly, he rasped, "What the fuck are you talking about?"

She blinked and looked away. "Mitch…came on to me."

His jaw locked. "Did he fucking touch you?"

"No," she quickly said. "Nothing like that. He just…asked me out."

"Oh, nothing like that, he just asked you out, knowing full

bloody well you are *my wife!*" He was on his feet and pacing without realizing he'd stood.

"I handled it. I told him he was not only disrespecting you, but me and my family by even asking such a thing." She looked away. "I told him we couldn't work out together anymore."

"I'll kill him—"

"Finn, please don't make this any worse than it already is. It's still my gym."

He shook his head, trying to quell the rage burning to spill out. "He *knows* you're married! I've met him, invited him to O'Malley's with us. What kind of fucking man does that?"

"I know! Which is exactly why I told him it was disrespectful."

Fear had him panting. His palms broke into a sweat as his knuckles cracked. "Did you…consider it?"

Her lips parted. "God, no. I swear to you. I *love you*, Finn. Our family, our children, even our stupid dog. I will never leave you or the life we made."

How had this happened? How had he dropped his guard so much that another man would even consider it possible to tempt his wife to stray? "This is my fault."

"No—"

"Don't make excuses for me, Mallory. I should have been there. We used to go to the gym together."

"That was before we had kids, Finn."

"My mother can watch the kids."

"But sometimes packing them up is more of a hassle then just leaving them home. And this is my fault too."

He frowned. "How?"

She fidgeted, wringing her hands on her lap. "I've been… lonely. I know I'm hardly ever by myself, but sometimes…I miss you, Finn. Us. I miss adult time." Her face lowered, her expression hidden by her hair as she whispered, "We go days without touching each other."

He rounded the bed and dropped to his knees, taking her hands in his and kissing her fingers. "Philly, I'm sorry we've let things get to this. It has nothing to do with you, I swear it. Life just caught up with me and I lost track. Every damn day I look at you and want you more than the day before."

She sniffled and a tear fell on their hands. "I want you too. We have to take more time for each other, Finn. I don't want to wait years before Gianna becomes a big sister, but at this rate, I don't know if that will *ever* happen."

"It will." He leaned forward and kissed her. "My aunts are always offering to take the kids and my mum never minds. We have to stop trying to do everything ourselves. I don't know how or why we got that way, but if leaning on others a little more gets us back to where we were, then I'm game."

She nodded. "I compare myself with others too much. I look at Ashlynn and Kelly and I see this serene couple. Then I look at our life and there's cereal spilled all over the table and the dogs eating the couch and Gianna's naked again."

He laughed. "That's life, Philly. Kelly has one kid. Let's see how he does with two. You had twins. When me and Luke were born, my dad says my mum nearly lost her mind. Boys are tough. Twin boys are tougher. And Gianna is going to grow up into a powder puff linebacker the way things are going. And you know what? I love it. I love the chaos, the shouting, the mayhem, and even the insanity of bath time, because *we* made that, Philly. You and me."

Her glassy eyes met his. "I love you, Finn."

"I love you too. I love you more than the air I breathe. I want to kill that fucker for even thinking he could take what's mine."

Her fingers sifted through his hair. "I know I can sometimes be a basket case, but I need you. Otherwise I get lost in my head and it isn't always a pretty place. You keep me grounded and make me believe I can do this."

He kissed her nose. "I'll always pull you back. Always."

He eased her to the mattress and stripped her out of her dress. Their motions were hasty as they were starved for each other, their need bone deep and something only each other could satisfy.

As he made love to her, he vowed to never let things get this far again. He reclaimed her, over and over again throughout the night.

Perhaps he needed to be reminded not to take her for granted. They rarely fought and laughed every day, but he would be lost without her and he'd fight to the death to keep her. She was his. His Mallory. His Philly.

Maureen sighed and tossed her arms beside her on the bed. "Well… I suppose your doctors would have a thing or two to say about that."

Frank chuckled. "I'm not dead yet, woman."

"No, you certainly aren't." She rolled to her side and ran her fingers over his chest. "I've missed you."

He turned and quietly studied her. "You have no idea how much I missed you, too, love. If taking better care of myself is the price I have to pay in order to feel your body wrapped around mine, then I'll eat turkey bacon and salad for the rest of my days."

She grinned and curled into his side. "It's July."

His fingers laced with hers. "Aye."

"The children have worked so hard putting everything together. I can't wait to see everything they've planned."

"It should be quite the event."

"Aye."

They lay in silence for some time, her mind going over the past forty years. Try as she might, it was impossible to summarize all the ups and downs in one evening. "We've had quite the go of it, Frank. Do you have any regrets?"

His lashes lifted. "No, Maureen. My life has been one long line of blessings. The tears only make me appreciate the good times more."

"You are a romantic soul, Frank McCullough. I'll not tell the other boys to protect your reputation."

"I don't know what you're talking about, woman. I'm a lumberjack, born and bred to hunt, fuck, and feast like a carnivorous man."

She chuckled. "You're a big softy."

He rolled farther to his side, pinning her with his arms around her face. "Bite your tongue." His mouth pressed softly to hers. "I'm a McCullough."

"Aye. *My* McCullough."

"Mum..."

Maureen frowned as someone poked her shoulder and giggled.

"Is she breathing? Mum, wake up."

More giggles.

Maureen squinted her eyes in the dark and gasped. "What the hell are you all doing in my bed?"

"It's your wedding day," Sheilagh hummed.

"Wha—" She glanced around the room. Mallory, Sammy, Kate, Becca, Ashlynn, Rosemarie, and Colleen were all crowded around her. "It's dawn."

"Happy birthday, Mum," Kate said and the others echoed.

"Shhh…we'll not tell anyone just how old I am."

"Aye, but you're no spring chicken," Colleen cackled. "We got our work cut out for us. Up you go."

They yanked away her covers and she frowned. "Where's Frank?"

"Already at Luke and Tristan's," Sheilagh said. "Alec's making all the guys a big breakfast."

"And who will be feeding us?" They all grinned. "Oh, no. I'm not cooking on my wedding day."

They laughed and Rosemarie said, "I've already taken care of it. Wash up and come get some coffee. My minions are below and I can't leave them unsupervised for long."

Maureen frowned, counting her daughters. "Who's missing?"

Becca grinned. "Nikki and Carla are here for the party. They're dying to see you so don't take long."

As they shuffled out Maureen went to use the bathroom. When she returned to her room in her nightgown, Kate waited on her bed. "Why aren't you down with the others, Katie girl?"

"Sit down, Mum."

She slowly sat beside her eldest daughter. "Is everything okay?"

"Yes." She took her hands. "I love you."

"I love you too, dear."

She reached beside her and picked up a small wooden

box. "Do you remember when I married Ant, how you told me marriage wasn't perfect and loving a husband meant holding something in my heart too big to cram into any box?"

"Did I say that? That's rather lovely."

Kate smiled. "Yes. And you were right. I've loved him on days I didn't like him. I've given more thought to what he and my children need than anything I could possibly want, because at the end of the day I just wanted them to be happy. I learned to laugh at life and roll with the punches. And through it all, I had you setting an example for me. You and Daddy make it look so easy."

"Oh, honey, it's not, but thank you. You're very sweet. Truth be told, your father's lucky I didn't poison him long ago. But I love the bugger and I don't know how to live without him. He's a slob and can be a grouch, and hardly says more than the two or three words that need saying, but he's mine and I wouldn't have chosen differently no matter how big of a pain in my arse he can be. Love is messy and I've been in it with him since I was just a girl." She smiled. "I like the mess. It tells me I'm still living."

She opened the ornate box. "This is yours. You gave it to me on my wedding day and now I'm giving it back to you." She held the old garter. "It's not so new anymore, but it's blue."

Maureen tried not to laugh as she gently took the lace piece. They each stared at it for a moment. "Perhaps it's more of a wristlet..." she muttered, noting the slender dimensions.

Kate snorted. "Yeah, it wouldn't fit on my thigh either. Was I ever really that skinny?"

Maureen shook her head. "I'm lucky if I remember yesterday. You can't expect me to remember your damn size, Kate."

They laughed and Maureen hugged her. "Thank you. Every bride needs something old and blue." She glanced at her chest. "Perhaps I'll stuff it in my bosom."

"There you go."

There was a knock at the door and Sheilagh peeked in. "Kate, Becca needs you to help her with something."

"Okay." She kissed Maureen's cheek. "Today's going to be great, Mum. We have everything ready, so try to relax and enjoy it."

"I will, dear."

Kate left and Sheilagh took her spot on the bed. Maureen glanced at her enormous belly and snorted. "Are you going to be all right in this heat, love?"

Sheilagh shook her head. "It's ridiculous. I was supposed to go early. Never once did I expect to be a week late."

"Brat. Your water will probably break right in the middle of my wedding and there will go my thunder."

Sheilagh affectionately nudged her with her shoulder. "I'm praying that doesn't happen."

"Pray harder. Though that would be an excellent story." They laughed and sighed. "So… are you all planning on making me emotional today?"

"Yup."

"Well, let's have it."

Sheilagh smiled, showing signs of her mischievous self. "I couldn't think of something old, new, borrowed, or blue…so I got you a flask of Tullamore Dew." She withdrew a silver flask with a tiny blue ribbon tied around the cap.

"This *and* your poetic words?" Maureen laughed, taking the whiskey. "I believe this will come in handy today."

"I figured. I, on the other hand, will be sober as a saint."

Maureen placed a hand on her daughter's stomach. "I'm so proud of you, Sheilagh. You made a decision and you stuck with it. You've also shared a bit of your heart, letting others share this incredible gift with you. It's not something every woman could do."

"I know it doesn't make sense to everyone, but… I wanted my own and Alec tried. It wasn't right that Luke and Tristan got turned down."

She nudged her with her shoulder. "Who would have thought you'd actually be carrying Tristan's baby after all?"

"And yet I've still never seen the man naked," she joked and they both laughed.

When the giggles faded, Maureen said, "Alec is a good husband and he's where you belong."

"I know. I've never looked back since meeting him. He's the other half of my soul."

"It shows, dear. It shows."

There was another knock on the door and Becca stepped in. "Am I interrupting? I can come back."

"Nope. We're good," Sheilagh said as she awkwardly tried to stand. Becca rushed to her aid and helped pull her to her feet. "I'll be downstairs."

Becca came in and delicately sat by her side, her head resting on her shoulder. "I love you, Maureen."

Maureen kissed her blonde head, loving her for her sweetness and gentle manner. "I love you too, Becca." She patted her hand. "You're family."

She faced her. "When I first met you, I fell in love with you on the spot. I've never really talked to you about my family, but losing my mom was like losing a piece of my heart. You've always treated me like a daughter and that has meant more to me than I could ever say."

"You're one of my daughters, Becca. Family."

She smiled. "I want to give you something new, if you

don't mind. I'd like to stop calling you Maureen and start calling you…Mom."

"Oh, Becca, nothing could make me happier." She kissed her cheek.

"I hope you have the best day ever, Mom."

"It's already more special than I dreamed."

She nodded. "I'll send Sammy up."

As she waited, she found herself blinking back tears. She was indeed blessed.

She glanced at the flask and the clock. "Oh, to hell with it." Unscrewing the cap, she took a quick swig, tightening the top just as Sammy entered.

"Knock-knock."

"Come in, Sammy."

"I have something for you."

Maureen grinned as she sat down. "You're all spoiling me rotten and it's not even eight in the morning."

"You spoil us year round. It's nice to give a little back after all you've done."

"Taking care of all of you is all I know. It's what I'm good at, I think."

"You're more than good at it, Maureen. No one could do what you do. If you believe anything, believe that. *You* are the glue that holds us together."

Her face heated. "You're going to make me cry, love."

"Well, don't cry." She reached in her pocket. "I have something for you, something old. I saw it at an antique shop and thought of you." Sammy opened her fist and dropped the small item into Maureen's palm.

"Oh, Sammy…" The tiny pendant was not fancy metal, but nonetheless lovely. The bronze metal formed an intricate tree of Celtic knots.

"You *are* family, Maureen. This tree has a branch for all seven of your children. It just…reminded me of you."

She was consumed by unexpected emotion. Suddenly, the significance of the day struck her. It wasn't about a party or fancy clothes. It was about all they had made from their love and devotion.

She nodded, blinking back tears. Her voice cracked as she whispered, "We sure have grown something beautiful from our love."

"Yes."

Trembling with emotion, she kissed Sammy's cheek. "Thank you for this, Samantha. Thank you for being a part of our family tree, for loving my Colin so, and giving me beautiful grandbabies. You're one of us and that's just as it should be. I love you, dear."

"I love you too."

Soon after Sammy left Mallory came in. Things were better since Maureen eased up on her meddling. Mallory sat beside her and she waited.

"You're a pain in my ass, Maureen…"

"It's my job to be, love."

"You know I love you."

"I know. You're a tough cookie, Mallory, stronger than all the others. I know you don't see yourself that way, because you like to count your failures, but believe me, you *are* strong. No failure has ever been enough to break your spirit. You always pick yourself up and try again. You're unbeatable in my book, and just what my Finnegan needed. A good, solid woman."

Mallory sniffled, catching her off-guard. "I'm not that tough."

"Why are you crying, love?"

"Because…you're so good to me and I don't always show how much you mean to me, but you do, Maureen. You mean the world to me."

"Oh, sweetie, don't cry." She pulled her into her arms. "There, there, love. It's okay."

She sniffled again and wiped her nose. "I didn't get you something old."

"All right."

"And I didn't get you something blue."

"Okay. You don't have to give me anything."

She sniffled again. "I don't have anything for you to borrow."

"I have everything I need, love. Please stop crying."

She wiped her eyes. "I have something new for you, though."

"Oh?"

She nodded and met her stare. "I'm pregnant."

She jumped. "*What?* Truly?"

"Yes. And as a wedding gift, I'm telling you first. Even Finn doesn't know yet."

Her chest swelled with happiness. "I'm the first to know? But I'm always the last to know anything."

"I know. And I know you're going to tell everyone before I get a chance to tell Finn, so I'm asking you to just give me five minutes to run over to Luke's and break the news."

"Oh, Mallory…this is such incredible news! And I'm the first to know! Are you happy, love?"

"I'm very happy," she said, her glassy eyes smiling. "Nothing compares to this feeling." She sighed. "I should have known better than to think I stood a chance against a McCullough man."

She nudged her. "They're very virile."

"You aren't kidding."

"I'm so glad to see the two of you have worked things out."

Mallory smiled. "Life gets complicated sometimes. I never doubted Finn's love and affection, but having a family is exhausting. We were both burnt out."

"Oh, you don't have to tell me. And twins are tough."

"You aren't kidding. Thank you for pushing us in the right direction. As much as I grumble I really do appreciate your intentions."

Maureen smiled. "My son has never loved someone the way he loves you, Mallory. He's more like his father than any of the rest of them. They don't always express themselves when it comes to matters of the heart, but they love fiercely. It takes a tough woman to hold faith in such an unspoken thing."

"Thank you."

"Go on and tell Finnegan. I'll keep your secret."

Mallory raised a doubtful brow.

"For a few minutes at least. Be quick."

"Happy anniversary and happy birthday, Maureen."

"Thank you, love. And thank you for my incredible gift. We're truly blessed."

She nodded. "We are."

Voices talked over one another as they all crowded into Luke's den, each man hovering over his own plate as Alec manned the stove.

"Are you nervous, Dad?" Braydon asked as he inhaled a strip of crispy pork bacon.

"I think you should give me that bacon."

His son chuckled. "Not a chance. Eat your egg white omelet."

"There's turkey bacon over here, Frank," Tristan called.

"The person that invented that should be shot."

Tristan eyed the plate. "Yeah."

Mallory walked in and all the men hooted and hollered. "No girls allowed, lassie!"

"Unless you're the stripping sort," Kelly called.

Finn tossed the pastry he was gorging himself on at his brother's head and smiled. "What's up, Philly?"

"Um…can I speak to you for a minute?"

All the men booed as if he were in trouble.

"Shut up," Finn called, as he took his wife through the connection into the nursery and shut the door.

Frank glanced at Bray. "You really did a nice job with Alec and Devil's house."

"Thanks. Now she's just got to spit out the kid and their home will be complete."

"Easy now. We don't need anyone's water breaking today."

Luke blanched and pushed his plate onto the coffee table.

Frank frowned. "You okay there, sport?"

He took a long sip of orange juice and still appeared a little pale. "Yeah, just a little queasy."

"Aw…he's got sympathy pains," Kelly teased.

"Leave him alone," Tristan chuckled, coming to sit on the arm of Luke's chair. "We're all just a little nervous. Sheilagh's the size of a house and six days overdue. It's like waiting for a bomb to detonate."

Alec mumbled something from the kitchen and Frank turned. "What was that, Alec?"

"I said your daughter's a sweet little angel."

The men all laughed.

There was a howling shout from the other part of the house and they all turned and the door burst open. Finn stepped out, his face split with a wide grin. "I'm going to be a father again! Did you hear me? My woman is pregnant!"

They all cheered and Frank put his plate aside, walking over to his son who was being bombarded with hugs and slaps on the shoulder. He hugged his boy tight. "Congratulations, Finnegan."

"Thanks, Dad."

Turning to Mallory, he held out his arms. "And you…" She smiled and came to him, hugging his middle tight. "Are you happy, lass?"

She hummed and squeezed his ribs. "Very."

"Then I'm happy. Congratulations, Philly."

"Thanks, Frank."

"You better go tell your mother-in-law."

"Already taken care of. Telling her first was my anniversary slash birthday gift."

"Bet that made her day."

She smiled up at him. "Not as much as renewing her vows to you will."

Finn edged Mallory closer to him and beamed as he wrapped his arm around her shoulders. "Can you believe it? Four, we're gonna have four!"

"Three more and we'll be neck and neck," Frank teased.

Mallory scowled. "Settle down."

Finn kissed her cheek. "I love ya, Philly."

There were quiet moments with that one, moments when Frank noted her vulnerable side as she let down her guards. Finn did that to her and it reminded him so much of himself and Maureen.

Mallory left to return to the women and the mood had lifted with the happy news. "She's a good girl, Finn," Frank said quietly to his son.

"She's the best. I don't know how I got so lucky, but I must have done something right."

"Do you realize," Colin said, "we're all expecting children in the next year?"

Everyone sobered and got quiet. "Holy shit," Bray whispered.

Frank tried to do the math, but his mind was too distracted with other things. "That's a lot of McCullough."

Nodding, they all grinned and grunted with masculine pride.

"Well, not all of us," Ant said. "Kate's finished. We tapped out at four."

Finn's eyes glazed over. "Four."

Kelly put his feet on the coffee table. "We sure are a virile bunch."

"Oh, will you look at the lot of you, all sitting around strokin' each other's egos," Colleen said as she came in carrying a box of boutonnieres. "Good thing you were all born with such broad shoulders so you could haul around that lousy pride. I've never seen a group of men with such big—"

"Cocks?" Kelly called out.

Colleen rolled her eyes. "No." She dropped the box on the table. "Here. Each one's labeled. I've shown Luke how they go, so make sure you get them on the correct lapel and don't crush the petals, you hear? Frank, yours is the one with the green ribbon."

Tristan inspected the box. "These look great, Col."

"Your jackets are in the van, but I'll need a hand getting them out. Grab them now, because I have to go check on Paulie and Liam and the kids. Italian Mary's at my house doing Mum's makeup and I want to make sure she doesn't have her looking like a drag queen."

They went to unload the van and Colleen grabbed Frank's sleeve, stalling him. "You ready for today?"

"Aye."

She smiled at him, a soft show of feminine grace hidden in her fiery eyes. "We're getting' old, Frank."

"You don't have to tell me."

"Sometimes I still feel like we're careless kids kicking around Center County without a worry in the world."

Frank had always cared. He'd always been so focused on making it, surviving and succeeding at being a good man. "Sometimes it's nice to look back at how far we've come, Col."

Her smile was the sort that told of deep satisfaction. "Aye.

What would we have done without you, Frank? You and Maureen were meant for each other. You've given her forty years of loyalty and love, and I thank you for that. And you've been a brother to the rest of us, always there when we needed anything."

"That's what family does, Colleen."

She nodded. "I wish my father could have seen the incredible man you grew into, Frank. I don't think he'd be usin' your balls for target practice anymore."

He chuckled. "No, I don't think he would."

"I wish my mother was aware enough to understand what's happening today. She and Maureen were always closest and I know she'd have really loved being a part of all this."

"She still is, Colleen. She may not know what's going on, but she knows she's surrounded by love and warmth. She doesn't have to know each of us to know what family feels like."

She smiled. "That's a nice way to put it."

He hugged her. "I'm a day late, but happy anniversary to you too. I owe a lot of my happiness to you and Paulie."

She shrugged. "My baby sister stole my thunder once more. Lucky for her, I'm the loving and forgiving sort. Besides, I had my big wedding. It's her turn now."

"Thanks, Colleen. For everything."

The men returned carrying pressed kilts and jackets all wrapped in slick plastic from the cleaners. She turned and shouted, "You hang them up somewhere so they won't get wrinkled, you hear me?" She winked at Frank. "Good luck today."

"So long as she's there to meet me half way everything will be fine. How is my blushing bride?"

She giggled. "They're primping her like she's on her way

to meet the great and powerful Oz. Wait until you see her, love. We've even managed to paint her nails."

He arched a brow. "My wife?"

"Aye, your wife."

CHAPTER 17

*A*s the sun rose high above the white fleecy clouds, situated in the soft blue sky, Colin shut his eyes and prayed. Gratitude for his family's health and the bountiful life he'd been given, first and foremost in his thoughts.

The lake rippled softly as leaves fell from the trees along the bank. The still afternoon was indeed the perfect setting for a wedding.

"It feels like yesterday that I was walking down this aisle."

He turned and spotted Sammy making her way between the many rows of white wooden chairs. "One of the happiest days of my life."

She came to his side and slid her fingers between his. "Mine too."

Colin squeezed her palm as they stared at the dock in the distance. "Do you remember the first day we met?"

"I do. You all made me play baseball."

"I still remember the thrill that cut through my belly when I saw you nail that ball." He laughed. "You didn't run."

"I did too. It just took me a few seconds to get over the shock that I didn't strike out."

He kissed her cheek. "I recall discussing literature with you and being shocked your favorite was *Peter Pan*."

"It still is."

"You've grown up, Wendy."

She smirked. "And what do you know, I found a boy that wasn't afraid to love."

Facing her, he took her hands and met her gaze. "I've never regretted a single day we shared, Samantha. You're still that fire, burning in my heart, imprisoned in my bones."

"Oh, Colin…I have no regrets either. This mountain, your family, your parents, our children…it's more than I could have ever imagined, and it's so incredible because of you. I love you."

He kissed her. "I love you too." Turning toward the lake, he whispered, "Since your parents are staying with us, how about you and I swim out to the dock tonight after the party? Just the two of us, like old times."

Her gaze softened. "You have yourself a date."

Already, his body tightened with the slow burn of anticipation.

"Do you have everything you need for the ceremony?"

"I think so. All that's missing are the three hundred kilted maniacs."

"They'll be here soon. I'm going to run home and change into my gown. My mother took Lula to the beauty parlor with her so at least I don't have to deal with her hair."

He pressed a soft kiss on her cheek. "I'll see you at the ceremony."

She nodded. "And then at the dock tonight."

"Tonight," he agreed.

MALLORY STARED in the mirror and sighed contently. She'd worked so hard to get back to a point with her body that she was happy, but nothing could compare to the happiness of carrying a child again.

Her hand brushed over the satin bodice and rested on her lower abdomen. She joked with the others, teasing them about how potent McCullough sperm could be, but the truth was, every child came from love and the night she and Finn made this child was one she'd never forget.

He'd held her and looked into her eyes and she'd finally admitted her motives at the gym were not purely health related. She'd been sad and missing her husband, needing to hear his voice and see his face a bit more than usual.

The gym had been an outlet for all her doubts and the slight depression she feared falling into without him. Finn had told her that he, too, felt the distance. It was life. That was all there was to it. But sometimes confusion morphed into unintentional mishaps.

She recalled the way he'd held her that night and every night after. They'd made some compromises, moving the children's bedtime to thirty minutes earlier and starting the boys on chores around the house. Gianna was still young, but she was also learning to help out in little ways. All of this added to their time together, as a family and apart from the kids. And there had been many, many times.

"Whatchya thinkin' about?"

She jumped and spun toward the door. "Speak of the devil."

Finn shut the door and grinned. "You were havin' dirty thoughts. Look at you, your cheeks are all flushed and your eyes are dark." He stepped in front of her and ran his finger inside the seam of her bodice. "You look sexy as sin in this dress."

She glanced at his kilt. "You naked under all that plaid?"

"But of course."

Their eyes met and he softly kissed her, his hand cupping her belly. "I can't believe we're having another one."

She sighed happily. "Me neither. The kids don't know yet."

"Little buggers."

She slid her arms around his waist and his dress jacket pulled tight. "Shouldn't you be with the guys?"

"I wanted to check on my lady. I brought you something." He held up a box.

"Finn… what is it?"

"Nothing much. Open it."

Lifting the lid she gasped. "You got me sneakers." They were flats laced with McCullough tartan. "I love them."

"I figured you would."

She glanced at the heels in the corner and bit her lip. "But the other ones are so pretty."

"Well, wear the heels and then when your feet hurt you'll have a backup. But I want the heels back on for tonight. Aunt Colleen offered to keep the kids overnight."

"Really?"

He nodded. "Locusts do nice things sometimes."

She pressed a kiss to his cheek. "You know I really love your family."

"I know." He turned and caught her mouth. His lips twisted over hers, pulling and coaxing her closer. His hand slid to her ass and squeezed. "Do we have time—"

"No. My hair's all done and I'm not messing it up. For once I'm not covered in paint or puke or poop and I plan to stay pretty for at least a few hours."

"You're always pretty, Philly. Always."

Her heart warmed as she smirked, but she wasn't giving in—not yet. "You'll just have to wait until tonight."

"Gah, you're rotten."

"I'll make the wait worth your while."

"Yeah?"

She turned and shot a promising glance over her shoulder. "Yeah."

"There's a handsome man," Ashlynn said as she pinned Nate's kilt and adjusted his clip on bowtie. She stood and brushed the wrinkles from her gown, so naturally beautiful she still took Kelly's breath away.

He entered the room and grinned at his son. "Look at you, my little man."

"Daddy, we match!" Nate called.

Ashlynn turned, her smile full of affection. "He looks so cute."

Kelly smiled. "Your dad's here, Ash. He's going to take Nate over to the lake."

"Okay. I have a basket of toys to keep him occupied during the ceremony. Let me get it."

Kelly caught her arm and kissed her. She leaned into him and moaned as he pulled away. "You look beautiful."

She glanced down at her dress and fidgeted with her bust line. "My boobs are bursting out at the seams."

He grinned. "I like it." He gazed hungrily at her body. "Makes a man want some cobbler."

She playfully pushed him away. "You already had some."

"That was this morning. Cobbler for breakfast. Cobbler for lunch. Cobbler for dinner."

"Well, the bakery's closed until after the party, mister."

He followed her to the kitchen where she gave Roy instructions for Nate. Once her father left and they were alone, he caught her in his arms and kissed her again. "Kelly, we're going to be late."

"We've got plenty of time."

Her hair, held in a simple headband, filled his fingers. "Wherever you go…"

"I'll go," she finished, the familiar line, something they'd shared since the beginning.

"And where ever you stay…"

"I'll stay," she whispered, meeting his gaze with understanding.

"Stay with me a few minutes longer, Ash. Let me enjoy my wife before the day takes off."

She pressed her cheek to his chest and sighed happily. "Okay."

His fingers found the zipper at the back of her dress and slowly lowered it. The gown fell in a swish of crinoline and satin to the floor and she stepped out, scooping it off the ground and laying in on the kitchen chair.

"God, you're beautiful."

"So are you," she whispered.

He removed his jacket and set it on the back of the chair. Slowly, he stalked her, not stopping until he had her up against the wall, his mouth trailing kisses over her collarbone and sending goose bumps up her arms. "I love you, Ash." His hand pressed softy to her belly where she was just starting to show. "I love our life."

"I love you too, Kelly."

Though they had somewhere to be, he would not rush. Perhaps it was the significance of the day, or perhaps it was the soft way she'd dressed their son, with such love and affection. All he knew was that he wanted her and intended to have her to himself a little longer before they met up with the others.

His hands cupped and caressed her and soon he was filling her, right there on the floor of the kitchen. She clung to him, so responsive and true. In all of his life, he'd never imagined a bond as honest and raw as theirs could exist.

What they shared was genuine. It was love and it was without condition. When she looked at him, she still seemed to see the parts of his soul the rest of the world missed. And not a day passed that he didn't count his blessings, her and Nate among the greatest of them all.

"THIS IS RIDICULOUS."

Alec chuckled. "I'm a Brit dressed as an Irish clansman. Do you care to dispute which of us looks the most preposterous?"

Sheilagh turned and huffed, her arms handing on either side of her rounded belly. "I need you to lace me up. I'm the only girl that needed an adjustable back. I feel like a heifer."

"Turn around." He laced the bodice and tied a small bow. "This dress is rather Victorian."

She wobbled to the chair and sat with a huff. "Can you get my slippers?"

He glanced at the dainty shoes in the box. "Aren't you wearing these heels, love?"

Yanking up the gown she kicked out a foot. "Look at my feet, Alec. Look at them! I'm hideous and my ankles look like Pop-eye's arms."

He chuckled. "I'll get the slippers."

When he returned, he found her sulking in the chair. "Sheilagh, love, you're going to ruin your makeup."

"Fuck my makeup." Her eyes turned on him, showing signs of fear he hadn't seen there in some time. "Alec, I'm scared."

He stilled as he skated her slipper over her toes and secured the heel. "What do you have to be frightened of?"

"By the end of the week I'm going to be a mum. Either that or I'm carrying some alien being that has set up base in my uterus."

He chuckled. "You'll be a fine mum, Sheilagh. Look at how much your nieces and nephews adore you."

"I'm not like Kate. She got all my mum's maternal genes. I got the crazy parts."

He tipped his head in consideration. "Well, Tristan's a rather calm gent on most days. His DNA will balance everything out."

She met his gaze and gave a sad smile. "Sometimes I still wish it was you and me in here," she whispered, touching her belly.

"I know, but look at the incredible gift you're able to share this way. Sheilagh, I'm far past the age of tackle football and Cub Scout hikes. Our child will have three strong men in its life and one incredibly resilient mum. I'm grateful we can give him or her such a loving family. That baby will belong to all of us, he will have your fiery spirit and Tristan's easy manner, my wit and Luke's determination. Don't underestimate nurture's power over nature. I'm just as much a father to this child as the others."

She sighed. "What if my water breaks right in the middle of everything?"

"Then we go to the hospital and welcome our child into the world."

Her lips pursed. "You're so calm about all of this."

"I've been through this before, don't forget. You'll be fine, love. Have a little faith in you." He frowned. "Speaking of… Where is Wes?"

She grinned. "Oh, I introduced him to Becca's friend Carla."

His eyes went wide. "The crazy one?"

"She's harmless."

"Sheilagh, Wes has a very low tolerance for—"

"He needs to get laid, Alec, that's all. Carla will keep him occupied while he's here."

He sighed. He'd be lying if he denied finding some amusement from the idea of crazy Carla getting his son to loosen up. "I suppose you're right."

"Of course I am. Now help me out of this chair. I have to pee before we leave."

He helped her up, but held onto her hand. When she turned, he kissed her. "Sometimes I consider our life here and wonder how I survived without you all those years. I'm addicted to your madness, Sheilagh."

She grinned. "It's good stuff. My mum always said it's the craziness that keeps us sane. We've stocked up."

He laughed. "I've noticed. Go on and finish up. I'll track down Wes and the other one."

He searched downstairs for his son, but didn't find him. "Wes?"

There was a clatter in the kitchen and he turned. Carla spun away from his son and quickly wiped away her smudged lipstick. "Hey, Mr...Alec."

Wes's hair was sticking out every which way and he looked like he'd been through the wringer. "Hey, Dad."

I'll be damned. "Well..." There was really nothing he could say. "Will you be driving to the lake with us?"

"Uh...no, I think Carla and I will drive separately."

He understood immediately that this little rendezvous was far from over. It actually pleased him to see his son enjoying himself for a change. "Suit yourself. The ceremony starts in less than an hour."

"We'll see you there."

He grinned as he took the steps to check on his wife. The little vixen was right.

LUKE BROKE into a sweat as he tried for the third time to adjust his tie.

"Having trouble?"

He sighed and faced Tristan. "Yes." His gaze traveled down his husband's body. "Jesus…"

Tristan grinned and quietly tied his bowtie, the scent of his soap and aftershave climbing into Luke like a potent aphrodisiac.

"I love seeing you dressed like this. Only thing better is you in a baseball uniform."

He chuckled and adjusted the knot. "Good?"

Tristan nodded. "Good." His hand brushed down his chest. "You ready?"

"Yeah. I just have to get my speech."

"Already got it." He patted his sporran.

Luke leaned forward and kissed him. "What would I do without you?"

"Plenty, but you'd be miserable."

He chuckled. "So true. Shall we go check on Mum?"

Tristan grabbed his hand and took a moment to admire their matching wedding rings. "Will we do this in forty years? Renew our vows?"

A familiar peace washed over him, removing some of his nervous tension. "We can do it every year, cowboy. My loves far from fading."

Tristan stepped close, wrapping his arms around him and resting his head on Luke's shoulder. They swayed as if dancing in the silence. "Sometimes I think about how hard you fought this," he whispered.

Luke's hand flattened on his back. "There was no stopping the things you made me feel."

"Same."

Luke confessed a large source of his stress. "I'm worried about Sheilagh. Today's going to be a lot for her."

Tristan's gaze met his. "Do you think she's going to go into labor?"

"There's a good chance."

He laughed quietly. "We could be fathers by the end of the day."

"I know. It's surreal."

"Well, then we better get started. There's a lot to get done today."

Sliding his hand into Tristan's, they shut out the lights and made their way to the big house. Sheilagh and Alec were locking up as they stepped onto the drive.

"Are you taking Mum?" his sister asked.

Luke nodded. "You look beautiful, Devil."

She blushed. "Thank you." With a sigh, she said, "You boys look quite dashing as well."

They glanced at Alec and snorted. "How you holdin' up, Alec?" Tristan called.

"Bloody Christ, I'm in a skirt. I feel almost as ridiculous as a Texan might."

"It's not about the kilt, it's about what's underneath," Tristan called. "This Texan's doing just fine."

Alec held the door for Sheilagh and gave them the finger.

"Come on," Tristan said, pulling Luke toward the big house.

MAUREEN TURNED and slowly faced the mirror. "Oh, my…"

"Is good, yes?" Italian Mary adjusted a few of the trimmings making up the lace bodice of her gown and fit the veil to Maureen's hair.

"It's magnificent. Thank you, Mary."

She nodded, her red lips hiding a satisfied smile. "I'll go get your mother."

Maureen's gaze vainly returned to her reflection. She grinned at her painted nails. Never in her life had she felt so delicately feminine.

"This way, Mary, watch your step." Italian Mary ushered Maureen's mother into the room.

"Hello, Mum." She held her breath, waiting for any signs of recognition.

Her mother sat in the rocker and Italian Mary excused herself. Maureen smiled sadly. "You have a wonderful friend in Mary, Mum. I hope you realized that at some point."

Her mother stared blankly ahead as Maureen gathered her full skirt and crouched beside her rocker. "Mum… I wish you understood what was happening today. Your grandchildren worked so hard to make this nice for Frank and I." Her throat tightened as she blinked. "They've really thought of everything. My only wish would be that you could share in the happiness with us."

Her mother's fingers slowly ran over the lace trimming at her wrist. "You're a pretty lassie."

Maureen laughed, glad to hear her speak, but heartbroken with the disconnect of her mother's memories. "I wish Daddy was here."

"There's going to be a party," her mother said.

"Yes, Mum, a splendid party full of love and family. I'll be the bride and this time all of my loved ones will be there." She sighed. "Maybe even some looking down from heaven."

"Maureen?" Rosemarie stepped into the room. "It's time. Luke and Tristan are ready to drive you to the lake."

She kissed her mother's cheek and stood. "I love you, Mum."

Her mother's hand tightened on hers. "You remind me of a woman I once knew."

Sucking back her tears, she whispered, "You remind me of the same."

"Come on, Mum," Rosemarie softly said, carefully guiding their mother by her shoulders. "Colleen's going to drive you to the lake."

Taking a quiet moment to collect herself, Maureen glanced around the room and collected her bouquet. On second thought, she reached into her satin bag and pulled out the flask Sheilagh had given her, taking a steady sip of the good stuff.

"Hoo… just as Liberace said, bottoms up." She twisted the cap on and carefully took the stairs.

Luke and Tristan's voices spoke softly and then quieted as she stepped into the den. "Well…I'm ready," she said.

"Oh, Maureen…" Tristan stood. Luke slowly stood as well, his face a blank look of awe.

"Do I look all right?"

"Mum…" Luke noticeably swallowed. "You look *stunning*."

Her smile grew. "I feel rather pretty in all this fluff and lace. Look, the girls even painted my nails. And I have heels on!" She kicked out her foot to show off her green satin kitten heels.

"You don't look old enough to be celebrating your fortieth wedding anniversary, Maureen."

"Oh, aren't you sweet, Tristan. Keep tellin' lies and you'll get a black spot on your tongue. What's say we have a toast before we go?"

"Are you sure that's wise, Mum? The ceremony starts in twenty minutes."

"Then we better hurry. Tristan, get my good stuff under the sink next to the Windex. I need to fill up my flask anyway."

"Mum, are you already drinking?" Luke asked with a look of concern.

"I may have been born an O'Leahey, but I'm a McCullough by injection. It's my wedding day. *Of course* I'm drinking!"

Tristan poured three glasses and they held them together. "To Maureen and Frank, may they know another forty years of happiness. Salute."

They tipped the drinks back and hollered as the burning whiskey hit their bellies. "Let's do this," she said with a grin. "It's my first real wedding and I don't want to be late."

BRAY SMILED as he left Hunter at the piano and the soft tune of *Wild Horses* echoed across the lake. "He's all set."

Becca smiled, pride shining in her eyes as she watched her son play. "Look how happy he is."

Bray pulled her close, fitting her small body against his front and resting his chin on her shoulder as he held her hips. "It's amazing how far he's come, how far we've all come."

Her fingers closed over his, pulling his palm to her belly.

"It's amazing how much you can accomplish when you're surrounded by such love, how small the fears become."

His lips pressed to her pulse. "Thank you."

"For?"

"Letting me love you, giving me a family to care for, moving to the mountain with me, and always supporting my dreams."

She turned and wreathed her arms around his neck. "The mountain *is* home, Braydon. No other place could hold this much magic. Look around. Look at your incredible family and how they all pulled together to do this for your parents. It's like living in a love story, but with more cursing and too many sex jokes."

He chuckled. "Promise me something."

"Anything."

"Meet me here in forty years so we can do what they're doing today."

"I'll meet you here in thirty-eight. We already have two in the bag."

He kissed her. "Then thirty-eight. Promise."

"I promise."

"Bray?" He turned as Kate called his name. "Luke and Tristan just arrived with Mum. It's time to get started."

He drew in a long breath and turned back to Becca. "I'll see you at the altar."

"I'll be looking for you." She brushed a soft kiss on his cheek and left with his sister.

The men lined up beside Colin with their backs to the lake. "I've never seen so many hairy knees in my life," Bray joked as he fell in line beside Kelly.

"One stiff breeze and boy will the lassies in the front row be gettin' a show."

Bray snorted and glanced at his father. "You ready to see

your bride, Dad? Any cold feet? Finn's got a getaway car ready just in case."

His father shifted his shoulders, folding his hands at the base of his back and puffing out his chest. "The only direction I'll be runnin' is toward my wife."

They all smiled and faced the dunes as the music shifted and the first of the wee McCullough's appeared, dressed as clansman, a future generation of heartbreakers in training.

CHAPTER 18

There seemed to be pollen in the air, because Frank's eyes were suddenly itching for a swipe. His grandchildren, dressed in shades of blue and green with accents of McCullough tartan, marched in orderly disarray down the aisle as Hunter played a beautiful rendition of *Somewhere Over the Rainbow.*

"Look at them," Kelly chuckled. "Precious little devils."

"I remember when all of you were that age."

Becca came around the corner, her gold gown glittering in the sunlight, green shoes peeking out with each step. He glanced at his sons, Braydon's gaze turned soft as he smiled at his beautiful wife.

Next came Ashlynn, her beauty so unrefined and natural. Kelly's lips parted as his steady stare turned heavy and he muttered a curse and something that was likely inappropriate.

Sammy followed, her freckled cheeks tight with a smile and her hair twisted off to the side. All of them were so very different, yet equally lovely. Glancing at Colin, he smiled. This was where his son belonged, not far away from home, but here, with the rest of them, a part of the family.

Mallory turned the corner and Finn drew in an audible breath. The possessive glint in his son's eyes was so familiar, something they had all been known for. Mallory winked at them and took her place on the other side of Colin, who would be doing the ceremony.

Ah, and then there was his Devil. Her hair, fire and spice, fanned behind her as she made her way down the aisle. Dear Lord, she was ready to burst. She stepped in front of him and pressed a kiss to his cheek. "I love you, Daddy."

"I love you too, Devil. You look so much like your mother."

She smiled softly and took a seat beside Roy, the Dougherty's, and Alec's son, who seemed to be keeping company with Becca's friends.

His gaze lifted just in time to see Katherine make her way around the bend. His heart trembled. She was his first. He could still recall how sweet she smelled and the way her tiny body weighed in his arms the day they brought her home from the hospital.

Swallowing back a lump in his throat, he blinked as she too pressed a kiss to his cheek. "You look great, Dad."

"I love you, Katie girl."

"I love you too."

The music faded and everyone stood. He breathed in a tight breath as the tune of *When Irish Eyes are Smiling* began. The crowd gasped and he craned his neck, dying for just one glimpse of her.

And there she was.

His breath left in a whoosh as her eyes met his and held. His Maureen, his one true love. The tightness in his throat became too much as his vision blurred. Blinking away his unshed tears, he licked his lips.

"Dad, where are you going?" one of his son's hissed, but he was too enchanted by her spell to answer. He'd always meet her halfway. So long as he was alive, his love would never walk alone.

Her gown was all beaded silk and her hair was spun into some fancy twist with Irish lace coming down past her shoulders. He walked slowly, never once lifting his gaze from hers. She was a vision.

When he met her halfway, just as he always had, she smiled and whispered, "Frank, love, I think you were supposed to wait up front with the others."

"No, love. You're too pretty to be walkin' alone. Let me take you there."

Her cheeks blushed a soft shade of pink as she slipped her arm through his. Their children smiled, many—even the men—wiping away a tear or two. When they reached the front, he laced his fingers in hers and squeezed tight. "You're up, Colin."

His eldest son cleared his throat and the music faded. It seemed they all let out a collective sigh.

"Forty years," Colin started. "We are here to celebrate forty wonderful years shared by my parents, Frank and Maureen McCullough. Falling in love is easy, but staying in love is the trick. When I look at my parents, their love is obvious. It's genuine and evident in every teasing glance, every cutting jibe, and every little laugh.

"I grew up in a house full of love and laughter. I don't know how families manage otherwise. Though there were sad times, they were few and far between and always over-shadowed by the jubilance that seemed to grow within the very walls my father built. He built that home for her, for us, for the dreams they once shared. Today, we celebrate the fruition of all they created, all their dreams that have come true. Because they loved—without apology—without conditions—but with all their hearts."

Frank glanced at Maureen as she dashed a tear away with her thumb. *I'll be damned, those nails* are *polished.* He reached into his breast pocket and removed his kerchief, gently slipping it into her hand.

"Thank you, love. It must be my damn allergies," she whispered. "I'm sorry, Colin, dear. Continue."

"Frank, will you continue to have Maureen as your wife, to live in this loving and happy marriage?"

"I will," he rasped.

"Maureen—"

"You call me Mum."

Laughter chortled softly and Colin cleared his throat. "Mum, will you continue to have Dad as your husband, to live in this loving and happy marriage?"

"Well, I'm used to him now," she joked and batted her eyes. "Of course I will."

"Dad, have you prepared your vows?"

He turned, facing his wife and cleared his throat, then cleared his throat again. "Maureen...you're a lass like no other. You're as unstoppable as the wind and as wild as the sea. Your heart is an unfathomable gift you share with every person you meet. I consider myself blessed, as you have shared that gift with me for forty beautiful years. You have honored me, cherished me, and loved me beyond measure. Though you've never obeyed a single person besides yourself, you've never gone against me either. You are my soulmate in this life and the next, and I thank God every day for bringing you to me.

"I promise to always love you and hold you fast. No

matter how quick you're runnin', I'll never let you stray too far from my side. You're as necessary as air to me, and our children and grandchildren. I could never love another as fiercely as I do you. I give you my vow and my heart, for all of eternity."

"Oh, Frank…" She sniffled into her kerchief and giggled. "I think you've been savin' up your words for the past forty years to say just that. Now you've gone and knocked all my common sense away and I've forgotten what I wanted to bloody say." She blotted her eyes and laughed. "Jesus Christ, I'm speechless."

The crowd burst into laughter and Maureen reached into her flowers and pulled out a flask. Frank frowned. "Are you drinkin', woman? The ceremony's not finished yet," he hissed.

She rolled her eyes. "Well, you're not gonna go spouting off all sorts of poetic words and expect me just stand here unaffected. For the love of Mike, you've shocked me. Give me a moment to find my bearings." She handed the flask off to Luke. "Hold that, love."

She blew out a breath. "Now, I'm ready." She smiled and took his hands in hers. "Frank, you're a pain in my arse, but my pain, a pain I can't live without. I love you to a fault, more than I've ever loved another—but somewhat equal to the amount I love Kate, Colin, Luke, Finn, Braydon, Kelly, and Sheilagh."

"Focus, Mum."

"Right. I love you. They may just be three words, but our story is forty years long and I promise to give you an eternity more. You made me promises and fulfilled them all. The dreams we lost, we made up for in other happy times. You've given me more joy and more laughter than any one person deserves, and I hope I've given you the same. I promise to love you far beyond my last breath, to honor and respect you well into my next life. And should we find heaven, we'll find it together, but I'm pretty sure we're already there."

"Your hands."

Frank turned his palm, keeping his fingers laced with hers. "Hold me fast, love, and don't ever let go," he whispered as Colin wrapped their entwined fingers in tartan.

"Repeat after me," Colin whispered and together they repeated.

"We swear by peace and love to stand, heart to heart, and hand to hand. Holy Spirit, hear us now, confirming this, our sacred vow."

Their hands remained fastened as they lowered their arms.

Colin spoke so all could hear. "It is a sacred thing we celebrate by the water today. With the passing of time, your skin has changed, but your hearts have only grown fuller. What was once chaste, now knows no bounds. There is no faking a love such as this, no truth forsaken in the presence of such affection. And as years go by, tears will sometimes come, but I have faith there will be more joy than sorrow, so long as you hold fast to each other and never let go of the incredible love you share."

He smiled. "Mum, Dad, today you have renewed the promises you vowed forty years ago. You have symbolized the renewal of your vows in a tying of hands. It is with great pleasure, that I conclude the ceremony, renewing the marriage that has joined you and forever binds you as husband and wife. You may kiss the bride."

"Come here, woman," Frank gave their bound hands a tug and caught her in his arms, dipping her back and sealing his lips to hers. The cheers echoed across the lake as he took his time kissing her well and good. "I'll be hard pressed to get you out of that gown, lassie—though you are prettier than ever in it, I prefer you in nothin' at all."

"Frank!" she clucked as her blush darkened.

Returning to his full height, he lifted their bound hands and shouted, "My beautiful wife!" The guests let out whistles and cheers as the piano played again.

O'MALLEY'S HAD NEVER SEEN a crowd like this, Maureen thought as she sat under the tent in the parking lot amongst her many relatives. The place had been transformed with tables and slipcovered chairs, all decorated fancier than any wedding she'd ever attended.

"This is quite spectacular, Rosemarie."

Her sister smiled around the mouth of her beer bottle. "Aye. Your children have outdone themselves."

"You haven't seen nothin' yet," Sheilagh commented, her face poised in front of an oscillating fan, hair blowing in a cloud of red. She'd insisted on the fan the moment they arrived at the reception and Alec along with the rest of them accommodated, knowing she was a ticking time bomb they had to keep comfortable over the next few hours.

"Frank, where are the boys? It's almost time to eat and I haven't seen them in some time."

The girls snickered. "They'll be here," Sammy said.

"You all look like you're up to something."

They all turned away, smirks tight like cats stuffed with canary feathers. She glanced back at her groom. "Don't think I didn't notice your new jacket, Frank. You're as handsome as ever."

He took her fingers and kissed them. "And I noticed how lovely your fingernails are."

"Well, this is probably the first day in my entire life I haven't washed a dish. Look, the polish isn't even chipped— oh, bollocks! Never mind."

The microphone squeaked as the DJ lowered the music. "Oh, there's Luke. Is he going to make a toast?"

"Something like that," Mallory said, a shit eatin' grin on her face.

"Can I have everyone's attention, please?"

The mob continued to talk over him. "He'll never get them quiet."

Luke rolled his eyes. "We're out of whiskey!"

Silence.

He chuckled. "Just kidding. But now that I have your attention, I'd like to say a few words." He reached behind him and lifted a glass. "Mum, Dad, today was beautiful. I think I speak for everyone when I say, the love you celebrate was as evident as ever.

"I've watched you all my life, and always envied what you shared. It took me a long time to realize you didn't love each other for the way you looked, or the possessions you claimed, but for the bond you shared. We have a unique family, each one of us sharing a bit of the other, be it the color of our eyes, our stubborn streak, or our dry sense of humor. All of those traits come from you, both of you. I think it's a testament to the example you set that in a clan the size of ours, we've all found our own version of happily ever after."

He paused and grinned. "But it's just the beginning. Mum, Dad, you've worked hard to raise us well, and I think we've all turned out all right—even Kelly." The crowd chuckled and his smile turned nostalgic as he softly said, "Even me."

There was a moment of silence where every memory seemed to fill Maureen's heart, the good, the bad, and the surreal. She pressed her fingers to her lips and blew a kiss to her sweet son as she took Frank's hand and squeezed.

Luke caught the kiss in a fist and brought it to his heart, meeting her blurry eyes and smiling softly. "Thank you for everything. There has never been a day you turned us away. You've always been there when we needed you and for that, I know, we are the luckiest kids in the world.

"It's time to enjoy and take a bite out of life, Mum and Dad. I hope the next forty years are even greater than the first. To start you off on the right foot, this September, we're sending you to Ireland."

Maureen gasped. "Did you hear that, Frank? Ireland!"

Luke grinned. "And as a special treat, we've planned a little something for you today. We love you, Mum and Dad. Thank you for everything you've done and continue to do. Salute."

"Salute," the guests echoed.

"Let's get this party started McCullough style!" he shouted and everyone cheered. Turning to the DJ, he said, "Hit it."

Very rapid electrical guitar began to play accompanied by a sort of chanting. She glanced at the girls who were all frowning. "This is *not* the song they were supposed to use," Sheilagh said.

Sammy grinned wide as Mallory snorted. "This is AC/DC's *Thunderstruck.*"

Heads bobbed, but Maureen failed to recognize the lively tune.

"Let's hear it for the McCulloughs!" the DJ called as Finn came out, shirt unbuttoned and rolled to the elbow, bowtie wrapped around his head like a character from *Mad Max Thunderdome.*

"Oh my God," Mallory gasped and snorted.

He pranced onto the dance floor like a peacock, arms held wide as he clapped to the beat, hands meeting above his head. The crowd followed his rhythm and started clapping to the beat.

"Oh dear," Ashlynn muttered, cupping her fingers over little Nate's eyes as Kelly darted onto the dance floor.

"Where the hells his shirt?" Maureen cried, wide eyed as her son paraded in all his tattooed glory to the sound of the heavy music.

Tristan swaggered out next, a grin on his face as his head bobbed to the beat. Slowly, he slid off his jacket and tossed it aside. He reached in the waistband of his kilt and pulled out Luke's Irish cap and popped it on his head. The DJ tossed him a microphone and he proceeded to lip synch to the screeching vocals of the lead singer and the crowd went nuts. *"You've been...Thunderstruck!"*

Luke came out next, also shirtless, as he clapped along with Finn and got the guests out of their chairs, yelling the chanting chorus of, *"Thunder!"*

The girls all cracked up as Alec seemed to be pushed into the mix, still dressed in his jacket, tie neatly in place. He shifted from foot to foot as the others danced wildly.

"Oh, that poor man," Becca said, sympathetically.

Maureen looked around. "Where's Colin?"

Suddenly everyone screamed as Colin—her sweet, good, Colin—slid onto the stage, prancing like a possessed gazelle doing some sort of Michael Flatley impression. "Sweet Jesus! Is he River dancing?"

The boys fell into a line just as the song built and the drums pounded and suddenly they were all doing an Irish jig. Maureen's mouth opened in a wide smile. "Look at them Frank!"

"It's like a train wreck. I can't seem to look away," he mumbled.

She glanced at her daughters. "Did you help them plan this?"

"This was all Luke and Finn," Ashlynn said, pointing to Mallory.

"Look, there's Kate!" Sheilagh called, a huge grin on her face.

"Well, I'll be..." Her eldest daughter cavorted onto the dance floor and twirled laps around her brothers as they formed a sort of line to show off her fancy moves. "Look how fast her feet are moving."

They formed a circle and kicked and time suddenly stilled, the loud music fading as her mind drifted into slow motion, savoring the incredible moment. As if their smiles all held in a freeze frame of elated joy, she glanced at her husband, laughing at their children's expense.

Her daughters were all wearing expressions of pure amusement as her boys and Kate... well they looked to be having the time of their lives, putting on an unforgettable performance.

She slipped her hand into Frank's and glanced at her grandchildren, laughing at their parents and having a ball.

Maureen's lips pressed tight, as her lashes grew damp. Soon enough they'd all be grown and discovering who they were.

"They grow up so fast, Frank," she whispered, drawing his attention to the wee ones.

"Aye." He smiled, releasing a satisfied breath. "We did good, Maureen. We did good."

Blinking away her tears she nodded. "Aye." The song ended and every guest shot to their feet and cheered. Wedging her fingers between her lips, she whistled and cheered. *This* was her clan.

EPILOGUE

lexis Luka Devereux McCullough was born on June
twenty-sixth at four thirty-two—one full week after
schedule. The mob of Irish maniacs arrived at the hospital,
overwhelming the staff just before dawn. Many came in their
pajamas and most had severe hangovers. But it was a day to
remember as another redheaded lass was added to their clan.

Maureen fell in love on the spot, as she had with all her
other babies. Luke, Tristan, and Alec fawned over the sweet
girl, speaking softly as they straightened her little blanket
and turned the strawberry curl at the top of her hair just so.

Sheilagh was relieved, though the hard part was far from
over. Her daughter's eyes were blue at the moment, but soon
they'd be green like the other O'Leahey women and she
would be tough like every other one before her. Her daughter's beauty enchanted her fathers and Sheilagh pitied the
boys that would someday come knocking.

It seemed, sometimes, memories could knock the breath
out of a person, which often happened as Sheilagh thought

back over her life. She may not have done everything right, but there was not a thing she didn't put her whole heart into doing.

As the room quieted and she held her daughter, mesmerized by her perfect little fingers and tiny little nose, she smiled. "I want you to know that there isn't a thing you can do to make me stop loving you. If you're ever sad or feeling alone, I want you to come to me, because I'm your mum, and if anything, mums are the toughest people in the world." She kissed her head and whispered, "You're daddy's a big softy—all of them."

She shut her eyes, basking in the contentment she'd longed to find and finally owned. How true it was, about mothers. If not for hers, she'd never have had the faith she needed to do all the wonderful things she'd done.

"Are you sleeping, dear?" Maureen whispered as she stepped into the room. "I brought you some ginger tea."

Lifting her lashes, she smiled. "No, Mum. I was just sittin' here thinking."

"You look so happy, love." She placed the tea on the bedside table and kissed Alexis's soft hair.

"I *am* happy, Mum. Happier than I ever thought I could be."

Maureen sat and sighed, a peaceful smile curving her lips. "Me too, love. Me too."

The End

Want more edgy romance from Lydia Michaels?
Read Intentional Risk now!

Kate McCullough has always been a good girl, but when one bad choice lands her in a heap of trouble, her entire world changes in the blink of an eye. If not for her accidental friendship with Anthony Marcelli, she'd be lost.

Captivated by her wild charm and natural beauty, Anthony wants more than friendship from his best friend, Kate. She's the strong-willed sort, and Anthony quickly learns that loving a McCullough woman is never without drama. Refusing to give up, he risks everything to prove they belong together—even if that means going toe-to-toe with the craziest McCullough of all—her father.

Read Intentional Risk next!

Lydia Michaels has a gift for you!
Subscribe to her mailing list and receive 7 FREE books!
Click here to stuff your Kindle with freebies!

Free Books Here!

Do you follow LYDIA?
TikTok @LydiaMichaels
Instagram @lydia_michaels_books

BOOKS BY SERIES

Many First in series books are FREE

Grab them here!

MCCULLOUGH MOUNTAIN

Almost Priest *

Beautiful Distraction

Irish Rogue

British Professor

Broken Man

Controlled Chaos

Hard Fix

Intentional Risk

JASPER FALLS

Wake My Heart *
The Best Man
Love Me Nots
Pining For You
My Funny Valentine
Side Squeeze

CALAMITY RAYNE

Calamity Rayne Gets a Life *
Calamity Rayne Back Again
Calamity Rayne Gets Hitched
BONUS: Calamity Rayne Veiled & Railed
Calamity Rayne Over the Moon
Calamity Rayne Knocked Up

THE SURRENDER TRILOGY

Falling In
BreakingOut
Coming Home

Ruthless Billionaires

One Billion Secrets *
Two Billion Enemies

MASTERMIND

Blind
Untied

NEW CASTLE

First Comes Love *

If I Fall

Shattered Vows

ADDICTED TO YOU

Crush *

Bang

Throb

THE ORDER OF VAMPIRES

Original Sin *

Dark Exodus

Prodigal Son

Immortal Bastard

Primal Kill

Blood Moon

STAND ALONES

La Vie en Rose

Simple Man

Sugar

Breaking Perfect

Hurt

Protege

ABOUT THE AUTHOR

To receive Lydia's Newsletter and 7 FREE Books, click
HERE !

Lydia Michaels is the bestselling and award-winning author of more than forty novels. She writes heart-clenching, unpredictable romance with dark elements and high heat. Her work is character-driven and bursting with broken heroes and badass females. With a sweet spot for overbearing, territorial types, her deeply emotional books are spicy, emotionally satisfying, and guaranteed to leave readers with many book hangovers.

Lydia is the consecutive winner of the *2018 & 2019 Author of the Year Award* from *Happenings Media* and the recipient of the *2014 Best Author Award* from the Courier Times. She has been featured by *USA Today*, *Romantic Times Magazine*, the *Women in Publishing Summit*, and more.

Michaels started her author career in 2007, becoming a recognized presence and advocate within the publishing industry. She is the CEO of LMC Consulting, a certified author coach specializing in character and plot development, and the founder of the *East Coast Author Convention*, the *Behind the Keys Author Retreat*, and www.LydiaMichaels-Books.com.

She is happily married to her childhood sweetheart. Her favorite things include cooking Italian cuisine, hosting extravagant dinner parties, sipping espresso martinis, listening to her husband play piano, and escaping to her coastal home on the Jersey Shore. She's an LGBTQ ally, a BLM supporter, a firm believer that the patriarchy must end (women's rights are human rights), and an advocate for pediatric cancer research.

LYDIA

Follow Lydia Michaels on social media!
Facebook | Instagram | TikTok

THANK YOU FOR YOUR REVIEW!

Reviews help authors so much! If you left a review for this book, I greatly appreciate it!
Thank you,
Lydia

Click here to leave your review!

LYDIA MICHAELS
FREE BOOKS
CROSSOVER CHARACTERS
INTERCONNECTED STAND ALONES
SMALL-TOWN Hotties
McCULLOUGH MOUNTAIN
Visit the Mountain
Jasper FALLS
FREE
BROTHER'S GIRLFRIEND
FRIENDS/ LOVERS
BAD BOY/ VIRGIN
TEACHER STUDENT
LGBTQ M/M
IT'S COMPLICATED
HOW IT STARTED
SURPRISE PREGNANCY
FREE
SECOND CHANCE
FAKE DATING
OPPOSITES ATTRACT
BOSS + NANNY
ENEMIES/ LOVERS
SECOND CHANCE

www.ingramcontent.com/pod-product-compliance
Lightning Source LLC
Chambersburg PA
CBHW061048190726
48286CB00006B/1658